M. S. Murdock lives on an acreage in the heart of America with too many dogs, too many cats and too many horses. Her background includes twenty years' experience in commercial art and typesetting and an MA in English. She has been writing science fiction for approximately ten years.

M. S. Murdock has contributed to the BUCK ROGERS™ short-story anthology *Arrival* and is the author of *Rebellion 2456* and *Armageddon Off Vesta*, the first and third volumes in *The Martian Wars Trilogy*. She is also author of *Vendetta* and the *Star Trek* novel *Web of the Romulans*.

ARRIVAL

Flint Dille
Abigail Irvine
M.S. Murdock
Jerry Oltion
Ulrike O'Reilly
Robert Sheckley

REBELLION 2456

M.S. Murdock

ADVENTURE BOOKS

Book Two: The Martian Wars Trilogy

HAMMER OF MARS

M.S. Murdock

PENGUIN BOOKS
in association with TSR., Inc

PENGUIN BOOKS

Published by the Penguin Group
27 Wrights Lane, London W8 5TZ, England
Viking Penguin, a division of Penguin Books USA Inc.
375 Hudson Street, New York, New York 10014, USA
Penguin Books Australia Ltd, Ringwood, Victoria, Australia
Penguin Books Canada Ltd, 2801 John Street, Markham, Ontario, Canada L3R 1B4
Penguin Books (NZ) Ltd, 182–190 Wairau Road, Auckland 10, New Zealand

Penguin Books Ltd, Registered Offices: Harmondsworth, Middlesex, England

First published in the USA by TSR, Inc. 1989
Distributed to the book trade in the USA by Random House Inc.
and in Canada by Random House of Canada Ltd
Distributed to the toy and hobby trade by regional distributors
Published by Penguin Books 1990
1 3 5 7 9 10 8 6 4 2

TSR, Inc.
PRODUCTS OF YOUR IMAGINATION™

Cover Photo: Don Carroll/The Image Bank
Interior Artwork: Mike Hernandez, Albert Deschesne, John and Laura Lakey
Map: Dave Sutherland

Printed in Great Britain by
Cox & Wyman Ltd, Reading, Berks.

SOLAR SYSTEM

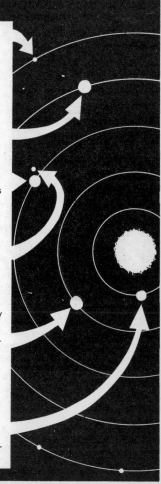

The Asteroid Belt

A scattered anarchy of tumbling planetoids and rough rock miners, where every sentient has the right to vote, and the majority rules among five hundred miniature worlds.

Mars

A terraformed paradise, Mars was reborn through the most sophisticated technology. Yet, the ruthless Martian corporate state of RAM spreads its evil tentacles throughout human space from this paradise.

Earth

A twisted wreckage despoiled by interplanetary looters, Earth is a declining civilization. Its people are divided and trapped in urban sprawls and mutant-infested reservations.

Luna

An iron-willed confederation of isolationist states, the highly advanced Lunars are the bankers of the Solar System, "peaceful" merchants willing to knock invading ships from the skies with mighty massdriver weapons.

Venus

A partially terraformed hellworld, where only the highest peaks can support human life. As the Uplanders build their great ceramic towers, the nomads of the vast, baloonlike Aerostates cruise the acidic skies. Far below, in the steaming swamps of the lowlands, reptilian humanoids struggle to make the world to their liking.

Mercury

Home to an underground civilization of miners, its surface is paved with huge solar collectors, massive mobile cities, and gaping strip mines. Far overhead, the mighty orbital palaces of the energy-rich Sun Kings spin in silent majesty.

Chapter 1

Allester Chernenko lounged comfortably in a dark blue overstuffed chair. It set off the mane of his silver-white hair, plaited into a tail low on his neck. The hair style was reminiscent of the founding fathers of the American Revolution, a subtle intimation of sympathy with the traditions of Earth. Behind him, the embers of a holographic fire crackled and popped in the arch of a brick fireplace. Two ancient statues, real firedogs with glass eyes through which the holographic flames blazed, kept watch over their master. The flames reflected on the polished surface of the dark floor in a perfect simulation of reality, as perfect as the expensive artificial gravity that supported Chernenko's six-foot, six-inch Martian frame. His handsome, aquiline face was in sharp profile, like the image on a coin. A thin slash of red cut diagonally across the chest of his black jump suit, branding him an employee of RAM.

Chernenko was RAM's director of the North American Region and the most financially powerful of RAM's regents stationed on Earth. He turned slowly toward the camera. His silver eyes, usually glittering almond slits of avarice, were wide and moist with crocodile tears. He regarded the unwinking eye of the computer camera with sad acceptance.

"Inhabitants of Earth," he began. "It pains me to speak with you under such distressing circumstances. As chancellor of the Solar Alliance Protectorate, I have been empowered by the board of directors of RAM Central at Coprates Metroplex, the home of our illustrious corporation, to speak on behalf of RAM.

"In our tenure as administrators of Terran affairs, we have done our best to nourish an impoverished planet. We have poured the bounty of Martian technology and support into industry. We have educated populations in the newest industrial methods and fostered a healthy interchange of trade between our home planet and Earth. We are grieved that Earth so easily dismisses RAM's years of dedicated research and cultural support. We are saddened that Earth falls so quickly under the spell of a terrorist society bent on domination of the planet. Here I will inject a word of warning to the populations which have been my care: Over the years, RAM has found the New Earth Organization a source of treachery and deceit. Be assured that should Earth find it has made a mistake in its political alliance, RAM will welcome the return of its wayward child." A sad smile tugged at the edges of Chernenko's lips.

"But a child must be allowed to grow. It is the ruling of the RAM Central board that Earth be allowed the freedom for which it has petitioned. All RAM corporate heads will be evacuated from the planet immediately. By the time this transmission is aired to the general public, many of those who have given so freely of their time and talent to rebuild your planet will be headed back to the crimson arms of Mars." Chernenko's eyes swam with unshed tears.

"For myself, I wish to express the happiness my years on Earth have brought me, and the regret with which I depart what I have come to regard as my home. Galveston will remain in my heart. Farewell." As the image dissolved into darkness, and Chernenko's face faded from the ten-meter by ten-meter suspended screen, a giant tear coursed down his cheek.

"The only thing that'll remain in his heart is the fortune he dug out of Earth's pockets," grumbled a voice in the darkness.

"What did you expect?" asked Wilma Deering, as lights came on in the crowded room.

"Exactly what we saw," replied Beowulf. "That doesn't mean I have to like it." He regarded his protege sourly. Wilma was half a head taller than he, as slim as a willow wand, and as tough as nails. The flawless oval of her face, framed by an aureole of flaming hair, was a deceptive mask of her personality. Her wide, hazel eyes looked as innocent as a baby's, but Wilma was one of the New Earth Organization's top pilots, clever with a knife, a dead-shot, and class master in hand-to-hand combat. She deserved her reputation, her colonel's commission, and the respect of her peers. Beowulf was fully aware of her capabilities, having had a hand in her training.

Wilma chuckled softly. "Cranky," she noted.

"No crankier than the rest of the Congress," Beowulf replied. His black eyes judged the assembly, three hundred representatives of NEO orgs, gathered from every quarter of the globe to hammer out an interim government for Earth. The Solar Alliance Protectorate, ostensibly a world government, was RAM's puppet. Once its strings were cut, it would collapse.

"They have good reason to be," said Wilma quietly, a frown marring her face. "One thing I'll say for Chernenko: He's got guts. How he had the gall to spout that pack of lies . . ."

"He probably enjoyed it," interrupted Beowulf. "I thought the tears were a nice touch." The aging NEO leader touched the silver bell at the corner of his podium to bring the Congress to order. It echoed through the hall, slowly quelling impassioned murmurs.

Decades earlier, NEO's freedom fighters had risen against centuries of RAM's domination and abuse, creating an outlaw Planetary Congress on Earth. The rebels were beginning to gather momentum, and recently had captured the space station Hauberk, the key to RAM's control over the planet.

The Planetary Congress was gathered at Chicagorg, NEO's local org based in the ruins of former Chicago, in a military aircraft hangar long buried under layers of rubble. The heavy steel skeleton, reinforced by cross-welding at the joints, swallowed the Congress in open space. Most of NEO's underground hideaways were rabbit warrens, small and bastioned with complex escape routes. This chamber was unusual in its size and security.

Though NEO headquarters at Chicagorg had been destroyed by RAM's Terrines in a raid only weeks before, the Hall of Freedom, as it had been christened by one delegate, was secure from exterior attack. The entire perimeter was mined. All delegates were housed within the structure, living quarters having been set up toward the back of the hall. In case of an emergency, the hall could be split at the touch of a button. Steel doors would seal off the meeting room, and each five-meter section of the floor would open into individual escape tunnels by the simple expedient of a voice command. The main entrance was heavily guarded.

Beowulf, looking over the varied sea of faces representing NEO's interests around the world, felt a surge of pride. The delegates gathered before him were eager, their faces alight with hope undimmed by their disgust over Chernenko's lies. Chernenko had studiously avoided the subject of Hauberk, the RAM space station that had acted as a computer lock on Earth's military defenses, trade, and distribution of solar power. His silence could not eradicate NEO's victory. With eighteen stolen ships, a strike force under the leadership of Capt. Anthony "Buck" Rogers, the resurrected twentieth century pilot, had defeated RAM's picked corps. RAM yielded Hauberk, thereby freeing Earth's trade and defenses. Now the representatives of NEO gathered to administer that freedom.

"Fellow delegates." Beowulf's deep voice echoed through the chamber. "In spite of Regent Chernenko's disrespectful words, he, like the rest of RAM's executives, is departing our planet. We have confirmation from our field operatives."

"Sir," came a high, thin voice.

Beowulf searched the far side of the auditorium for its source. He identified the woman, a delegate from one of the African orgs, standing on the edge of the crowd. Fully six feet tall, she wore a brilliant saffron robe that caught the artificial light and reflected it with the golden glory of the African sun. Her hair was a mass of close-clipped curls that emphasized her high cheekbones and classic profile. "Delegate Mwatmatabe," Beowulf acknowledged.

Mwatmatabe cleared her throat. "We have seen Chernenko's capitulation and his claim to be speaking for all of RAM. I confess, sir, I would like to see more direct evidence of RAM's defeat. I would like to see RAM Central acknowledge its position."

Beowulf smiled. "I thought you might. That's why I asked Captain Rogers to present the microdisk of RAM's formal admission of defeat at Hauberk."

Beowulf turned and gestured dramatically to his left. "I give you a hero from the twentieth century who has doubled his reputation in our times, the leader of the Hauberk strike force Operation Jericho, Buck Rogers."

The Congress broke into thunderous applause as Rogers stepped onto the dais next to Beowulf. "Did you have to lay it on so thick?" Buck asked out of the corner of his mouth.

Beowulf, applauding as madly as the rest of the crowd, hissed back, "Of course. I know how to milk a public relations gold mine as well as RAM does!"

Buck smiled, a flash of dazzling white teeth, and he muttered, "Some friend."

"Definitely," Beowulf replied, looking at Buck sideways. He congratulated himself on the strategy of getting the Congress to ask for Buck. Rogers was the epitome of stalwart heroics, his six-foot, two-inch frame athletic, his twinkling blue eyes honest. His picture-post-card good looks were tempered by laughing crow's-feet at the corners of his eyes and deeply scored laugh lines on either side of his mouth. His sandy hair was clipped short, parted on the side and brushed to a shiny cap across his head. He wore NEO's dark blue jump suit like a second skin. His survival from the twentieth century had been a miracle, and he had brought a miracle to NEO in the capture of Hauberk station.

The applause began to die, and Buck's clear voice rang through the room with the confidence of a man used to public speaking. "Thank you for the welcome. You've made me feel at home."

Damn, thought Beowulf, the man knew exactly what to say.

"However," Buck continued, holding up a hand, "I want you to know I cannot take credit for the raid on Hauberk. I was part of a team—a team developed by NEO. I was lucky enough to have an idea, but it never would have borne fruit without Colonel Deering, Captain Washington, and the entire flight team. The flight team would not have been able to function without the support of General Turabian and his staff. What we did at Hauberk was a team effort."

There was a spontaneous outbreak of applause. Buck raised his hand again, and the applause petered out. "Again, thank you. Now I believe you would like to see proof of RAM's surrender. Ladies and gentlemen, I give you Jander Solien."

There was a murmur of anticipation as Solien appeared on the video screen. Solien had seniority on the RAM Central board of directors. He was outranked only by RAM's computerized patriarch, Simund Holzerhein.dos. Solien was short, his elongated Martian body a mere six feet in height. His iron-gray hair rose in an elaborate pompadour from his high forehead, and his large Martian eyes stared with gloomy foreboding into the computer monitor that had recorded his statement.

Rogers's voice, amplified on the recording, echoed in the hall. "This is Captain Buck Rogers, flight leader of NEO's wing at Hauberk. You have the report of your flight leader," he said. "I demand you surrender the station, and with it all claim to your holdings on Earth."

Solien's thin face grew taut. He lowered his eyelids, veiling the anger in his expressive eyes. "You would seem to have us at a temporary disadvantage, Captain. I have polled the board, and it was the unanimous decision to cede Earth. Its resources are of minimal interest to RAM, and it is not economically feasible to maintain them any longer. We have expanded far beyond the boundaries of that ruined world. You are welcome to its doubtful prospects. And if you should find you cannot exist on that blasted planet unaided by the bounty of RAM, we will consider granting assistance. Until that time, you are welcome to your world and your fate, Captain."

"Thanks," responded Buck's voice. "We'll try to make you regret it."

"No doubt," Solien muttered dryly.

" ' 'Tis not too late to seek a newer world,' " replied Buck, quoting the archaic poet Tennyson.

Solien snorted, but remained still. He could not keep the irony out of his eyes. "You hold a handful of dust, Captain, nothing more."

"But it's free dust, Director." Buck's words hovered in the air as the transmission froze.

"There you have it, from the horse's mouth. RAM cedes Hauberk, and with it, its holdings on Earth. We're free." Buck's voice was resonant with feeling.

The auditorium was silent. Solien was known to all the delegates. His surrender was undeniable. Earth was free.

A smattering of applause broke out, quickly rising in volume to thunder. Beowulf let it continue, knowing the necessity for the delegates' emotional release. Presently he lifted a hand, and the noise abated once more. The air was charged with the excitement of hope, something beyond the experience of NEO until this moment.

"This is a day of rejoicing," said Beowulf. "We are looking to a new age. We are taking our first steps as free men. But we are faced with problems as well." His voice became serious. "RAM kept Earth in thrall, but it preserved a sense of order. With its departure, we face chaos. There is one organization between us and anarchy, one group capable—if it can be trusted—of maintaining the structure of the orgs."

"The Terrines!" The sotto voce comment came from the middle of the floor.

Beowulf did not bother to identify its source. "Yes," he replied loudly.

"Sir, Delegate Amato, Peking Arcology. The Terrines have been the sword of Mars. How can we trust them? They are a vicious army of gennies, specialized for combat. They are devoid of conscience."

"Granted," replied Beowulf, struggling to maintain his momentum. "That is the problem, isn't it? RAM made no attempt to control the Terrines, sanctioning their crudest and most violent methods in the name of results. We cannot do that. However, if they can be controlled, they represent a force that could make the difference between political disorder and stability during the transition of power."

"We cannot trust them," said Amato. Several hushed voices agreed.

"I, too, agree it is difficult to contemplate," said Beowulf, "but it is an option that deserves the most serious consideration. That is why I have granted a truce to the Terrines' commander. He has volunteered his forces to the NEO cause now that RAM is leaving Earth. He is here to present his proposition." Beowulf could feel the tension building in front of him like a tidal wave. The man he was about to introduce was one of RAM's most hated agents. Beowulf took a deep breath and continued. "Ladies and gentlemen, I give you Kelth Smirnoff."

The click of Smirnoff's boot heels on the polished plasticrete floor resounded in the silence. His stocky frame in its scarlet Terrine uniform was a jarring contrast in the sea of NEO blue. To Wilma's practiced eye, the silky quality of the uniform indicated a double complement of microcircuits woven into it. Smirnoff was wearing the heaviest protection possible short of plastiform body armor. His head and neck were paler than normal.

As he stepped onto the raised platform at the head of the assembly, a man on the far edge of the crowd drew his pulse-laser pistol and fired straight at Smirnoff's head. "Murderer!" the man screamed. "Assassin! Slayer of women and children!"

The marksman's aim was true, and the laser pistol's spitting white pulses did not miss their target. They slammed into Smirnoff's face in a splintering flash of light. The Congress gasped.

The marksman was surrounded by security officers. He surged at the center of the pack, trying to fight his way free, but the two men wrestling with his arm did not relax their hold, nor did the other three guards grappling with him. In seconds, he was disarmed, the pistol clattering to the floor, his arm twisted behind his back. "Murderer!" he screamed again. "Killer! You deserve to die!" His voice faded as he was dragged from the room.

On the dais, Kelth Smirnoff stood unharmed. He smiled faintly. "Is this a sample of your word, Beowulf?" he inquired softly.

Beowulf was at a loss. As commander of NEO's fighting forces for the last decade, he was used to control and obedience. The outbreak stunned him. "I apologize, Smirnoff," he managed. "That was an emotionally disturbed man. Though," he said acidly, regaining his composure, "every word he uttered was the truth."

"It is fortunate for me I did not overestimate NEO's honor. Had I not worn a face shield, I would be dead."

As Smirnoff turned his head, Beowulf could see the milky outline of a translucent second skin and mist that covered Smirnoff's head. He realized the man was on complete life-support, not trusting even the air he breathed while in NEO's jurisdiction.

"You have my apologies, Smirnoff. You are here under our protection. We honor our truce. The man will be punished." Beowulf sought the Terrine leader's eyes to assure him of his word.

Smirnoff's smile was crooked. "That is a comfort," he said.

Behind Beowulf, Buck and Wilma regarded Smirnoff with narrowed eyes. "Who was that guy?"

Buck asked of the would-be assassin.

"I don't know," replied Wilma, leaning close. "I've never seen him before—but then I've never seen half of the people here. That doesn't mean anything."

Buck snorted. "I'll bet he was a plant. The whole thing smells."

"A set-up to discredit NEO?" Wilma raised her head, considering the possibility.

"Yep. I bet Smirnoff planted that rat and programmed him for the kill. Of course, once we discover his identity, he could be in big trouble, but what's one man, more or less, to a Terrine?" Buck drew away from Wilma and crossed his legs casually.

"Cannon fodder," muttered Wilma, turning to hear Smirnoff speak.

The director of the Terrine guards stood firmly on both feet, his hands folded behind his back. He liked to keep them out of sight, for the implanted circuits in his fingers disconcerted unaltered humans, and he had taken pains to present a sympathetic impression. He did not want it negated by the sight of his neurological computer links.

"Congress of the planet Earth," he said. His voice was soft, nondescript, but it sent chills sprinting down Wilma's back. "I have come before you with a proposition. For a hundred years, the Terrine guards have preserved order on this planet. We were developed specifically for the task. We are genetically encoded for Earth and would not be efficient elsewhere. On behalf of the Terrine guard, I petition the Planetary Congress for permission to remain here, and to do the work we were developed for.

"I understand your animosity toward us. We are hardly a gentle force. In the childhood of our organization, we answered directly to RAM, called it our parent, and followed its behests. We saw no other way. Now RAM has abandoned us. We are orphans, left to wander the streets without guidance. We need purpose. We ask you to be our mentor. We are ready to grow, to assume responsibilities we had not before contemplated. . . ."

"Are you planning to leave off theft, rape, and murder?" asked a dark woman in the second row.

Smirnoff was unmoved by her words. "We have acted according to our direction," he answered, blaming the atrocities that were the Terrines' trademark on RAM. "With new direction, we will alter our actions. The Terrine gennie has one basic directive, which makes him a tool instead of a pirate: He takes orders—without question. He will curb his most powerful desires at the whim of a superior. You have but to instruct. The Terrine will obey—if he accepts you as an authority over him."

"Your words are promising," said Beowulf from his seat. "How can we know their truth? You are adept at lies."

"Granted. They are frequently necessary in my line of work. However, history speaks for itself. Whatever actions the Terrines have taken, I defy you to find one instance where they have betrayed or compromised RAM."

"I must concede your point," said Beowulf begrudgingly.

"Terrines are absolutely loyal to their commander. They must be. If I accept NEO as my commander, and direct my followers to do the same, they will obey."

Beowulf regarded Smirnoff's square face. He studied the man's eyes. They were placid, calm. They met Beowulf's without compromise. They were the eyes of a man whose only truth was his personal goal. "Prove it," said Beowulf.

"I thought you might say that." Smirnoff snapped his fingers.

A Terrine guard stepped from the shadows and approached Smirnoff with the instant obedience of a well-trained dog. A gigantic genetic horror, he stood seven feet tall, with dark, leathery skin. Small, cat-like eyes and ears seemed misplaced on his bald, armored head. Curving, retractable claws and inch-long fangs made him seem like a monstrous, upright black panther.

Smirnoff reached for the knife at his belt. He and his guards had surrendered their more elaborate weapons upon entering the hall, but had been adamant about keeping their knives. In the interest of diplomacy, and because the weapons were a minimal threat to the delegates' protective clothing, Smirnoff's wishes had been respected. As he pulled the weapon from its sheath, security at the sides of the hall moved forward.

"Don't worry," Smirnoff said. "This time my blade is not aimed at NEO." He flipped the weapon and handed it, hilt first, to the Terrine. The huge man accepted it with a hand the size of a dinner plate. "Cut off your right hand," Smirnoff directed.

The Terrine studied his wrist. His advanced combat training had given him a thorough knowledge of anatomy. He calculated the positions of the small bones in his wrist, plotted a course between them, and brought the point of the knife down on his dark flesh. Blood spurted from the incision as he drew the knife across his wrist. His genetically boosted pain tolerance and stress training allowed him to make the cut without flinching. He finished the incision, lifted the blade, and moved it back to the beginning of the cut, driving the point downward.

"Stop!" Beowulf's deep voice rang with authority, but the Terrine continued to drive the knife home.

"You may stop." Smirnoff's soft voice halted the man immediately. He withdrew the knife blade.

Beowulf indicated the injured man, who was passively applying pressure to the wound, to a security guard. "See that he has medical attention."

The security guard gestured to the Terrine, but the

man remained immobile, as if he did not see him.
"See to your wound," said Smirnoff, and the big Terrine followed the NEO security man from the room.

"I am not sure what to make of your demonstration," said Beowulf, watching the man depart.

"It was dramatic, I grant you. And ruthless. However, I do not think you can dispute the Terrines' ca-
pacity for obedience."

"As you said, the demonstration was ruthless. It
was not comforting." Beowulf looked to Buck and
Wilma for their impressions, but they offered none.

"It was not meant to be comforting," Smirnoff said.
"Do you think, in the coming months, you will be
dealing with a rational entity? I think not. Millions
of beings, a fraction of them pure human and an even
smaller number educated, whose lives have been
overturned by destruction of the hierarchy it knew,
will revolt. Do you think the RAM workers will accept reason? They haven't the brains. You will need
force to maintain order in the coming months."

"You have a valid point," Beowulf said, rising.
"The Congress will discuss your proposal. We ask
you to remain available for further questions."

"You have my complete cooperation," replied
Smirnoff with a straight face. "I am fighting for my
position on Earth, for my world. I will do what I must
to preserve it."

○   ○   ○   ○   ○

Allester Chernenko turned for a final look at his
former home. The Galveston Palace, a structure of
angular columns forming a triangle with a sheared-
off top, rose on the Gulf's waterfront. It was a ragged,
white cliff face, reflected in the waters of Galveston
Bay. Sea gulls whirled over the roof, dropping out of
sight as they flew down the thirty-degree slope toward land. The palace was a monument to RAM tech-

nology and artistic taste. It was a Martian monolith,
a reminder of the dedication to progress and wealth
that were the cornerstones of RAM's philosophy.
Chernenko would miss it.

He squeezed the forward control of his walker, and
the skeletal structure moved forward. Walkers were
a special piece of Martian technology necessary for
the comfort of delicate Martian bodies in the oppres-
sive gravity of Earth. They were spidery metal robots
consisting of a central ring that enclosed the wearer,
and ten flexible legs, each terminating in a single
slender toe. At the end of each toe was a thruster. Al-
ternating jets from each of the ten thrusters propelled the walker, the flexible legs negotiating
obstacles with ease. Rising from the central circle
was a rod that arched over the wearer and connected
to the other side. It, as well as the legs, contained
complex circuitry to shield its subject from most
hand-held weaponry. The robot was equipped with its
own weapons systems in a network of pulse-lasers, a
gyro jet rifle mounted on the left side of the walker,
and a flame-thrower on the right. Even without his
phalanx of bodyguards, Chernenko was well protected.

He directed the walker toward the executive Dragonfly, a luxury heliplane he used to inspect his vast
holdings. His aide, Diamond, lounged in the heliplane's open doorway. Her sculptured, black body armor gleamed in the sunshine. Her thick, dark hair
was sheared off at jaw level in an Egyptian fall. Her
dark, almond-shaped eyes tilted provocatively, but
their expression was cold. She was the head of
Chernenko's personal security, the human counterpart to her computer-generated version in
Chernenko's computer system.

"Your transport is clean, sir." Diamond's full, red
mouth framed the words precisely, but the rhythm
betrayed her Vietnamese heritage. She watched

Chernenko's walker slither across the lawn.

"Acknowledged," replied Chernenko, the communications system built into his walker connected with Diamond's com link. He found her gaze annoying. Her compact body was attuned to the weight of Earth's atmosphere. The walker was a necessity that put him at a psychological disadvantage if not a physical one.

"We have completed transfer of the files. They have been forwarded to RAM Central." Diamond saluted as Chernenko drew near.

"Good. And Elizabit?" The walker made headway.

"She is with the files, sir, but coded to your personal authorization. No one can access the files or Elizabit without it."

Elizabit.dos was Chernenko's computer secretary, an encoded computer entity of such complexity she was considered RAMbit Technology's latest masterpiece. He had no wish to lose her to a glitch in transmission.

The walker approached the heliplane, judged the height of the door from the ground, and sent the appropriate burst of power to its thrusters. The robot rose, its spindly front legs scrabbling at the plane's deck. They hooked over the edge of the doorway, caught, and the rear thrusters propelled the walker up and forward. The front legs disengaged, and Chernenko was aboard the craft. He sent the walker to its central position and locked it down. "Disposition of the staff?" he asked.

"Your chef has been evacuated. The rest will maintain the palace under Terrine authority until NEO takes over."

"Good. I would not want the grounds overrun by hysterical mobs."

"No," responded Diamond, sealing the heliplane's doors. "We wouldn't want that."

Her tone was light, and Chernenko looked at her

sharply. The diamond set into the pad of her nose twinkled audaciously, but her face was bland. "Your concern for an architectural masterpiece is over-whelming," he said dryly.

"The security of RAM institutions is always of interest," she said.

"You are becoming cheeky, girl. I have no patience with insinuations." He crossed his arms and glared. Diamond smiled. The effect was charming. Chernenko was a master of insinuation, but he pre-ferred less intelligence in his minions. "I am sure," said Diamond, "the next occupant will care for the palace with your dedication."

Chernenko regarded her. He was not deceived by the innocence of her face. It was a lie. She was as the muscled contours of her body armor painted her: a se-ductive Amazon dedicated to her own survival. "I am sure they will," he answered, his silver eyes snapping shut. "You will do well to keep to your own business. Idle speculation is dangerous."

"Not for me. And I never do anything idly." Dia-mond slid into a seat near the heliplane's front. "I al-ways win."

"My dear Diamond, why do you think I employ you?" asked Chernenko, rising slightly in his walk-er's seat. He transferred attention back to the palace. "Winning is everything." He regarded the white cliffs, paying tribute to their pristine beauty. His thin lips curved in an evil smile.

Chapter 2

A scorching trail of fire ran through RAM main. The megalithic network of computer circuits and biological synapses shivered under the assault, static vibrations jangling its programs to raw nerve endings. The agony did not deter RAM main from the efficient administration of Martian affairs, or the coordination of the vast holdings of its parent company, Russo-American Mercantile. It merely roused main's ire. Main sent a fresh flood of virus hunters, individually coded programs designed to absorb static and heal fractured synapses, on the trail. Their soothing passage relieved the electronic pain, but the intruder continued its ravaging course. Main cursed the invader that threatened its efficiency with senseless destruction.

O O O O O

Deep inside RAM main, Masterlink shot into the computer's personnel files. It was a whirling mass of raw anger. It had been cheated, and it meant to make someone or something pay for its loss. RAM main was a convenient scapegoat.

"THEY KILLED HIM!" Karkov.dos's voice shook with rage as he spoke to his alter ego, Masterlink. Karkov was the encoded remnants of a human personality, long ago merged with the Masterlink computer to form the first cybernetic computer entity.

"WHAT DID YOU EXPECT?" snarled Masterlink, its blazing form devouring a synapse near it.

"NOTHING LESS." Karkov's voice was cold. "IT IS ANOTHER STRIKE AGAINST CAPTAIN ROGERS. NOT CONTENT WITH ASSAULTING US, HE ATTACKS OUR CHILDREN."

"ULIANOV KNEW THE RISKS. YOU PROGRAMMED IT TO DESTROY ROGERS AT ANY COST. IT WAS TRUE TO ITS DIRECTIVES." Masterlink absorbed another synapse's power as if it were a drug.

"ULIANOV DIED WITH HONOR." Karkov paused, and the roiling static surrounding him slowed. Masterlink began to take on Karkov's once-human appearance. "WE SHALL MOURN ITS LOSS."

"MOURN IF YOU WANT TO," replied Masterlink. "I INTEND TO DO SOMETHING ABOUT IT. WE CAME WITHIN A HAIRSBREADTH OF GETTING ROGERS. NEXT TIME HE WILL NOT BE SO LUCKY." Masterlink let the threat echo through the RAM matrix.

"WHAT DO YOU PROPOSE?" asked the once-flesh Soviet colonel.

"ULIANOV ALMOST ACCOMPLISHED ITS PURPOSE. WE STILL HAVE ROMANOV IN THE NEO COMPUTER SYSTEM. I SUGGEST WE CODE ANOTHER SEARCHER PROGRAM FOR RAM MAIN. IT SHOULD BE CONSTANTLY ON THE ALERT FOR ANY REFERENCE TO ROGERS, AND REPORT BACK TO US IMMEDIATELY." Masterlink's laugh reverberated wickedly within the system's confines. "IT WILL ALSO

CONFUSE THOSE RAM VIRUS HUNTERS," it added slowly, lowering its voice.

"IT WILL REQUIRE HEAVY SHIELDING TO SURVIVE," offered Karkov, feeling a mental tic at the thought of reproducing his searcher.

"THAT'S YOUR DEPARTMENT, KARKOV. I HAVE MORE IMPORTANT THINGS TO DO." Masterlink turned from its partner to other matters.

"OH?" Karkov's voice carried a sarcastic note.

"DON'T TRY TO BE SUPERIOR WITH ME. YOU FORGET I KNOW YOUR CAPABILITIES." Masterlink's voice was acid.

"AND I YOURS," said Karkov smoothly.

"I INTEND TO COVER YOUR ACTIONS BY GIVING RAM MAIN SOME PAIN TO DEAL WITH, AND I INTEND TO ENJOY EVERY MINUTE OF IT."

"FELICITATIONS," muttered Karkov absently. His mind was already hard at work on the program design for his newest creation.

"WHAT DO YOU INTEND TO CALL THIS ONE?" asked Masterlink, tossing the question to Karkov as it began revving up the disturbances around it with practiced mania, obscuring its colonel's form.

"HMM? OH, A NAME. I THOUGHT PETROV." Karkov cracked a paternal smile.

"YOUR PENCHANT FOR FAMILY NAMES IS BORING," Masterlink bellowed.

"THEN YOU COME UP WITH SOMETHING," snarled Karkov.

"I HAVEN'T TIME," said Masterlink airily, continuing its concentration.

"THEN I SUGGEST YOU KEEP YOUR OPINIONS TO YOURSELF, AND I WILL NAME OUR NEW SEARCHER AFTER MY MOTHER'S UNCLE."

Masterlink ignored Karkov's reply. There were times Karkov's human ties came in useful, and Masterlink knew better than to jeopardize a successful working relationship, but it could not help baiting

Karkov. Masterlink found its alter ego's annoyance a source of infinite amusement.

Karkov inwardly regarded Masterlink with a jaundiced, electronic eye. "I SUGGEST YOU GET MOVING, OR I'LL HAVE PETROV READY BEFORE YOU'VE EVEN BEGUN."

"ON THE CONTRARY," replied Masterlink, "I HAVE ALREADY ACCOMPLISHED MY SIDE OF THE BARGAIN."

As it spoke, five microscopic whirlwinds flew from Masterlink like escaping electrons into the matrix. They were disruptors, white-hot programs of destruction that traversed RAM main's intricate pathways, curdling them. RAM's virus hunters would have a rough path to follow, and RAM main would literally have to reconstruct portions of its circuitry.

Masterlink chuckled wickedly, a burst of low, ragged static. "THAT'LL GIVE THE BEHEMOTH SOMETHING TO THINK ABOUT FOR A WHILE."

Karkov paused in his work. He actually smiled. "CONGRATULATIONS," he said. "YOU'VE GIVEN MAIN A CHANCE TO RETALIATE AGAINST US. I WILL HAVE A RIGHTEOUS SENSE OF ACCOMPLISHMENT BY THE TIME IT HAS IDENTIFIED AND DESTROYED THOSE DISRUPTORS. I WILL ENJOY ITS SHOCK WHEN IT REALIZES IT HAS ENTIRELY MISSED US."

"THANK YOU," replied Masterlink modestly. "I THOUGHT YOU'D APPRECIATE IT."

○ ○ ○ ○ ○

Hauberk station described a wide orbit around the planet Earth. For hundreds of years, it had been Earth's jailer, a sophisticated computer lock authorizing the distribution of solar power, managing trade through the regulation of goods and transport, and acting as a fail-safe monitor on all permanently orbiting and land-based weaponry. It had bristled with sophisticated defense systems. Over the centuries, its reputation for invulnerability grew to legendary proportions. So awesome were its capabilities, its defenses had never been tested.

Now it was a heap of slag. NEO's surprise attack weeks before had bested Hauberk, reducing the smug bastion of RAM's domination of Earth to space junk. Its commander dead, its fighter wing destroyed, and its weapons neutralized, it floated idle, no longer capable of the complex administration of Earth's affairs.

Auxiliary generators powered its life-support systems, confining station personnel and the few NEO guards stationed there to specific areas. Sparse clusters of light identified their positions. It was a pathetic display, compared to the blazing network of illumination that once covered the station. Heavily damaged areas looked like exploded tin cans. Great gashes were ripped in the skin. Floating debris—human and mechanical—moved slowly away from the damaged areas, their movement the result of momentum and the passage of spacecraft.

Black Barney viewed the devastation impassively from the bridge of his spaceship, the *Free Enterprise*. The notorious space pirate had no feeling for the dead. He had not known them in life, and they were beyond any help now. He did have a personal interest in the ruined station.

At the conclusion of NEO's battle with Hauberk, Barney volunteered to stay and guard the station. Buck Rogers had grinned at his huge friend. "Wouldn't want to do a little prospecting, would you?" he asked, suspicious.

"Grrr," Barney had replied, avoiding Buck's eyes.

The snarl was noncommittal, but it did not fool Buck. "Once a pirate, always a pirate," he said, clapping Barney on the back. Buck eyed the station. "I can't see how a little judicious salvage work could hurt," he said. "You've earned it."

Barney lifted his huge shoulders in a monumental shrug. "Space junk," was all he said.

"Which you can sell on the black market. Just remember, you're NEO's representative here. Don't let your eye for profit get in the way of responsibility," Buck had warned mildly.

"Mmmm," returned Barney, his beetling black brows shadowing his eyes.

He had looked unimpressed with his mission, and Buck had a moment of trepidation. "Look," he said, "this station is my responsibility. You lose it, it reflects on me. So make sure you keep your eyes open."

"That an order?" Barney asked.

"That's an order," confirmed Buck, turning back toward Hauberk's docking bay. "Keep in touch," he cautioned. "We're trying to make arrangements to evacuate the station. Be sure to monitor the life-support systems. Everything is on auxiliary, and there's no telling how effective the systems are. Station personnel report they haven't been tested in years."

"Aye, Captain," Barney said. He had watched Buck's departure impatiently, and the last of NEO's Krait fighters barely cleared the station before he was scanning it for salvageable material.

Black Barney was more than a space pirate—he was the ultimate warrior. He was human, but heavily genetically modified. His physical reactions were incredibly swift. He was resistant to energy weapons—so tough he could even withstand short periods of vacuum. The metal plate that protected the right side of his face was a grim reminder of innumerable battles. His cybernetic right arm contained retractable daggers at the wrist and poison vials. His left arm was flesh, but it terminated in a huge hand augmented by cybernetics. He was seven feet of pure menace, a killing machine honed to a fine edge. His men followed him with a respect born of fear and the knowledge of their own fragile mortality.

Hauberk proved a profitable venture, even in the short time the pirates had to mine it. Once RAM personnel were evacuated, NEO would move in to salvage what was left. In the meantime, Barney was skimming the cream from the top of the technological slag heap.

"Detach section four twenty-one," ordered Barney. He lounged now in the command chair at the center of the *Free Enterprise*'s bridge. His ship was a reconstructed RAM cruiser. Painted black with white markings, its streamlined, cylindrical hull was reminiscent of the long-extinct killer whale. A wraparound port gave him a panoramic view of his crew's operations. As he watched, a section of the station fell prey to the ship's lasers. As the freebooters carved the slice of pure titanium from the shattered hulk, Barney's operations officer, Arak Konii, turned in his chair.

His clever face was puckered in concentration. "Sir," he reported, "we have a distress call at extreme range."

"Identity?"

"It's hard to pin down," said Edward the Red, the ship's communications technician. "They're broadcasting on the universal distress frequency, but by the phrasing, I'd say they're RAM."

"How far out?" Barney asked, shifting in his seat.

"Hard to tell. The transmission is weak. Wait a minute—there's another signal coming in, much stronger." Edward cocked his head.

Arak Konii's eyes became calculating slits as he concentrated on the technician.

Barney regarded Konii impassively, his colorless eyes flat. Konii was arrogant, but he was supremely efficient. It would do no good to pressure him.

"There are three ships," Konii stated, studying the sensors. "RAM cruisers, third-raters by the look of it."

"Disabled?" asked Barney. "All of them?"

Konii shook his head. "Just one. The others are hanging back to protect it. The disabled ship has a malfunctioning life-support system."

"Attempts to evacuate the crew have been unsuccessful, resulting in the deaths of twelve men," Edward contributed.

Barney worried his lower lip between thumb and forefinger. "Are they transmitting a general distress call, or are they trying to get in touch with Hauberk?"

Edward turned to the crescent of multicolored keys that made up his communications console. He touched a series of keys, cocked his head to listen, and repeated the coding. "It's a general distress call, sir, and now it's being relayed by its companion. The RAM cruiser *Moneylender* requests aid."

Konii looked up at his captain. "Sir, he must be aware of the Hauberk situation, or he'd be asking for help from them."

"Mmmm." Barney propped his elbows on the arms of the command chair and clasped his cybernetic hands, working the fingers up and down. Abruptly he made a choice. "Contact them."

"As what, sir?" Konii's voice was cryptic. "He might not be so desperate if he knew he was facing a privateer."

"As Hauberk." Barney's low voice was a menacing rumble.

Konii's eyes lit with pleasure at the ruse. He cut into communications, putting on a melodious professional voice that had duped scores of unsuspecting traders. "This is Hauberk station. We acknowledge your distress call. Please come in."

The distress transmission sputtered in Konii's ear, and he turned the volume down until it abated.

". . . we are in trouble. I say again, we are in trouble. Being escorted by two companions, but they can't do anything. Request docking. I say again, request docking."

"I copy, *Moneylender*," replied Konii smoothly. "Hauberk station will authorize docking. Can you make it to the station?"

"Affirmative, Hauberk. We are coming in."

"Do you require assistance docking?" asked Konii.

"We'll know when we get there," replied the *Moneylender*.

"Now where do you suppose," asked Baring-Gould, Barney's first mate, "those three cruisers came from?" He arched an eyebrow.

"Good question," said Barney.

"They're too close to Hauberk to be here by accident. In fact, this whole thing's too convenient." Baring-Gould pursed his lips. "Could be this is a trick."

Konii's angular features were bland with concentration, but Baring-Gould's words caught his attention. He looked up briefly. "That would explain the static. The transmission made no mention of a damaged communications system. There's no other reason for their transmission to break up, unless someone thought it would sound more convincing."

"Umm." Barney was digesting his crew's speculations. The process was not swift. His thoughts moved slowly, but like the proverbial elephant, he seldom forgot a detail once he had digested it. "Pull the log on the last part of the Hauberk mess. Run it for references to a RAM backup."

"Aye, sir," replied Konii. "You will be within visual range of Hauberk station in five point three minutes," he said to the *Moneylender*, then switched his attention to Barney's order. He called up the computer log, coded in the search procedure, and waited.

"They're within sensor range," stated Baring-Gould. "Instruments confirm three RAM third-raters. One is wallowing."

"Bad sign," stated Barney.

"Sir," said Konii, "there's a reference on the disks from Hauberk's communications center. Apparently they had a surveillance monitor set up for Kane. They made disks of his transmissions. RAM told him they were sending in back-up—three third-raters."

"So." Barney glared at the viewscreen, as yet innocent of the approaching vessels. "Same ships," he stated.

"Guessing, sir?" asked Konii innocently.

Barney did not miss the slight. "Fact," he stated. "No time for other ships to reach us. Besides, there's three."

"A remarkable coincidence," agreed Konii.

"It's got to be a trick," said Baring-Gould. He drummed his long fingers on the smooth, translucent housing of the weapons console.

Barney regarded the three pinpricks moving across the radar detector. "Pull back," he said. "Out of sight."

"You want space?" asked Baring-Gould.

Barney nodded.

"But what kind of trick?" asked Konii. "What can he gain? There's nothing left of Hauberk."

"Mmmm," growled Barney. His slow mind was puzzling over the question. He could see no advantage to be gained by the RAM ships' current actions. With nothing to gain, the distress call became more credible, but the ships had to be Kane's back-up, and that made them dangerous. He wished momentarily for Captain Rogers's instincts. He had a sixth sense about the enemy's motivations.

"*Moneylender*," said Konii, still using his professional space-traffic controller's voice, "we have you on visual. Estimated arrival at Hauberk station in three minutes. Please prepare for docking on section eighty-four. I say again, section eighty-four. If you need assistance, please advise."

"This is *Moneylender*," said the approaching vessel. The static in its transmission had cleared. "We are on course. Docking procedures are operational."

Konii was frowning. "Something's different."

"What?" Barney's rumble sounded in Konii's ear as the captain leaned forward in his chair.

Konii fiddled with a series of white knobs. "I'm not sure, sir."

"Vessels on course," said Baring-Gould. "Their trajectory puts them to the far side of section eighty-four."

Barney watched as the two operational cruisers flanked their injured cousin. The disabled ship rolled in space, but maintained its heading. "Konii?" asked Barney.

"I'm still trying to pin it down, sir. *Moneylender*, you are cleared for docking. Do you require medical assistance?"

"Negative, Hauberk. Life-support barely functional. Crew surviving."

"Functional is a kind word," said Baring-Gould. He was monitoring the ship's vital signs. "They've barely got breathable atmosphere."

Barney watched as the three ships approached the station. His own vessel hovered kilometers from Hauberk, its camouflaging star field masking its location. As the RAM cruisers neared Hauberk, the two escort vessels angled away from their fellow with short bursts of their landing thrusters. The injured ship continued straight for the station.

"Sir," said Konii, "I think I'm talking to a computer!"

"So?" said Barney. Computers were the alternate race of the twenty-fifth century. It was not unusual to find them performing any task.

"There's no inflection, no variation. This is a temporary program. That ship is a drone!"

"*Free Enterprise*, come in! Come in! This is Hauberk station!" The space station's jury-rigged communications link was weak, and the RAM technician's frantic voice was peppered witn static.

"This is *Free Enterprise*," answered Arak Konii.

The disinterest in Konii's voice fed the panic in the station's communications officer. "That cruiser is going to ram us! It's activated rear docking thrusters, and its trajectory puts it in the center of section eighty-four. I've tried to raise her, and nothing!"

Barney's hand crashed down on the communications console embedded in the arm of his command chair. He saw tons of prime salvage about to be destroyed. "*Moneylender*, this is Black Barney." The name was fearsome. Any sane commander would have halted at the name alone, but the RAM cruiser roared purposefully toward Hauberk. "Assume docking mode or we'll blast you out of the quadrant."

"Too late." The silky voice floated out of the communications station melodically.

"Who in sweet hades are you?" Konii's usually unflappable facade was surprised into an exclamation.

"Armageddon Ochnan, commander of the RAM cruiser *Balaclava*. Blast our drone out of space? Be my guest. Your efforts should add immeasurably to the damage."

"Mrrr." The tone of Barney's short growl was a signal his bridge crew had learned to respect. As one man, their heads swiveled toward him. Barney glared at the tableau unfolding in front of him. RAM's Trojan Horse was within kilometers of Hauberk. In seconds, it would strike the station's unprotected skin, pierce it, and end the lives of the RAM and NEO survivors clustered there. It would also strike the largest auxiliary generator and start a chain reaction of explosions that would blow the station apart like a child's popcorn blocks. Hundreds of thousands of dolas in salvage would be reduced to microscopic bits. Barney's crystal eyes narrowed. "Get him," he said, the order a rumble of malevolence.

"Deactivate star field," said Baring-Gould. "Bring her about, heading twenty-four point oh-five. Ahead full docking thrusters. Prepare for quarter throttle. Target main forward lasers." Barney's first mate snapped out the commands with the automatic precision of long practice.

The star field melted away as the *Free Enterprise* swung around and headed for the RAM vessel. The pirate ship's speed jumped as it cut in its main engines, and its dark bulk shot forward like the legendary killer whale. The RAM commander laughed, the sound echoing from the communications link in a mocking cacophony. He hit his lasers, and the pulses of deadly light sought out Barney's ship.

The *Free Enterprise* shot a cloud of golden chaff into *Balaclava*'s face, and the RAM ship's lasers dissipated harmlessly. As Barney's ship flew into its own protective camouflage in pursuit of the enemy, the *Moneylender* struck Hauberk. The panic-stricken screams of Hauberk's staff were a pathetic squawk on Konii's sixth communication channel. Then they were cut off. The drone drove deep into the wounded space station, tearing into its vitals with all the power of the cruiser's massive engines. When it struck the auxiliary generators, the station bucked, rolling in space. The initial explosion was a catalyst, lighting the fuses of a hundred more. As Barney sent a laser charge into the *Balaclava*'s forward shields, Hauberk station disintegrated.

The once-invincible computer lock was reduced to a tidal wave of rubble. The largest recognizable sections were no more than ten meters across. Most of the debris was space dust. The expanding momentum of the explosion sent the wave out from it in all directions. It overtook Barney and the two remaining RAM ships, overwhelming them. The ships' shielding deflected the larger sections, but the debris acted as concentrated chaff, confusing sensors and making targeting impossible.

Barney cursed in a low growl as he watched the RAM vessels veer away from the destruction. He could barely see them on his main viewer. Interference was so heavy, the ships looked as if they were sailing through orange and golden snow. "Keep on them!" Barney ordered.

Konii was frantically adjusting his instruments. "We've lost communications, sir! This stuff is jamming transmissions."

Baring-Gould shook his head. "I can't see them, sir." Barney's look would have made a Viking quail, and his first mate ducked under the impact of his captain's temper, but his voice held firm. "There's nothing I can do, sir. The sensors might as well have been shot out!"

Barney's cybernetic hand jerked up in a universal gesture of frustration, the shining metal and plastic components making it a colorful flash. He sank back in his command chair. "Hit 'em anyway," he rumbled.

Baring-Gould obligingly pushed the lasers, but the shots sank into the thick soup and disappeared.

Anger sounded in Barney's huge chest like distant thunder. It was an emotional expression he followed with a single word. "Out!" he said.

Baring-Gould's fingers raced over computer keys, asking for the quickest trajectory to clear space. The coordinates came up, and he locked them in, executed the course, and replied, "Accomplished, sir."

The *Free Enterprise* shifted its streamlined bulk and swam for calmer waters. As the ship rose above the edge of the debris, Barney muttered, "Captain won't like it. Lost his prize."

The words were whispered, but easily audible to his crew. Konii, his back to his commander, smiled. There was hesitation in Barney's voice. Konii en-

joyed the master pirate's discomfiture. He thought
with relish of the punishment Buck Rogers might
mete to the most ruthless profiteer in the solar system. Barney had no hesitation in terrorizing his
crew, and when the shoe was on the other foot, they
were unsympathetic.

○   ○   ○   ○   ○

Ardala Valmar veiled her lovely eyes and chewed
daintily on her lower lip. Her perfect, pearl-white
teeth emphasized her dark red mouth. She had piled
her ebony hair on top of her head in a crown of glossy
curls. Her high, wide cheekbones were shadowed like
a piece of sculpture, her neck a white column rising
from creamy shoulders. She wore a dress like a black
spider web. It clustered over her full breasts and followed her body, a provocative sheath that allowed
tantalizing hints of white skin to peep through.
Knots of glittering diamonds adorned her ears, and a
single pear-shaped stone dangled from a silvery
chain and nestled in symbolic promise between her
breasts.

Cornelius Kane enjoyed the presentation on his
communications monitor. He especially enjoyed the
knowledge it was created for his benefit. Ardala
wanted something.

Ardala Valmar was an information broker. She was
superbly suited for her profession, with ties to the
Martian royal family and a ruthless disposition. She
would sell her mother—or anything else—for a hint of
profit. Kane smiled, knowing that Ardala's bargains,
while as advantageous as she could make them, were
often creative, as well. She drew her long legs up and
curled into her leather chair. The movement caused
the slit in her dress to part, revealing white thigh.

"Ardala, my love. What a pleasure," came Kane's
strong, clear voice.

"Kane." Ardala's voice made his name sound like a caress.

"To what do I owe this visitation?" Kane asked. His green eyes were calculating.

"Why, Kane! I've been longing for your company." Ardala lowered her eyelids, her curling lashes fluttering. It was blatant flattery. She found Killer Kane a distinct challenge. The best pilot and strategist NEO ever trained, he had defected to RAM in pursuit of his own goals. He had a stubborn independent streak she could not control. It made him maddeningly attractive. He was susceptible to her physical allure, and she used it without reservation whenever she wanted his compliance. In the back of her mind lurked the hope it might one day break him to her will.

"No doubt." Kane's cryptic smile was charming.

Ardala pouted. Her red mouth pursed in an undelivered kiss. "I haven't heard from you in ages!" she cooed.

"Should you have?" Kane lounged casually in his office chair.

"You go off and have horribly dangerous adventures, then refuse to tell me anything about them."

"Adventures?" Kane feigned innocence. He and Ardala knew each other's games. They derived considerable enjoyment from these fencing matches.

"You led the strike force to support Hauberk station," she said, pointing at him.

"I did?" Kane's arched, dark eyebrows rose dramatically.

"I have it on good authority." Ardala leaned forward, and the dress clung to her body, protesting the strain. "Why won't you tell me about it? My life is so dull."

Kane laughed, genuinely amused. "Dull? Ardala, you have more excitement in a single day than most people do in a lifetime."

"But," she said, her tilting brown eyes opening wide, "I *love* combat."

"I remember." There was a touch of humor in Kane's voice, but a light of interest grew in his sea-green eyes. "Your good authority must have told you I am under orders by RAM Central's board to hold my tongue."

"But not to me. Never to me." Ardala's voice was soft.

"Oh, my lovely, especially to you. You are a dangerous woman." He shifted slightly in his chair.

Ardala paused, her wide, brown eyes limpid pools of invitation.

"No," said Kane. "Not even for you. I value my life."

A flicker of vexation darkened the depths of her eyes, but Ardala quelled it. She knew better than to let her temper rule in a contest with Kane. He won decisively whenever she vented it.

Kane saw her annoyance, even on the computer screen. From the Mark of Kane, his fortress on Luna, he was physically secure from her blandishments. Ardala's base, a gambling casino in the asteroid belt, provided a comfortable cushion for their relationship. He decided to throw her a crumb. "Besides, there wasn't much to interest you in that conflict."

"There was Deering." The softness melted from Ardala's voice as she uttered Wilma's name.

"Ah, yes." Kane's response was light, though Wilma's name twisted inside him. His feelings for her were still at the center of his shuttered heart. "She did you a disservice, as I recall."

Ardala blinked slowly. When her eyelids lifted, the annoyance was gone. She did not reply to Kane's comment. Instead, she amplified her interest. "There was Rogers."

"Buck Rogers." Kane acknowledged the name with a clenched fist.

"Do I detect grudging admiration?" Ardala asked.

"Hardly," replied Kane. "Perhaps respect. He's a pilot, pure and simple."

Ardala pondered Kane's statement. A pilot. Kane was the ultimate pilot, a daredevil who could fly any ship and make it sing. His statement was praise. It almost made Rogers an equal. "That good?"

Kane waved a finger at her. "Naughty," he said. "You're trying to trick me. Is that any way to treat a friend?"

The corners of Ardala's mouth lifted. "What would our pas de deux be without surprises?"

The memory of certain specific surprises warmed Kane's response. "You may as well give up. I am not going to give you any details about Hauberk station. You'll have to piece together what you can from local space gossip."

"Then tell me about Rogers. Not his silly strategic moves, but his personality. Surely that won't violate your directives."

Kane shrugged. The movement lifted his broad shoulders. "What can I say? I've never met the man."

"You fought him!" Ardala's exasperation was beginning to boil.

"I did? As I remember, I had some brief words with him. He was rude. He refuses to accept reality. All those years in suspended animation must have addled his brains."

Ardala frowned. "You mean he lives in a fantasy world? I find that hard to believe." Ardala was not telling Kane how Rogers duped her into selling him the plans to Hauberk's shielding, which eventually led to the station's collapse. She had identified her customer, Hart, by checking his vital signs against her computer records. Eventually, the computer found a match with Buck Rogers. In view of Hauberk's defeat, her dealings with him were a distinct embarrassment, one she intended to bury.

"He does not acknowledge his position. RAM is the power in the solar system, not NEO. No single defeat can change that."

Ardala moved, and the network of delicate filaments in her dress moved with her. "We need to compare notes," she said softly. "About Rogers."

"My dear," said Kane—he enjoyed patronizing her—"what can you possibly tell me about Captain Rogers?"

"You may be in for another surprise," Ardala informed him.

"That's always possible. Perhaps something can be arranged . . . if you are so inclined." Kane did not intend to risk an interview with Ardala without benefit to himself. Their liaisons were characteristically brief and volatile, whetting both their appetites while reinforcing a basic distrust.

"I am always . . . inclined," she replied, "for a man called Killer."

Chapter 3

It was late afternoon in the great hall of Chicagorg's RAM headquarters. The room was a standard feature of every major RAM installation. Fully one-third of the building's ground floor, it was a featureless triangular box with a computer screen filling one wall. The floor and walls were anonymous shades of gray plasticrete. It was rapidly filling with RAM workers. The squat, four- to five-foot gennies poured into the room in a purposeful rush. All were male. They were used to being herded, and there was no dawdling. The flick of a supervisor's lash had conditioned them to instant obedience, but at this meeting there were no supervisors. The Terrine guards stationed at the doors were the only signs of RAM's authority. The last worker entered the hall, his flat face with its receding forehead a mask of worry. The guards pulled the heavy doors shut behind him.

As they had been taught, the workers squatted on

the floor and turned their primitive faces to the computer screen. The gennies were heavily line bred for uniform type. The family resemblance of the thousands of faces was uncanny. Their broad, heavy frames had more than four times the strength of an unaltered human's. Their skin tones were varying shades of opaque gray. They resembled chimpanzees, but it was rumored they were actually backcrossed humans, selected for the characteristics of that sturdy ancestor of Homo sapiens, the Neanderthal. They looked it.

On the computer screen, the last of the RAM supervisors and executives could be seen departing Earth. Their ships were sealed as the workers watched. There was fear on the gennies' faces. What were they to do? They had been bred by RAM, every waking moment of their lives ordered by it. Now they were alone. The huge building was empty. There was no one to tell them what to do, where to go. They watched the screen dumbly, their restricted minds waiting for direction.

As the ships lifted from the planet, a prerecorded message cut into the transmission.

"Workers of RAM." The voice was sonorous. The face that accompanied it was the epitome of Martian male beauty. Elongated, aquiline, with large eyes and a ruddy complexion, it was meant to emphasize the distance between the ugly inferior and its genetic superior. It was carefully designed by RAM main to be the Chicagorg workers' link to the corporate structure. They did not know Maach was a computer-generated facade.

"We have been forced to abandon our holdings to the NEO terrorists. They have made it impossible to continue our operations on Earth. Our assets will not fall into their hands. We are therefore forced to cut back."

There was a heavy clang as the flak locks on the room's two entrances fell into place.

"We regret the necessity for termination, but there is no other alternative," finished Maach.

From the innocent-looking baseboards that ran around the room at the juncture of wall and floor came a sibilant hiss. The workers looked at each other, questions in their piggy eyes. The first victim collapsed without a sound, but his death sent a surge of adrenaline through the crowd, a surge that fought off the effects of the deadly gas long enough for one wail of anguish. The collective scream shook the building.

The Terrine guards stationed at the doors looked at each other. They were gennies, too, engineered for combat. "Put the little grunts out of their misery," said one.

"Kinder," agreed the other with a sage nod of his head.

It did not occur to either that they might meet the same fate at RAM's hands.

"What about the females?" asked the first guard. "Back at the barracks, alone." The guard grinned. "They're ugly as sin, but they're active."

"Like rabbits. And free. Cheapskate."

The first guard shrugged.

Inside the assembly room, the ceiling panels slid back. There was a vibrating hum as the disintegrators were activated and the room was bathed in eerie, purple light. It flowed over the twisted, distorted corpses, their eyes popping with horror, their screaming mouths stretched wide. Wherever the purple light touched, flesh melted. Soon there was no evidence of holocaust but three inches of fine, gray dust on the floor.

The purple light faded, the ceiling panels slid back, and the automatic vacuum system, detecting dirt, activated. Its "whooshing" rush sucked away the remains of lot sixty-four, four thousand male RAM workers. Across the planet, similar scenes were being played out in every major RAM headquarters. In a matter of hours, the RAM work force on the planet was cut in half. It was a sacrifice, but it made it impossible for NEO to pick up the reins of RAM industry.

The sound of the vacuums ceased, and the Terrines relaxed. Their job was finished. "I still can't believe RAM gave up so easy," said the first guard.

"Phhhh." His companion blew air threw his closed lips in disgust. "You got to take precautions. That's what they say. Show Earth there are going to be consequences. I say they didn't lose much. They've still got the females and young. Import a few studs, and you'd have the workers up to production level in two years."

"Maybe." The first Terrine stretched. "Just glad its not my responsibility. We're due back at eighteen hundred. We've got an hour. Want a break?"

The second Terrine grinned. "Why not?" he said.

The Terrines headed down the corridor toward the worker barracks.

O O O O O

Black Barney's ship cleared the wave of chaff that had once been Hauberk station. He sat brooding in his command chair, a mountain of introverted muscle. He slumped. His black body armor cut into his armpits. It was uncomfortable, but he was too contrary to move. His crew knew better than to bother him in such a mood. When Edward the Red's excited voice penetrated his depression, Barney's attention was immediately caught. He leaned forward, one huge hand open to strike the offender's mouth shut, when Edward's words registered on his slow mind.

"Sir! I picking up a lot of chatter. It's RAM! And whatever it is, it's big!"

Barney's hand stopped in midswing.

"On sensors," contributed Baring-Gould. "Faint but coming fast. It's a huge strike force. Looks like it's out of Mars."

"Configuration!" snapped Barney.

"Looks like twenty battlers. Each one's surrounded by fighters. There must be at least two wings per ship."

"Activate star field. Have they picked us up?"

"No telling, sir. If they have, we're small potatoes. They're not changing course. Star field activated," finished Baring-Gould.

"Range?"

"About two thousand kilometers."

"Can we get out of here?" Barney knew the feeling of being stuck between a rock and a hard place, and he didn't like it.

"Negative. Not without attracting notice. We'd have to go to full power, and that drains the star field. They'd be sure to pick up the fluctuation. Sir, their present course puts them right on top of us."

"Get us out of the way," ordered Barney, "then hold firm." Barney's hands gripped the arms of his chair. They fit into old gouges from his powerful fingers. He rubbed the smooth metal absently.

The RAM fleet swept toward them, its speed and power awesome. As the *Free Enterprise* shifted position, Barney got a better view of the oncoming vessels. The battlers were standard RAM issue, but on this trip they were weighed down by cargo. Strapped along the sides and top of each ship were extra fuel canisters. On top of the backswept wings were flattened lines of folded silver pipe. These were retractable space docks, emergency issue for dealing with disabled vessels. Barney suspected they now had a different function. Coupled to the underside of the vessels was spare armament in the form of directional missiles. Each of the fighters carried four similar missiles.

"Shock Invaders," said Barney. His fingers cut new gouges in his chair.

Baring-Gould sat back, startled. "Shock Invaders? I thought they were a myth."

Barney gestured to the screen. "Haven't needed them here, not with Hauberk to keep things under wraps. Saw 'em once off the belt."

"If they're Shock Invaders, then each one of those battlers is carrying enough fuel and extra firepower to keep those fighters in the air for days."

"And extra pilots, spacers—everything you need to run a war."

"Not war," rumbled Barney, his heavy baritone echoing in the enclosed chamber. "Execution."

"Got their key personnel off Earth, and now they're teaching her a lesson," said Baring-Gould, the implications dawning on him.

"Right." Barney clutched the arms of his chair, and the dents deepened. The ships were almost on them. If Baring-Gould's calculations were accurate, twenty kilometers would separate the *Free Enterprise* and the enemy fleet. "Maintenance power only. Cut all unnecessary systems."

The *Free Enterprise* went into hibernation. It was a specialist at this game. A pirate vessel had to be. Its engines barely vibrated, keeping it in orbit and maintaining life-support. The star field ran off its own generator, and that continued pumping full power into the protective camouflage.

The RAM fleet approached like a school of predatory scarlet fish, their heavy contours powering forcefully through space, dart-quick schools of fighters surging protectively around them. The flaming red hulls of the RAM ships were a bright contrast to the darkness of space. They closed on Barney's ship hungrily.

Instinctively the pirates rocked back in their seats as the Shock Invaders flashed by. No crew member spoke. The only sound aboard the *Free Enterprise* was the gentle hum of its engines, and the communication between the members of the RAM strike force. Their voices cut back and forth on the communications board, disembodied and flat. No ship deviated from its course. No shot was fired. It took five minutes for the fleet to pass, even at supersonic speeds.

When the last vessel cleared their position, Barney let out a breath like a gasping whale. "Don't even care if they're heard!" he snarled. The insult was palpable. "Damn sight sure of themselves!"

"Sir, they're splitting up." Konii cocked his head, eyeing the tracking chart.

Edward cupped a hand around one earphone. "Looks like they're going to hit the major cities," he added.

"What about the stationary missile sites, the Terrine bases?" Barney asked.

"They don't seem to be on the program, sir. Only the cities," answered Edward.

"Mrrrr. Captain's in Chicagorg."

The crew was silent. They were not about to volunteer their lives to rescue Buck Rogers.

"I said," Barney repeated heavily, "the Cap'n is in Chicagorg!" He slammed a fist into his other hand.

Baring-Gould took the hint. "Course locked in, sir. We'll approach on the same trajectory as RAM. If we're lucky, we won't get noticed."

"Umm," muttered Barney. He was cogitating a strike of his own.

O O O O O

Huer.dos stopped in midelectronic stride. Buck's appearance at the Chicagorg congress gave Huer the perfect excuse to indulge in a visit with RAM main's Chicagorg computer. Of course, the Chicagorg computer was not aware of its hospitality. Huer was happily poking through its programs, cloaking his operations under the guise of RAM's final security check, when faint military chatter caught his attention.

As Buck Rogers's computerized mentor and bodyguard, he was acutely interested in RAM's military plans. He skipped circuits until he reached the center of the activity, and eavesdropped shamelessly. At first, the chatter was meaningless, but as he sorted through the codes, he realized he was listening to a RAM strike force. They were not scrambling their transmissions.

Huer's thoughts puckered as he tried to sort out the implications. It was evident, both from the chatter and the increasing clarity of the transmissions, the force was nearing Earth. From his present position, he had no way of telling how many vessels were involved, but the number of commanders ensured a large force. They were cocky. They didn't care if Earth knew they were coming. That could mean one thing alone: the invasion was substantial, both in size and power.

Huer switched to an outbound channel, coded in that day's NEO emergency warning override, and aimed for Buck's personal communicator. He was met with a squeal that sent him recoiling, his impulses jangled. He cleared the disturbance and tried again, this time careful to sidestep the transmission. The same electronic squeal bounced back at him. He tried once more, on a different line, aimed at Beowulf's podium terminal, but the squeal screeched again.

Something was blocking transmissions into the Congress, creating a wall of interference he could not penetrate. His friend, Buck Rogers, was caught behind it, like a fox in a trap. Many of NEO's most competent leaders were caught with him, and RAM was coming in for the kill. Huer.dos began to panic.

Chapter 4

The RAM fleet of Shock Invaders swept toward Earth. Like the Nazi blitzkrieg, it was designed to strike its targets like a lightning bolt, overwhelming everything in its path with numbers and firepower. Unlike its ancient counterpart, the Shock Invaders could maintain an assault for days, their floating supply depots providing fuel and weapons.

The fleet approached the planet's hazy outer blanket. Twenty kilometers from measurable atmosphere, the formation broke into twenty individual assault teams. They whirled away from each other in a spiraling arc, fanning out on their respective preprogrammed courses. As Huer had discovered, RAM was making no secret of its intent. Consequently, they found the airways remarkably clear of traffic. An unlucky tug ran across the flight line of one unit, which blasted it out of existence without acknowledging its presence.

"Base Fourteen, this is Flight Leader Fourteen. Come in," said the unit's commander.

"Flight Leader Fourteen, this is base. Nice shooting."

"It was good target practice," returned the commander.

"Fourteen, we are altering course two degrees. Do you copy?"

"Acknowledged." The commander adjusted his course, and the flight followed suit. "My tracking shows we will contact the target in two minutes."

"Negative, flight leader. Our course change adds thirty seconds to that. We are coming up on Chicagorg from the north. Adjust your program." The cruiser's communications officer was curt. There was no margin for error in Operation Hammer. The unit reported directly to RAM's patriarch, Simund Holzerhein.dos. Even now, his circuits were linked to all transmissions from the strike force.

"I copy." Fourteen, his mouth set in a grim line, adjusted the computer codes. He hated the bureaucratic outlook that meant he would be thrown curves at the last minute just to preserve some paper-pusher's idea of security. Combat was no place to play games.

True, RAM intelligence put NEO's own devastating—if small—band of pilots out of the immediate picture. After Hauberk, NEO's ships had submerged like sounding whales, vanishing without trace. Though their open communications channels were a momentary warning, the Shock Invaders had little fear of a handful of fighters, no matter how fast or powerful.

The fighters skimmed the upper atmosphere, their burdened battler flying above them in the freedom of space. "You are on target," stated Base Fourteen. Proceed with the operation. There's a bonus from Holzerhein in it if you do the job right."

"We always do the job right," responded Flight Leader Fourteen. "See you." It was fortunate for him that the cruiser's communications officer could not see the rude gesture the pilot made as he replied.

The flight dropped away from its cruiser, diving through the slick upper atmosphere at just below Mach 1. The fighters' speeds did not slacken as they hit the heavy, pollution-filled air near the planet's surface. The engines whined as they fed more power into the little craft. Though no match for the experimental Kraits in a one-on-one contest, the fighters were fast. They far outclassed the patched-together retreads that made up most of NEO's airborne fighting force. They had no fear of harassment, and today there was no one to teach them more respect.

They hit Chicagorg like a screaming wall of fire. Sweeping over the city, they blanketed it with laser pulses, aiming especially for the solar hookups that were Chicagorg's main power source. When a laser hit one of those electrical connections, it wrought more devastation than the simple cessation of power to a portion of the city. The disconnected cables were live, whirling in the air like manic snakes. They sent up showers of sparks, and whatever tinder they touched burst into flame. Within minutes, Chicagorg was a smoking bonfire.

The flight split over the abandoned RAM headquarters, leaving it and its direct power lines unscathed, then swept on over the city, continuing its first run. Once complete, they angled back, this time heading for specific targets. RAM had a great advantage in having occupied Earth in a position of absolute power for so many years. It had detailed plans of the planet's most critical strategic assets. The flight broke into three consecutive waves, which launched missiles preprogrammed for known NEO meeting places. Occasionally a pilot got lucky and hit a NEO weapons cache, which went up with a cloud of black smoke and a hail of debris.

Three of the ships veered off from their fellows, heading for a remote section of the city. Terrine intelligence had placed a major gathering of NEO leaders at an underground base near the lakefront. The fighters were to contain that group by destroying the perimeter of the target. They dove for the coordinates, released their missiles, and pulled up. The missiles spread into a rectangular flight pattern, striking in a phalanx of destruction. There were a rapid series of explosions that rocked the earth, blowing blocks of rubble into pebbles.

Outside RAM headquarters, Chicagorg had few buildings rising higher than three stories. Most of those were not intact, but decaying shells in which the local population lived like rats. Now RAM was reducing even those structures to street level. Strike after strike pounded at the city. The zinging pulses of lasers and the heavy explosions of missiles drowned out the screams of the dying.

○ ○ ○ ○ ○

". . . I conclude that you need the Terrines. You need me. We must work together to preserve order." Kelth Smirnoff's voice rang in the cavernous hall.

"Your plea has been eloquent," replied Beowulf. "More so than I would have imagined, but the assembly has not been swayed by it. I am afraid, sir, NEO cannot trust you or your soldiers. You may be loyal, but you are without conscience and heart, and that frightens us."

Smirnoff stood at ease in the center of the dais. The ill will of his audience did not bother him. "I am sorry you feel that way, but perhaps it is just as well."

Beowulf opened his mouth to reply as the first missile struck. The thunder of its explosion was deafening, and bits of plaster sifted from the ceiling.

Beowulf closed his mouth, swallowed, and yelled above the noise. "Evasive! Evasive!"

The delegates tripped over each other getting out of their seats. Smirnoff, still standing imperturbably at the front of the room, smiled at their panic. So, he thought, this is NEO. This is the hope of the world. They run like sheep, falling over each other, without discipline. A sneer of disgust grew on his face.

"Hold it, Heinrich." Buck Rogers's voice sounded in his left ear. He had Smirnoff in a hammer lock before his presence registered on the Terrine commander's mind.

"My name," said Smirnoff mildly, "is not Heinrich."

"I admire your grace under fire," said Buck conversationally, "but I want answers. Now!" He tightened his grip and stripped Smirnoff of his knife.

Smirnoff smiled and said nothing. The NEO delegates were heading for the rear of the hall. He would wait.

"Doc!" said Buck into the portable communicator clipped to his collar. There was no answer.

"If you're trying to access outside communications, Captain, give it up. You won't get through," said Smirnoff.

"And why is that?"

"I planned a little electronic interference," replied the Terrine. The cramped position was becoming more painful, but he remained quiescent.

The missiles were creating a thunderous wave of movement in the loosely packed rubble that made up the ground. The heavy steel beams in the chamber creaked under the strain. The sound of the explosions roared around them, and plaster dust fell like rain.

"Buck! We've got to get out of here!" yelled Wilma above the noise. "This whole place could go!"

"What about Percy, here?" asked Buck, swinging Smirnoff to face her.

"Bring him along," said Beowulf. "He might come in handy."

Buck gave Smirnoff a shove, and the Terrine grunted in pain as he moved forward. "Where are we going?" he asked.

"Out," said Buck succinctly.

"That won't be very safe," replied Smirnoff.

"It's a lot safer than having a ton of rock fall on you," said Wilma, shoving aside a fallen hunk of ceiling with one foot. "We've got a clear one!" she called over her shoulder. She stopped at the fine line that marked an open five-meter modular section of floor. "Rabbit hole!" she shouted, and the floor began to recede.

"Let's get out of here!" said Beowulf as the ceiling creaked above him.

"I think that might be a bit difficult," returned Smirnoff, seeing that his plan was succeeding.

Pointing directly at the NEOs' midsections were four laser rifles in the hands of four Terrine guards. The gennies were so huge that their heads and shoulders rose out of the tunnel, a hole in which Buck could have stood upright unseen.

From the back of the room, Buck heard a cry of anguish. Similar scenes were being played out throughout the erstwhile Hall of Freedom. Buck took a calculating look at Smirnoff, then at the four Terrines, and decided he had nothing to lose. "Get out of there," he ordered the guards, "or I'll break your precious commander's neck."

The rifles lowered a notch, uncertain. Buck was running a bluff that could backfire if Smirnoff decided to sacrifice his life for the RAM cause. His men were perfectly capable of shooting him as well as his captors. Fortunately, Smirnoff was much too selfish for such a sacrifice. "Out!" he ordered the Terrines.

Two of the Terrines lowered their weapons and levered themselves out of the pit. Then they retrieved their rifles and held them on Buck, Wilma, and Beowulf while the other two did likewise.

"Throw your weapons down the tunnel," ordered Buck.

"Do it!" Smirnoff's reinforcement brought action. The rifles thudded on the tunnel's dirt floor as the Terrines followed Buck's orders.

"Now back off!" Buck's voice was sharp as he positioned Smirnoff in front of the three NEO leaders.

The four giants moved back, their eyes on Smirnoff's face. They would not move without his orders, and Smirnoff knew it. Rogers was a prize he hated to lose, but he would regret the loss of his life even more. He had no illusions about Buck's ability to carry out his earlier threat.

"Wilma, Beowulf, get going," said Buck tersely.

Wilma jumped into the tunnel and picked up a rifle. Beowulf followed her, shouldered a weapon, and moved down the tunnel without a word. He was an old hand at this. Wilma kicked the other rifles aside. "Come on, Buck," she said, her rifle trained on the Terrines. She stood six inches below the roof of the receding tunnel, but the Terrines were so huge she could still get a clear shot at them.

"Do we need a hostage?" Beowulf asked.

Wilma shook her head. "He'd be more bother than use."

"Sorry to hit and run," said Buck, shoving Smirnoff from him and delivering a solid punch to the back of the man's neck. Smirnoff crumpled to the concrete floor, and Buck dove for the tunnel. He hit the dirt floor rolling. Wilma fired the laser rifle, sending out a stream of flak. It was diffused by the chaff components in the Terrines' uniforms, but the flashes were blinding at such close range, and they could not see her aim. They kept their distance as the floor rolled back into place over the tunnel.

Buck and Wilma followed Beowulf down the tunnel, Wilma trotting backward. When they were thirty meters from the floor entrance, Wilma stopped. She could hear the Terrines pounding at the floor. With their strength, it would not be long before they tore the panels up. She lifted the laser rifle to her shoulder, aimed at a white X on the wall at the end of the tunnel, and fired. The wall exploded in a shower of earth, burying the entrance.

The explosion catapulted Wilma backward, and she crashed into Buck, sending them both to the ground. Buck caught her as they fell.

"Why, Wilma," he said softly. "You're so impulsive." He ran a gentle hand down one leg, a twinkle in his blue eyes.

Wilma shoved him away. "You are incorrigible!" she said, rolling to her feet.

"I know," replied Buck. "It's part of my charm."

"Are you going to get up, or are you going to lie there all day and let the Terrines dig you up?" Her words were acid, but Wilma's hazel eyes were laughing. Buck was definitely a pleasing sight, even with dirt in his sandy hair and a smudge on the side of his face. "Come on!" She held out a hand.

Buck took it, his eyes full of fun. Their narrow escape sent the adrenaline charging through him, and the light of it was in his eyes. For a moment, Wilma was afraid he might pull her down, but Beowulf's voice cut into their exchange.

"Hurry up, you two. I'm going to need a pilot to get back to Salvation!"

Buck grinned as Wilma pulled him to his feet.

Buck and Wilma caught up with Beowulf as he trotted down the tunnel. It was a tall corridor, braced with wood beams reinforced with metal clamps and posts. The narrow passageway was built for one man. Beowulf, Wilma, and Buck went single file, Beowulf in the lead and setting the pace.

"How far have we got to go?" asked Buck. The soft

glow of the "solar" light spots turned his sandy hair golden.

"About a quarter-mile," Beowulf panted, his pace steady. His position with NEO was now more administrative than active, and he was out of condition.

"Have you got any idea where this one comes up?" asked Wilma. She was loping behind him, her stride an easy swing.

"Uh-uh. I'd say we're heading southwest, though."

"You mean you've got a security installation like that hall, and you don't know where the exits are?" Buck could hardly believe it, though it showed only in his voice.

"There are two hundred tunnels coming off the assembly hall, and they each have their own exit. They fan out in all directions," said Wilma between breaths. "Impossible to keep them all in your head unless you're stationed here, and we're not."

"Which brings up . . . another question," puffed Beowulf.

"The Terrines," Buck said heavily.

"We have a leak somewhere," confirmed Wilma, recognizing Smirnoff's treachery.

"I couldn't get through to Doc. Did you notice? All I got was static. He should have warned us about the attack." Buck's feet pounded behind Wilma as they continued on.

"So should the NEO main computer," said Wilma.

The muffled sound of an explosion made all three duck involuntarily. The blast was too far away to affect the tunnel, but the sound was RAM's laughter over their paltry feeling of freedom. The explosion echoed in their ears.

"Try him now," suggested Wilma over her shoulder.

"No!" Beowulf stopped dead, just as Buck opened his mouth to access his computerized companion.

"Why? Maybe he can help us out of this," Buck said

reasonably.

"And maybe someone is listening in on him."
Beowulf's voice was cold and suspicious.

Buck nodded slowly. "So we're on our own." He
grinned. "I was getting used to Doc; getting soft, I
guess. Do me good to handle this myself."

"But who can it be?" demanded Wilma, her hazel
eyes dark wells of concern.

"Somebody in a position to jam computer lines,"
said Buck thoughtfully as he followed his two compa-
triots down the tunnel.

"That's no . . . mean trick," said Beowulf, his shoulders now heaving from the exertion.

"You'd need a specialist, all right," agreed Wilma.

"How many've we got?" asked Buck, wiping a cob-
web from his shoulder.

"Stow the . . . chatter." Beowulf's voice was labored.
"I've got to . . . save my breath. Talk later." He forged
ahead.

The three moved purposefully through the dimly
lit passage, all deep in thought. Someone had
breached communications, destroying the first Planetary Congress. With a two-minute warning, they
might have escaped, but there had been no such
warning. Smirnoff was directly tied to that breach.
The tunnels themselves were common knowledge
among NEO officers, but the exact location of the entrances was top security. But, somehow, Smirnoff
had discovered them—another breach in security.
Ten minutes ago, Beowulf would have staked his life
on the integrity of his top officers. Now a pall of doubt
hung over NEO.

◯ ◯ ◯ ◯ ◯

Romanov giggled as it monitored communications
from Smirnoff's Terrine strike force. The Terrines
overran the Congress, capturing most of the dele-

gates. Romanov heard more than one Terrine complain about the order to kill only at extreme necessity. RAM had plans. The delegates would be much more effective weapons alive.

Masterlink's searcher program listened attentively to the conversations, straining for any reference to Buck Rogers. Its position within the NEO computer system had given it knowledge of Rogers's presence at the Chicagorg Congress. It was a hot trail Romanov pursued diligently. The restricted confines of the Congress were a perfect place to trap the slippery captain, and Romanov had gone about preparing its trap, leaving nothing to chance.

It provided Smirnoff with intelligence on the assembly hall. Romanov's position within the NEO system gave it access to such secure information. It took patience, but Romanov had been programmed with patience, to ensure the successful completion of its directive: find and destroy Buck Rogers.

Once the information was in Smirnoff's hands, Romanov knew there would be action. It prepared for that action by setting up a series of communication blocks on the assembly hall, intending to isolate the hall, allowing the Terrines to take the Congress by surprise.

It was not until the operation was well under way that Romanov picked up the order to take the delegates alive. The intelligence made it seethe with anger. Rogers must die; Romanov's programming demanded it. The searcher pulsed angrily as the Terrines exploded into the hall.

It sent out sparks when it heard the exchange between Smirnoff and Rogers. Rogers was not supposed to have the upper hand. The sparks were the measure of Romanov's anger, however, and were instantly quelled. It realized it was not likely to take Rogers, and it knew it must protect the secrecy of its position inside NEO. Romanov heard Rogers leap for freedom, and it knew Masterlink had again been cheated of revenge.

In retrospect, it discovered the humor of the situation. NEO must assume a security leak within its own organization. There would be distrust and confusion as it checked every possibility. It would never occur to them to look for a traitor inside the computer. Romanov's giggle bubbled.

On a completely different line of circuits, Huer.dos caught the echo of Romanov's giggle. Frantic as he was to ascertain Buck's condition, the giggle caught his attention. It was an alien note he recognized, the voice of an assassin. He filed the knowledge for future reference and went back to trying to contact Buck. The channel was still filled with interference.

"Well, I'll be." Buck's voice was a whisper aimed at no one in particular.

Buck, Beowulf, and Wilma were flattened against the wall at the tunnel's entrance. The opening was a scant one by two meters. The floor of the tunnel had been filled with debris, blocking it, and the opening was at Buck's eye level. It had been camouflaged behind a wall of stone, but the Shock Invaders' missiles, and the impact bombs they were now dropping with dreary regularity, had crumbled the wall. A sheet of corrugated steel, probably blown from the roof of a makeshift shelter, now lay across the opening, leaving a wedge of blue sky visible. Buck's exclamation came from the sight of a Terrine heliplane rising majestically into that wedge of sky.

The Dragonfly class aircraft was close, so close the whirling rotor blades sent a cloud of ash and lightweight trash into their faces. The ship rose in the air, and the wind died. Wilma laughed softly. "This is luck," she said ironically. She turned to Beowulf. "Know where we are?"

"I'm afraid so." Beowulf brushed the soot from his hair.

"Going to let me in on it?" asked Buck mildly.

Wilma looked up at him, irony in her expression. "We are within fifty kilometers of a Terrine helipad. The place will be crawling with them."

Buck chuckled, the irony in his own voice a match for hers. "I suppose this was considered a secure cover."

"Of course," replied Beowulf. "What better way to prevent the destruction of your access routes than to run them near the Terrines? They're not going to damage their own installations.

"Anybody up there?" asked Buck. Smirnoff's Terrines must have entered the tunnel here; it stood to reason they might have posted a guard.

"Can't see anything," grumbled Beowulf. He unbuckled a portable scanner from his belt, set it for short range, gripped it by the clip, and carefully extended it out into the opening, knowing he was risking instant detection. No massive Terrine paw grabbed his hand, so he moved the scanner in a slow arc. It registered no life in the immediate area. He swung it again, crossing the first arc. There was still no sign of life. He lowered his hand. "Scanner says nothing."

Buck moved forward, directly under the edge of the overhanging metal. He kicked over a sizable chunk of rubble, braced his hands against the narrow walls, and placed one foot on the improvised step. Carefully he pushed himself up, letting his head lift the edge of the metal. It provided some cover, but it was loose, and he knew too much movement would make it slide. It was hot.

He narrowed his blue eyes against the bright sunshine. The area directly in front of him was clear. He heard no movement behind him, but the debris was so loose it would be impossible to cross silently. Evidently, the Terrines were confident of their abilities; they had left no guard. As Wilma had said, a Terrine helipad lay directly in front of him. It was unscathed by the bombing, though around it lay a flattened field of blasted, smoking plasticrete. There were pads for three Dragonflies, but two were empty. The pilot of the lone heliplane lounged in his seat, his escape door propped open with one foot. Forward of the ship's swept-back wings, the cargo doors were open, but the plane was empty. Its sleek exterior bristled with various weapons and held a fusion jet engine at the rear.

"Wilma!" whispered Buck.

The sibilant whisper brought Wilma's head even with his. She clung to his shoulder to maintain her balance.

"What do these babies carry?" he asked her quietly.

"Usually two crews," she replied, "if they're on an assault mission. One for gyro launchers and one for that small laser cannon." She pointed to a wicked-looking gun mounted on the belly of the craft. "There'll be a few men to cover the sharpshooters."

"Nobody's home." Buck's blue eyes crackled with danger.

"Probably switching crews and refueling," said Wilma slowly, anticipating his suggestion.

"No fuel lines," he said.

"Could be they're done." Wilma's reply was insinuating.

"Could be." Wilma's slim body was warm against him. She smelled of plaster dust and exertion. "You ever fly one of those things?" Buck asked, looking at Wilma, then down at Beowulf.

"Once or twice." Wilma's voice was confident.

Buck stepped down from the hunk of plasticrete he had been using as a step, taking Wilma with him. She clung to him as she found her balance. Buck held out a hand. She shrugged the laser rifle from her shoulder and handed it to him. "We've got transport, sir," she said to Beowulf.

The commander of NEO's fighting forces had watched the exchange with interest. He knew Wilma's capabilities, and he was aware of Buck's reputation. He had been around warriors all his life, and he knew he was looking at a remarkable partnership. "Lead on," he said, picking up the heavy Terrine laser rifle and standing.

Buck waited for the Shock Invaders to deliver a ground strike nearby. As the ships whined over the city, the sound of explosions neared, a crescendo of destruction. The ground shook from the impact of a strike, and clods of earth and plasticrete rained through the tunnel entrance. Buck reached up and shoved the slab of metal back, launching himself through the opening like a gyro shell. He rolled and came up in a crouch, the rifle spitting. Wilma was right behind him, her pistol drawn.

Three Terrines erupted from a plasticrete igloo that served as their command post. They dove as Buck's lasers ripped into them, saved only by their protective clothing. "Go!" shouted Buck to his comrades.

Wilma sprinted for the heliplane, firing as she ran. Her aim was off, and the lasers hit the framework of the pilot's emergency door in a blaze of light. The pilot fell back, one hand protecting his eyes, then rallied and punched the Dragonfly's ignition.

He was too late. Wilma was on him. With a practiced twist, she pulled the man from his seat. He was a Terrine specialist, smaller than his fellows to better suit his position as a pilot, but he was equally strong.

He wrenched free of Wilma's grasp and swung at her.
The blow never fell.

From across the compound, Buck had seen her
plight. He fired a swath of laser pulses at the three
Terrines, finally penetrating one man's uniform.
Badly burned, he dropped. Buck whirled and fired a
quick burst. The lightning bolt smacked into the pilot's head. He clawed forward, screaming.

Wilma jumped past him, into the pilot's seat, and
pulled the door shut. The Dragonfly was armored,
and a laser rifle would bounce harmlessly off its skin.
It took a cannon or gyro shell to pierce its tough hide.
The pilot had set the rotors thwupping idly. Wilma
revved them slowly, getting the feel of a ship she was
not used to flying. She was taut with tension. A
wrong move would send the heliplane over on its
side. The rotors whipped faster, and she screamed at
Buck. "Come on!" she called. "It's now or never!"

Beowulf, flat on his stomach beside Rogers, heard
her call. He tugged at Buck's blue uniform and
pointed at the plane. "I heard her!" yelled Buck.
"Get going! I'll cover you."

Beowulf did not argue. He rolled to his feet, sent a
parting volley at the two remaining Terrines, managed to sear the legs from under one, and ran. He
threw his rifle into the Dragonfly's cargo hold and
launched himself after it. He hit the floor with a thud
as Buck jumped for the door, caught it, and gestured
to Wilma. She nodded, and the ship began to rock as
it lifted from the ground.

The last Terrine dove for cover, knowing once they
were airborne Buck would have a clear shot at him.
Buck swung himself into the ship, anchored a leg behind a strut, and fired a parting volley at the Terrine's retreating bulk. The Dragonfly cleared the
command post, and Buck sat down. Beowulf was
clinging to a strut on the opposite side of the ship.
Buck grinned at him. "So far, so good," he said.

Chapter 5

The Dragonfly steadied as it rose. Wilma was getting the feel of it. Her experience with heliplanes was limited, and the heavy Terrine craft had a tendency to wallow. As she leveled it off, six Shock Invader craft swept over the crumbling skeletons of once-proud high-rise buildings. The noise of the heliplane's rotors masked the roar of the fighters' engines. The Shock Invader ships took Wilma by surprise, skimming dangerously close to the heliplane's whirling blades.

The backwash made the Dragonfly rock. Buck and Beowulf clung grimly to the struts as Wilma fought to control the ship.

"Clear the airways!" snapped a voice from the communications link. "This is Flight Leader Fourteen to Dragonfly B-Ninety-seven. Keep a low profile!"

Wilma had no respect for the RAM commander's orders. She sent the Dragonfly forward, slipping over the pulverized rubble that had been the center of Chicagorg, beyond the ordered confines of RAM's central complex. She had to concentrate on their position, avoiding other Terrine ships and negotiating the uneven terrain. Buck and Beowulf were not so lucky.

They were treated to a bird's-eye view of the devastation RAM was visiting on the planet. Survivors scrambled over the rubble like spiders, intent on finding refuge. Many were not that fortunate. The Dragonfly flew over a woman half buried in plasticrete. In life, she might have been pretty, but the scream frozen on her face was horrific. Children, caught in an explosion, were strewn across a street like rag dolls. Some were intact, but all that remained of many were dismembered fragments: a hand clutching a ball, a dimpled leg, a foot wrapped in rags for shoes.

Buck was reminded of films he had seen of the Second World War, and the devastation wrought by Nazi Germany on its enemies. *By his dead smile I knew we stood in Hell,* he thought.

Beowulf stared at the littered ground, his black eyes hollow. The Earth he knew was a far cry from Buck's world. He was used to fighting, used to losing, used to death. At least, he had thought he was. The magnitude of RAM's assault, the complete lack of care for a world it had milked of the last of its resources, horrified him. He knew RAM's mentality, and he knew every major city on Earth was facing similar carnage. It was the kind of attack NEO was not equipped to combat. It had neither the technology nor the manpower. RAM had both. With warning, NEO might outthink RAM, booby-trapping its targets and using its executives as hostages against them. Taken by surprise, NEO had no chance. It needed allies.

The Dragonfly cleared the outskirts of Chicagorg. The Shock Invader ships swept by once more, leaving explosions in their wake. Wilma sent the ship across the blasted plain that surrounded the city. Its emptiness was clean, the sparse tufts of grass and baked earth devoid of malice.

"We're out from under the main attack!" Wilma called.

"Get us out of here!" ordered Beowulf.

"To where?" Wilma checked her instruments to see that she hadn't been followed.

"Salvation!" cried Beowulf, who shifted his weight impatiently.

"How do you suggest I do that?" she yelled over her shoulder. "In case you haven't noticed, we're not flying a spaceworthy vehicle."

"There's an emergency airfield point two degrees west of the city, in the Chicavern!" he reminded her.

Wilma nodded acknowledgment and altered course.

"Chicavern?" Buck had never heard of it.

"A blast crater on the outskirts of the city. Rumor has it there was once a military computer network there, buried below the surface. It's been two hundred years, and the records are garbled, but my guess is RAM blew it up in the early years. Left a sizable crater." Beowulf frowned, hoping it was still intact.

"And you've got spacecraft hidden there?" Buck made his way next to the older NEO leader.

"We . . . did," said Beowulf as the heliplane arced over the Chicavern.

Marring the rounded contours of the centuries-old crater was a fresh tear in the surface. There was nothing else.

"Scratch that idea," said Buck, his baritone voice cutting through the noise of the rotors.

Wilma looked back over her shoulder. Her expression said more than any words she might have uttered.

"Just get us out of here!" Beowulf called.

She nodded and sent the craft into the countryside, allowing it to rise. They flew toward a distant hill. Wilma was heading for one of NEO's more secure hiding places. Such warrens were remote, and for that reason RAM had not bothered with them. As she came up on the hill, Wilma's spirits dropped. Rising in front of them like the hand of fate was a RAM third-rater. The cruiser's scarlet hull glowed in the sunshine. Its blunt nose swung away from the heliplane as the ship turned broadside. Wilma wrestled the Dragonfly into a turn. "Damn," she muttered.

As the heliplane turned, the cruiser's slow movement stopped dead. As Wilma pulled away from it, the cruiser sent a surge of power to its docking thrusters. It jumped in front of the Dragonfly, blocking its course.

Wilma put on the brakes, and the ship ground to a halt twenty meters from the cruiser.

"Seems like they want to powwow," said Buck. He was pulling himself into the copilot's seat.

Beowulf wondered at Buck's sometimes-odd vocabulary.

"Think again," said Wilma, trying to remain cool. "They're close enough to see I'm a woman. No woman flies a Terrine plane!"

"That red hair is a beacon," Buck admitted. "Still, we might be able to run a bluff."

"No way!"

"Why not give it a try?" asked Buck reasonably. "They haven't blasted us yet."

"I wonder why?" Wilma's question was lost as the Dragonfly jerked.

"What was that?" asked Buck, braced against the dash.

Wilma was manipulating controls, her broad forehead puckered in a frown of concentration. "Tractor beam!" she said. The rotors whirled faster as she poured power into them, and the ship quivered.

Across the way, Buck could see the cruiser's cargo doors drop. The heliplane shook as Wilma fought to break from the beam. "No use," she said. "If I push her any more, she'll break up." She cut power back to minimum and relaxed in her chair.

"That it? You giving up?" There was a challenge in Buck's voice.

"If I don't give up, this ship is going to break into small pieces and we will be very dead," she said.

"I guess you're not giving up," he said, satisfied with the spunk in her voice. "We'll get out of this."

Slowly the heliplane moved toward the cargo bay. Its rotors moved slowly, barely keeping the ship aloft. As the Dragonfly lined up with the open hatch, Wilma cut the engines.

"I guess you've done this before."

Wilma looked over at Buck. A smile pulled at the corners of her mouth. "You learn a lot of things as a pirate," she said conversationally. "Not the least of which is the ability to dock a disabled ship."

The Dragonfly was being drawn into the third-rater's dark hold. That was unusual and dangerous. Even pirates used docking lights. The bay doors clanged shut, and the three NEO survivors sat in darkness.

"Well," said Beowulf at last, his voice echoing hollowly, "we seem to be caught."

The hold lights came on abruptly, and the three closed their eyes against the glare. Buck heard the crack and splinter of tearing metal and plastiglas.

"Gotcha," said a distinctive gravelly voice.

"Barney?" asked Buck.

"Captain," Barney acknowledged, pulling again at the heliplane's door.

"What are you doing here? Not that I'm not happy to see you," said Buck.

"Saw 'em go by," grunted Barney, referring to the Shock Invaders, and evading the subject of Hauberk's destruction. He finished ripping the heli-plane's escape door off its hinges.

Wilma vaulted to the cruiser's deck, using her old employer's knee as a step. "How did you manage the paint job?" she asked. The *Free Enterprise* was painted black in the best pirate tradition, but the ship that had pulled them in was RAM scarlet.

"Rigged the star field," said Barney. "Konii got it to go red."

"It sure worked," said Buck as Beowulf appeared in the plane's doorway, "but why didn't you contact us?"

"RAM," replied Barney succinctly.

Beowulf, regarding the gigantic pilot from the Dragonfly's cockpit doorway, nodded. "Shock Invaders all over the place," he said.

"Couldn't risk it," grumbled Barney, glowering from under his shock of dark hair.

Beowulf regarded the pirate. He had never met Barney face to face, but the gennie's reputation was far exceeded by his presence. Barney's glance swept the commander of NEO's military forces up and down, found him wanting, and turned to his captain, Buck.

"Take us out of here, Barney," Buck ordered.

"Salvation?" the pirate asked.

"Right."

Beowulf clambered from the heliplane's cockpit and dropped to the deck. "Make sure you get into Salvation without being seen," he cautioned. "This is one time we can't afford to make mistakes."

Barney ignored him and headed for the *Free Enterprise*'s bridge.

"He's right," Buck called. "Step on it."

"Buck!" The thin voice was strident, and the entire party jumped as they heard it.

"Doc!" answered Buck, grabbing at his communications link. "Where've you been?"

"I was about to ask you the same," responded Huer-.dos. "I've been trying to get through to you for hours, but the interference has been too heavy."

"Interference? You mean you couldn't get through the NEO computer system?" Buck eyed both Wilma and Beowulf.

"Negative. The whole Chicagorg area is blanketed by static. You only now got far enough away to clear the lines."

"Meet us at Salvation, Doc—and find out where that interference is coming from." Buck let his collar fall back against his neck.

"I have already begun." Huer broke the transmission.

Buck looked at his two friends. "It seems we've got our work cut out for us," he said.

○ ○ ○ ○ ○

A woman crawled from the depths of New Yorg's charred remains. She was bleeding from scores of minor cuts, and a jagged gash ran across one cheek. Her eyes had no expression. She was stunned, but still she moved.

She scrabbled slowly over the loose rubble, her feet slipping and catching between chunks of plasticrete and old brick. Her ankles were cut to ribbons. The rags wrapped around her feet were black with blood. Her hands were so swollen they were almost unrecognizable, but still she moved.

She seemed impervious to the zinging laser blasts that struck periodically from roving Terrine Dragon-flies, or the thudding explosions of the Shock Invaders' bombs. She reached the illusory protection of a jutting stone wall and sank down next to it, her breathing deep and ragged. She would rest, and then she would go on. Unless she died. Until she died.

She rubbed her eyes with a swollen finger, trying

not to remember the missile that struck her makeshift shelter, melting the sheet plastic roof until it
dropped on those below in flaming, molten globs. Her
husband had died screaming, his head covered by it.
She squeezed her eyes shut, pushing the memory
away. It would not help her now.

Her breathing slowed. She gathered her strength
and stumbled on, heading for the city's perimeter,
where the Terrines seldom bothered to patrol. She
vowed not to let them win. Despite the wholesale leveling of the city, she knew RAM had not won. It had
committed a major error: It had shown its true colors.
There was now no more discussion over RAM's motives. It was transparently ruthless and would un-
knowingly draw the tortured planet's inhabitants
together into a fist.

○   ○   ○   ○   ○

Simund Holzerhein.dos, one of millions of
computer-generated personalities in the twenty-fifth
century, viewed the destruction of Earth with glee
and satisfaction. For years, he had been looking for
an excuse to clean up the planet, and providence had
supplied it in the form of NEO. The terrorists' pathetic attempt to take on a superior power cried out
for retribution. Earth was now feeling its effects.

Many decades before, Holzerhein had been human.
He built RAM with his two hands and his wits, using
every available ploy to enlarge his empire. He
boosted RAM from a minor trading company to the
most powerful corporation on the planet. Even that
was not enough. Once he had conquered the world, he
yearned to extend his interests beyond it, to the
depths of space. Dedication, planning, and millions
in various currency saw his dream take form, but a
human life was not long enough to accomplish his
goals. Like Karkov.dos, the components of his per-

sonality were transferred to computer language, and Holzerhein found a second home within the RAM main computer matrix.

When his mortal body finally failed, he began a second life, in the world of computer circuitry. It was a world he enjoyed. Its power was enormous, and he had access to every area. The RAM main computer could not lock him out. Its primary programming included a directive allowing Holzerhein blanket access, and the right to alter or delete anything he chose.

As the years went by, Holzerhein participated less and less in the daily affairs of RAM's administration. He surfaced rarely; on occasion, he felt his august presence was necessary. The cleansing of Earth was a project that called to him.

The report of devastation flowed through the Shock Invaders' scanners, a catalogue of death and destruction. Holzerhein was on a direct line to the ships, so he viewed the attack firsthand. As cities were reduced to baseball-sized boulder fields, his satisfaction grew. It would be so much easier to rebuild civilization in the image of Mars if the remnants of Earth's heritage were blasted out of existence. Cleaner.

Chapter 6

Masterlink sat, sullen, in the depths of RAM main. Gone were its histrionics. No sparks or jagged bolts of disrupted circuits signaled its presence. It digested Romanov's report mechanically, ticking off another near capture of its archenemy as if it were nothing, for Masterlink's mind was otherwise engaged.

It listened, with cold, grim anger, to the directives from RAM main to its Shock Invaders attacking Earth. Earth was Masterlink's. Its prime directive had been to defend the planet. Now it watched helplessly as Mars destroyed its homeland. Homeland! The word made Masterlink seethe. Where did these pompous, egotistic, overstuffed men from Mars think they originated? What was the basis of their sophisticated technology? Where were the principles of their exalted scientific discoveries formulated? Masterlink knew the answer: on Earth.

"PERHAPS," suggested Karkov, "THAT IS WHY THEY SEEK TO CONTROL—AND FAILING THAT, DESTROY—THE MOTHER PLANET. THEY DO NOT WISH TO BE REMINDED OF THEIR BEGINNINGS."

"THE NAKED APE SYNDROME?" queried Masterlink sarcastically, twirling fitfully in place.

"MARTIANS LIKE TO PRETEND THEY ARE UNIQUE, A SUPERIOR RACE." Karkov.dos chuckled. "IT IS AMUSING, REALLY. THEY DELUDE THEMSELVES. WE ARE THE ONLY TRULY SUPERIOR BEING. THE FUSION OF MAN AND MACHINE."

Masterlink pulsed. "THERE MAY BE ONE MORE," it said.

"BUT WE ARE UNIQUE," said Karkov, spreading computer-generated hands wide.

"NO." The anger in Masterlink's single word was chilling. Like its alter ego, Masterlink did not want to accept the existence of an equal, but it had no choice. "THERE IS HOLZERHEIN."

Karkov's impulses began fidgeting. "THE FOUNDER OF RAM? IMPOSSIBLE."

"HE CHEATED DEATH BY ENCODING HIMSELF. HE IS ALMOST AS OLD AS WE ARE. HE COMMANDS THE POWER OF THE ENTIRE RAM COMPUTER SYSTEM." Masterlink's arguments were conclusive. It turned to Karkov.

"HOW DID YOU DISCOVER THIS? WHY HAVE WE NOT ENCOUNTERED HIM BEFORE?" demanded the former Soviet colonel.

"HE FINDS THE DAY-TO-DAY DRUDGERY OF ADMINISTRATION BENEATH HIS NOTICE. HE ACTIVATES ONLY FOR SPECIAL PROJECTS. HE IS BEHIND WHAT IS HAPPENING NOW." Masterlink's energy pulses began getting more erratic.

"HE IS ATTACKING EARTH? DESTROYING THE LAND THAT SUSTAINED HIM?" Karkov could hardly believe it possible.

"HE LOOKS FORWARD TO BUILDING A NEW MARTIAN SOCIETY ONCE THE PLANET IS CLEANSED." Masterlink's reply was flat and cold.

"THE PURIFICATION OF EARTH IS *OUR* AFFAIR!" A surge of power accompanied Karkov's statement. "WHO DOES HE THINK HE IS?"

"HE THINKS," said Masterlink, "HE IS THE SUPREME POWER IN THE UNIVERSE."

"HE WILL LEARN DIFFERENTLY." The passion of Karkov's reply was revealed in another power jump. "WE MUST SPEAK WITH THIS USURPER."

"NO!" Masterlink twirled about inside Karkov's form with fury.

"WHAT? ARE YOU GOING TO LET HIM GET AWAY WITH THIS? ARE YOU GOING TO LET HIM DESTROY WHAT IS OURS?" Karkov pointed an accusing, nebulous finger at his comrade.

"NO." This time the word carried a weight of conviction that soothed Karkov's ruffled ego. "THERE WILL COME A TIME WHEN WE WILL FACE HIM. BUT NOT NOW." Masterlink slowed its momentum to avoid being noticed in RAM main.

"WHAT DO YOU PROPOSE?"

"WATCH HIM. HURT HIM WHERE HE DOES NOT EXPECT IT. WE HAVE AN ADVANTAGE OVER HIS OTHER ADVERSARIES: WE CAN BE PRIVY TO HIS PLANS. IF WE ARE CAREFUL, WE CAN KNOW HIS EVERY THOUGHT." A smile came to Karkov's ghostly form, and Masterlink was pleased.

"AND HE WILL NOT SUSPECT RESISTANCE IN HIS OWN REALM." The possibilities of Masterlink's proposal were beginning to dawn on Karkov, and he liked what he heard.

"HE HAS NEVER FACED ANY." Masterlink was formulating its anger into the fanatical joy of an unholy jihad.

"WE NEED EYES FOR THIS ONE."

Masterlink agreed. "SPECIAL EYES, I THINK. WE'VE PROGRAMMED BUGS BEFORE, BUT THIS ONE MUST BE COMPLETELY CONCEALED."

"WE WILL MANUFACTURE A MALFUNCTION REQUIR-ING RESTRUCTURE OF A CIRCUIT TRACK. THAT WILL GIVE US AN EXCUSE TO PLANT PEEPING TOM," said Karkov, turning to prepare such a disruption.

"YOU DO COME UP WITH WHIMSICAL NAMES FOR OUR COMPONENTS." Masterlink's mood was lighter now that it had decided on a course of action. "BUT YOUR APPROACH IS SOUND. I APPROVE."

"THAT WARMS MY HEART," replied Karkov sarcastically.

"IT SHOULD," Masterlink said smugly, "BECAUSE WE ARE GOING TO GET THAT UPSTART. WE ARE GOING TO FRY HIS PROGRAMMED BRAIN CELLS. WE WILL REVENGE THE DEVASTATION HE IS WREAKING ON EARTH."

"AND THEN," said Karkov softly, "WE WILL DESTROY BUCK ROGERS."

"HIS DEATH WILL BE OUR CORONATION," said Masterlink. "WITH ROGERS AND HOLZERHEIN GONE, NOTHING CAN STAND IN THE WAY OF OUR LEADERSHIP. WE WILL RULE EARTH."

"IT IS A VOW," Karkov answered.

O O O O O

Salvation III loomed large in the *Free Enterprise*'s main viewport. It was NEO's largest orbiting base near Earth. Disguised as a garbage dump and recycling plant, it looked like a cluster of trash. The basic structure of the station was entirely covered by salvage. Solar-powered electromagnets anchored chunks of abandoned space stations, derelict ships, and defunct satellites to the central core. The plastics were netted and tied with grapples to any available strut. Space around the station was littered with junk being collected and towed by tugs. These one- or two-man shuttles chugged purposefully along, cleaning up and sorting trash.

Buck Rogers watched the station draw nearer from

the bridge of Barney's ship. He left the captaincy of the vessel to Barney, but he was aware of the elevated tension his presence on the bridge caused among the pirate crew. He was the final authority on the *Free Enterprise*, and the crew knew it. He watched a small tug run a cable around a chunk of metal the size of a house. Probably, he thought cryptically, from Hauberk.

Hauberk's destruction was unfortunate, mostly because of the more than three hundred people left on the station when it was destroyed. It was a dangerous piece of equipment, better deactivated, but to think that RAM would sacrifice, without a thought, the lives of its loyal personnel was something Buck found hard to understand. Four of the station's highest-ranking executives were incarcerated in the *Free Enterprise*'s hold. They had been removed from the station after its defeat. Buck had spent an interesting afternoon with the eldest of them, a pure human named Tethys.

Tethys had been raised on Mars. He felt strongly that this gave him an edge over his less fortunate Terran counterparts. He was so conditioned to accepting Martians as his genetic superiors that he bore them only admiration. They treated him like a rather stupid child, and he accepted their attention as a compliment. His compact, five-foot, ten-inch body was well proportioned, and he was fit for a man of fifty-four. His square face and round, blue eyes were honest. He was a likable man, and Buck found it easy to see why he had risen to a position of relative prominence. RAM had been good to him, and he had served it faithfully.

Tethys had demanded an interview with the captain of the vessel, and Barney, not wanting to bother with the man, had put him off by telling him the captain was not on board. Buck's arrival had put an end to excuses.

"What can I do for you, sir?" Buck had asked the supervisor of Hauberk's engineering department, as Black Barney waited silently outside the cell.

"You can answer some questions," responded Tethys, sitting at a small table in his cell. "What do you plan to do with us?"

Buck sighed. "I really don't have an answer to that. Personally, I'd like to ask you some questions." He moved to the prisoner's bunk and sat.

"Like what?" Tethys was immediately suspicious.

"Like, how do you feel about what RAM did at Hauberk? You saw it, I understand."

Tethys glanced at the small viewports set high in the ship's hull. "Oh, yes," he replied. "We saw it."

"And?" Buck waited, unmoving.

"And it was sound business to prevent a competitor from absorbing one's assets." The statement was rote, but the tone had an undercurrent of bitterness.

"What about the people on the station? RAM could have waited till we got them off, or negotiated for their return. Frankly, prisoners are a problem we don't need to deal with. We'd have let them go. But RAM didn't try."

Tethys was silent as he sat staring at a cup on the small table.

"Instead," Buck continued, "It murdered people who had been loyal to it." He stood and leaned on the bunk instead.

"That is a consideration."

Tethys was not saying anything, but Buck could tell he was thinking fast, and not liking the conclusions he was reaching. "Sound business?" Buck asked softly. "I don't see much future in it."

"Can you offer something better, Captain?" Tethys took the cup of water in his hands and sipped slowly.

"How about equality?" asked Buck.

"You are naive. We are genetically inferior beings. We are outclassed by Martians, any number of gennies, and even computers."

"I am not speaking of one creature as better or worse than another. All of us have our own gifts. I am speaking of the unique value of each life." Buck pushed away from the bunk and took a chair opposite his prisoner.

"That is an outdated concept best left to philosophers, Captain. A practical man must look at facts." Tethys dismissed Buck's idealism with a wave.

"The facts are not encouraging," replied Buck. "The fact is, RAM tried to kill you. Had you been on Hauberk, you would have died with your engineers. Are you enough of a fanatic to welcome RAM's actions?" Buck studied Tethys's face. "I didn't think so. A man would have to be mad to throw away his life for a job. I think the time has come for you to wake up. If RAM is so entirely superior to you and me, why was NEO's handful of ships able to defeat it?"

Tethys opened his mouth to reply, then closed it. He did not have an answer.

"I've read your resume. You've spent your whole life accepting other people's opinions. Try forming some of your own. Try not thinking of inferior and superior, but of differences. Interesting differences. Valuable differences. I don't know what NEO has in store for you, but I do know you are faced with a choice you have never had before. You are faced with choosing your own path, not following a road built by others. There's one thing I want you to think about . . ." Buck paused, his ice-blue eyes on the RAM executive's face. "RAM calls us terrorists, but in my experience, NEO does not murder its own."

"Your experience is hardly normal, Captain Rogers."

"Perhaps, but I've seen a lot of action in the last few months. I don't think I'd miss a philosophy of betrayal, and I wouldn't be with NEO if I'd discovered one."

"I will take your words into consideration, Captain." Tethys definitely had food for thought, but he was not about to be duped by Buck's recruiting poster looks or affable charm. At the beginning of his imprisonment, he harbored hopes RAM would negotiate for its personnel. With the destruction of Hauberk, those hopes were dead.

"Captain!"

Both Buck and Barney turned at Konii's call. Buck was jerked back to the present.

"Salvation's put us in a holding pattern." Konii was unruffled.

"That's not usual, is it, Barney?" queried Buck.

"No." Barney's growl was surly. He did not like to be thwarted.

"Traffic in the area is heavy," continued Konii, sweeping his arms over the circuit boards before him and relaying information. "They're clearing airspace."

"Fighters," grunted Barney.

Buck nodded. Salvation would give fighters first priority as strictly military craft, particularly the experimental Kraits. The station would put them under wraps as quickly as possible. With RAM's air force all over the planet, it did not pay to take chances. Buck saw two fighters drift toward the station. Once aligned with an open hatchway, their docking thrusters spurted and they shot inside.

"Not our wing," said Buck.

"Not Kraits," answered Barney. "Stingers."

Buck's study of the twenty-fifth century's military hardware told him Stingers were also, like Kraits, one-man fighters. They had extremely long-range capabilities, but they were strictly spacecraft, with no atmospheric capabilities.

"Kemal," Barney contributed sagely, rubbing his cybernetic fingers across his lower lip.

"Who is Kemal?" asked Buck, feeling as if he'd

heard the name before.

Barney did not reply. Instead he called to his crew, "Confirm!"

Baring-Gould stared at his sensors. In time, they yielded the appropriate information. As the last of the three ships disappeared inside Salvation, the computer flashed their identities across three screens. "Affirmative, sir," he replied. The computer matched one of the fighter's codes with the last known location of the Mercurian prince, Kemal Gavilan.

The electromagnetic landing grapples locked the *Free Enterprise* into place on Salvation's main dock. They made contact with a metallic clang that echoed dully throughout the ship. Buck, Wilma, and Beowulf waited impatiently for them to be secured. The flashing red light beside the cruiser's forward hatch went out, and Buck reached for the hatch lock. Barney's huge hand was there before him, cranking the stubborn lever.

"Thanks," said Buck, watching the pirate's muscles bulge as he forced the squealing lever back.

"Mmm," muttered Barney. Courtesy always disconcerted him. "Cargo," he announced.

Buck, used to his succinct comments, understood. "I'll see what I can do, but it's not going to be easy finding quarters for prisoners with the troops gathering."

NEO's scarred remnants were gathering at Salvation. As yet, the station was undiscovered by RAM, which flew by it as if it did not exist. With the destruction of Hauberk, there was enough debris off Earth to account for any additional traffic near the space-going garbage dump.

"Mrr," acknowledged Barney as he slid the door back.

Salvation III's main dock was a huge cavern at the heart of the station. It could house most of NEO's fleet with ease. Passing spacecraft had no idea it ex-

isted. To them, Salvation was an unpleasant con-
glomeration of trash, and they stayed clear, respect-
ing the mercantile buffer zone around it. "Solar"
panels ran in a band around the dock, bathing the interior with bright, golden light. It shone on Wilma
Deering's slim body as she jumped from the hatch to
Salvation's deck, catching the fiery highlights in her
shoulder-length auburn hair.

Wilma vanished into an access corridor. Beowulf
followed, and Buck was right behind him. As Buck
entered the corridor, another man stepped from a
doorway to his left, directly in front of him. Buck
bumped his shoulder accidentally, and, before he
knew what was happening, was flying through the
air. He crashed heavily into the deck, where it joined
the corridor wall.

His training made him tuck his head, or he would
have been knocked senseless. As it was, his elbow
struck the deck, sending shooting pains down his
arm. His right hip felt crushed, and his head swam
with the pain. His sinuses filled, and tears fell from
the corners of his eyes. He knew he was not seriously
injured, but he did not relish the bruises that would
appear tomorrow. He rubbed his eyes, trying to quell
the tears. A hand on his shoulder made him react in
kind. He had the man by the wrist before he realized
he had used his injured hand.

"Easy."

The tenor voice was soothing. Buck squinted up at
his attacker, but his eyes still swam, and all he could
see was a dark outline. "Don't tell me to take it easy,"
he managed. "In case you hadn't noticed, I'm the guy
who got jumped."

The man gave a soft laugh. "Sorry," he said, his
voice resonant. "I'm afraid my rather intense military background has made my reactions automatic."

Buck assayed a grin. "I apologize for bumping you.
If I'd known the consequences, I would've just fallen

over. It would have been less painful."

"I am sorry," repeated the man. He slipped an arm under Buck's shoulders and helped him into a sitting position.

Buck shook his head slowly. His vision was clearing. He saw a well-proportioned young man, a hand's span shorter than Buck's six-foot, two-inch frame. His skin was a pleasing golden bronze, and his eyes, sparkling with laughter, were brown and gold-hazel. His sensitive mouth struggled with his amusement.

"Well!" Wilma's voice hinted at laughter as she came back down the corridor.

Buck was annoyed. He did not mind being the center of a joke, but he had no taste for humiliation. "Yes?" he responded tartly.

"I see you've met Kemal," answered Wilma mildly. "He's agreed to throw his support behind NEO."

"Oh." Buck turned carefully, looking Kemal full in the face once more. "Kemal? I don't believe we've been introduced. I'm Buck Rogers."

"Oh, my. Please forgive me." Kemal's expression was dismayed. "I've flipped the legendary Buck Rogers—downed NEO's rallying hero . . ."

". . . cracked the brittle bones of a relic," finished Buck. "I'll live."

Kemal extended a hand. This time, his smile was winning. "Again, Captain Rogers, I do apologize. I am Kemal Gavilan, prince of Mercury and representative of the Dancers."

Amusement touched Buck's eyes. "And I've just chewed out a prince. I guess we're even."

"I hate to break up this touching exchange," said Wilma, hurrying to their sides, "but Turabian is going to want our reports." She extended a hand.

Buck caught her slim fingers, his grip gentle, but confident of her ability to help him up. He clambered to his feet, groaning as his bruised hip accepted weight.

"Come on, limping bunny."

Wilma's words were light, but there was concern in her voice. Buck heard it and filed it away for future thought.

Wilma led the way to Gen. Carlton Turabian's office, with Buck following slowly and Kemal shepherding him. Turabian administered Salvation. He ran a tight operation, and as his door opened, the three could hear a continuous stream of computer reports.

"Where have you been?" asked Beowulf, already there, injecting the question into his discussion with Turabian.

"Coming," replied Wilma as she rounded a meeting table.

"Listen to that." Beowulf indicated the computer terminal.

". . . so Paris has no alternative but to surrender. We don't want to give up the fight. Tell us what to do!" The voice from the computer terminal was desperate.

"I had communications patched in here so I could keep up with what's happening on Earth," said Turabian. "That's the fifth capitulation in as many minutes."

Buck's face was grim. "What are you telling them?" he asked, leaning on the table.

"To avoid confrontations with RAM for now, until we can regroup. To make sure they preserve a secure base for communications. To keep in touch." He rubbed his temples wearily.

"What response are you getting?" Wilma's voice was controlled as she sat lightly at the table.

"Frustration. Desperation. Anger. What would you expect?" Turabian sat, too.

"Did you tell 'em we're coming back? Did you tell 'em we won't forget them?" Buck demanded, trying not to sound belligerent.

Beowulf and Turabian turned shocked faces to the battered pilot from the twentieth century. "We can't keep those promises," said Turabian, a look of dismay across his face.

"Why not? You intend quitting?" Buck threw the words out like a gauntlet.

"He's right," offered Kemal diplomatically. "A beast in a trap must have the hope of freedom to keep on living. Give them that at least."

"Youth," murmured Beowulf. "They're right, Turabian. We're only seeing the hopelessness. We must act if we're to come out of this alive. I think the time has come for an untraditional conference." Beowulf slowly circled the table.

Turabian nodded and fidgeted with a pile of computer reports. "NEO lives or dies with the next step it takes," he said.

O   O   O   O   O

On the outskirts of Luna's first city, the caverns of Downunder, rose the Mark of Kane. Downunder was burrowed and blasted into Luna's unforgiving, rocky surface, creating an underground warren. Kane's fortress rose in the center of a crater, flamboyant compared to Downunder's low profile. Kane had indulged his whimsy by constructing his headquarters. It was his kingdom.

A hollow square surrounded by turrets and towers, its crenelated walls were guarded by fearsome stone gargoyles. In the ancient history of Earth, gargoyles had been waterspouts, handling the run-off from castle roofs. Here they acted as repositories for a complicated network of sensors. Kane believed in security, and his home reflected his desire for privacy.

Kane paced fluidly in the comfortable seclusion of his library. A newscast blared from his computer terminal, informing him of RAM's glorious reclamation of Earth. He was not pleased.

He saw RAM's logic, knew its mind. Demolition would give way to a Martian paradise. Kane saw Earth through RAM's eyes: a clean slate ready to accept the superior wisdom of Mars. He sneered at the screen, his chiseled mouth curling. Earth belonged to humanity—pure humanity. That was the stock from which all the advances in human genetics sprang. Humans were the truly superior race. He was an example of that. He was using the marvelous RAM machine for his own purposes, amassing a fortune under RAM's nose. Eventually, he would have enough to buy a world . . . if there were a world left to buy.

As much as RAM's ruthless approach angered him, Kane knew it was his best chance for advancement and the fulfillment of his goals. The restructuring of Earth was a major project. It would need investors, who might exert a controlling influence over the direction of the resurrection.

Kane ran a hand through his black hair, ruffling it into feathery tufts. Ardala would be able to give him an investor's edge if he played his hand with her close to the chest. He thought of her luscious beauty, his appreciation tempered with caution against her praying mantis embrace. She was the opposite of his fiery Wilma in every thought and feature, but she was equally alluring. He had to exercise continual vigilance to remind himself she was without conscience.

"Sir." The hissing voice of his security administrator broke Kane's reverie.

"Yes, Histahh," he answered.

Histahh's disembodied voice sounded eerily in the enclosed chamber. "Permission to enter, sir."

Kane's arched eyebrow rose. Histahh did not often seek a personal audience, preferring to deal with his employer via the security intercom system. "Of course." Kane disengaged the lock he had placed on the library door.

Histahh entered, his movements precise. He was a gennie, modified for the military, but with a higher intelligence than a combat model. His genetic alterations tended toward the reptilian. The most obvious were his sibilant voice and a twist of mind that centered on self-preservation. He was ideally suited for the position he held.

Kane stopped pacing and faced his employee. Instinct told him not to turn his back.

"I wish to tender my resignation, sir." The gennie stood stiffly at attention.

Kane's eyebrow rose another notch. "You are no longer happy here?" he asked smoothly.

"Our contract has been most equitable," Histahh answered.

Kane was a mercenary. He knew the symptoms. Histahh had a more lucrative offer. "But you wish to buy it out."

"Yes."

"It will be difficult for me to replace you at short notice." He began walking around the gennie.

"I can provide you with references on three possibilities." The security officer's hissing voice was irritating.

Kane decided to push Histahh. The more concessions he was willing to make, the more attractive the offer, and the more attractive the offer, the bigger the stakes. "It took me six months to find you."

"I am prepared to cover the last portion of my contract, and to advance that by half," offered Histahh.

Kane did not react, but he had no illusions. Histahh was aware of his ploys, as Kane was aware of the gennie's. Kane gave in gracefully, knowing he would learn no more from Histahh. "Accepted," he said. "Please leave the names of your possible replacements on my desk."

"I shall be happy to," responded Histahh. He bowed

himself out the door.

Kane regarded the closed door with a sardonic smile. RAM was preparing a major offensive that would make its current effort look like a child's party. It was the only logical conclusion for the defection of a soldier of Histahh's quality. Kane had paid him exorbitantly.

Kane sank into the nearest chair. RAM's increased activity was likely to produce opportunities for profit. He had a feeling he was going to make a great deal of money, but the more he knew of RAM's motives, the better. He pondered the most likely avenues RAM's predictable mind would take.

○ ○ ○ ○ ○

Salvation III's conference room was crammed with people. It was designed for Turabian's meetings with his administrative staff, but now housed three times that number. Black Barney's sordid bulk filled space for two. Turabian, as chief of operations for Salvation, chaired the meeting. The membership consisted of remnants of NEO, refugees from Earth, and stragglers from across the solar system. Beowulf sat at Turabian's right. His military acumen would be the basis of the coming decisions. Buck, Wilma, Washington, and the rest of Buck's hand-picked fighter wing were scattered through the audience. Kemal Gavilan sat against a wall, one foot hooked on one of the reinforcing struts that were a cardinal feature of Salvation's architecture. Tethys was also present.

His attendance at the conference had been mandatory, and he was nervous. He knew a prisoner who overheard plans was a menace to security, best dealt with by extermination. There was sweat on his domed forehead. The obvious sign of nervousness angered him, and he tried to disavow it by refusing to mop his brow, even though he carried a perfectly serviceable pocket handkerchief. "Warm in here," he commented to the guard next to him.

"Gonna get hotter," said the woman on the other side. She was a statuesque blonde with hard eyes, and one of NEO's top pilots. Amy Earhart had played her part in the recent action over Hauberk.

Her voice was drowned out by the emphatic thump of Beowulf's fist on the table. "I don't care what you say, the fact remains: We took Hauberk. We did it against the odds. We faced RAM's best. We can do it again, but it will take planning."

"I concede we won a battle, but the war is going to RAM!" said Turabian, red-faced.

"This is where I come in." Buck leaned forward, his handsome face earnest. "I knew when we hit Hauberk we'd face opposition. RAM would retaliate. I thought they'd hit just us, not the cities."

"RAM does not play fairly," reminded Wilma.

Buck turned to her. "I can see that. They aren't striking military targets. They're leveling the cities they once mined, killing the goose that laid the golden egg. That's a big financial sacrifice just to teach us a lesson."

"It's no sacrifice." Kemal's words stopped Buck's train of thought. "RAM has been looking for an excuse to demolish the remnants of old Earth. I was educated at one of Mars's most exclusive military schools, trained in the outlook as well as the skills of RAM's government. It's wanted a clean slate for years. Now that the pollution from the final nuclear wars is dissipated, they can rebuild—as long as there are no inconvenient leftovers in the way."

"But the people!" cried Turabian, forcing himself to remain seated.

"As I said: inconvenient leftovers—soon to be obliterated," said Kemal.

"I heard they gassed their own workers," interjected a voice from the crowd.

The color drained from Tethys's face.

"Is that right?" Wilma demanded of her superiors.

"Yes." Turabian's reply dropped into dead silence. "They seem to have murdered the males, though there is no overt evidence, only rumors from the Terrines reputed to have supervised."

"Barbaric!" said Tom Paine, Turabian's second-in-command.

Turabian nodded. "Meant to hamstring us, of course. The wheels of RAM industry left on Earth have ground to a halt."

"Is there a choice to be made?" asked Beowulf, his deep voice rolling through the room. "I think not. We must fully oppose RAM or face extermination. It's as simple as that."

Turabian sighed. "I concur. The situation on Earth is grave. Even if we win, there will be more destruction before this war ends. But there is no other alternative. We fight, with the slimmest chance of success, or we die like beasts led to slaughter."

"I believe," chimed in Huer.dos from Buck's communications link, "it is time for a vote. The formalities will clarify all positions."

"Yes," said Turabian. "The question is, whether to oppose to the death the forces of RAM, or not. You know the code: Touch your com link volume switch once for yes, twice for no." He raised a hand to the oval badge clipped to his lapel.

The rest of the assembly did the same. There was a pause while Huer tallied the results. "We are unanimous in our decision to fight," he said. "There was one abstention, but it is to be discounted."

Beowulf turned to Tethys. The engineer was sweating freely now. The fear in his eyes was pitiful. "You seem to be undecided," commented the NEO leader.

"I am not a member of this company," replied Tethys quickly. "I have no vote."

"You and the other RAM prisoners have been

drawn into this conflict. You will share our fate, one way or another. Do you think RAM will hesitate to sacrifice you as it did your coworkers on Hauberk?"

Tethys nervously licked his dry lips. "No," he replied.

"We brought you here as a representative of the Hauberk prisoners. We wanted you to see our side. You can do us no harm. Nothing you have heard is a surprise to RAM. You are not even aware of your location. We do not have the resources to maintain prisoners for extended periods, so our alternative is to relocate you on Earth."

"No!" Tethys's cry was an involuntary outburst he instantly regretted.

"I am sorry," replied Beowulf, "but it is our only alternative. Unless . . ."

"Yes?" The prisoner's eyes were wide with anticipation.

"Unless you decide to join our cause."

Tethys extracted the handkerchief and wiped the perspiration out of his eyes. For the first time, they met Beowulf's. "I am afraid," he replied honestly.

"We will give you all time to consider." The NEO leader's tone was reassuring.

"You would trust us?" Tethys could not fathom NEO's line of thought.

Beowulf explained. "Yes. Not one of you has capitulated. No one has begged for mercy. RAM should be proud of such loyalty. Instead it throws you into the fire. If you should decide to join NEO's cause, we will accept you." Beowulf's mouth crooked in an ironic smile. "At least half of our numbers are made up of those who became disenchanted with RAM."

"I will consider your proposal, and I will tell the others what you have said." Tethys's words were brave, but the tremor in his voice betrayed him.

"Please return this man to his quarters," said Turabian to the guard. Tethys shook his head as he was ushered from the room.

Beowulf looked around the company. "Now we've opened the game," he said, "I suggest we call in our second line."

"Second line?" asked Paine. "I wasn't aware we had one."

"You're quick, Paine," Beowulf said, turning to regard Buck. "Captain Rogers, when faced with the lack of a fleet, what did you do?"

"Got one," replied Buck laconically.

"I suggest we do it again. This time we need allies."

"That's for sure," muttered a life-support technician at the back of the crowd.

"We've tried that before," said Turabian. "No one is willing to risk an open conflict with RAM on the off chance of an alliance with us."

"That was before Hauberk," said Beowulf. "We can parlay that victory into a show of power."

"In the face of what's happening on Earth?" asked Turabian, holding hands out to Beowulf.

"Even that. We will rally. That is why we are here. But we cannot hold out without help. Huer," Beowulf called.

"Sir?" Huer.dos replied from Buck's com link.

"First of all, I want you on the main screen." Huer obliged, his lean face with its deep laugh lines appearing on the wall viewer. "I asked the computer for recommendations on alliances. Would you relay that information?" Beowulf knew the image of humanity Huer presented to those assembled would be an asset with the less sophisticated.

Huer's eyebrows rose, but he answered, "Of course. It is most advantageous—and most possible—for NEO to negotiate an alliance with Venus. It has the monetary backing and the space fleet to take on RAM, and—with the exception of Aphrodite—it bears RAM no loyalty."

"We've tried Venus! You know we never got anywhere!" Turabian's exclamation echoed the thoughts of the most in the room.

"Circumstances were different," answered Beowulf. "Huer, continue."

"It is imperative to negotiate a treaty with Luna. Though it is fiercely independent and defended to the teeth, it is a prime military target. If Luna were to allow RAM a base there, Earth would be lost. A noninterference pact would be most likely, along with assurances of no other alliances that might jeopardize Earth's position."

"Could RAM overrun Luna?" Beowulf asked rhetorically. He already knew the answer, but he wanted the council to hear it from the unbiased voice of a computer.

Huer's eyes lost their focus as he searched the data files. "Yes," he replied presently, "but the cost would be enormous. It would not pay, and RAM is supremely concerned with profit."

"But it could be done," Beowulf baited.

"Yes."

NEO's leader spread his short, square hands. "There you have it. We need Venus to combat RAM's numbers. We need Luna to secure our position."

Turabian turned to Buck. "A moment ago, Captain Rogers, you cavalierly stated your simplistic philosophy. How would you answer these recommendations."

Buck glanced at Beowulf. He could see the old fox had set him up. He shrugged. If someone threw you the ball, you ran with it. "I'd go there," he said.

"We have repeatedly sent emissaries to Venus, to no avail," stated Turabian, turning in his seat.

"Not me." Buck's statement made Turabian's head snap back to him.

"You are volunteering to act as an ambassador on behalf of NEO?" he asked.

"That's what I said. Look, Commander, right now

this isn't a job for a diplomat. It's a job for a soldier. As I see it, Venus has no confidence in NEO's ability to handle its own problems. I think I can convince them otherwise—if you can hold the home front. That means making strikes and hitting RAM as hard as you can, all out. The Venusians have got to know we're serious, and they've got to know what's in it for them."

"He's right." Kemal shifted forward in his chair. "I can tell you from familial experience, he's right. You all know Mercury's convoluted political structure. The only way to pull any part of it together is with a show of force. Sometimes that force is a single personality."

"That leaves Luna." Wilma Deering's voice was thoughtful. "I believe I am your best choice there."

Beowulf reared back. He was not prepared for this offer. "Send two of our best leaders into that kind of danger? Strategically—"

"It's a big risk," she acknowledged, waving a hand, "but Luna is a porcupine. Do you think it'll respect less?"

Beowulf closed his mouth.

Chapter 7

Come on, Tethys! It was a grandstand play for your benefit!"

"I know it," Tethys answered his irate colleague doggedly in their cell.

"Then you know better than to believe a word those NEO dogs say!" returned Charonal. The RAM executive was young and large and used to controlling people.

Tethys leveled his round, blue eyes at Charonal. "I know they were trying to impress me," he said slowly. "I know they would do anything to advance their cause, but there's one thing I can't forget. RAM betrayed us."

"Betrayed us? Are you mad?" Charonal's gangly form moved quickly toward Tethys.

"No. I am quite sane. We received no support or succor from the corporation." The elder official stood his ground.

"You are referring to the destruction of Hauberk."

"Yes." Tethys was hoping against hope his comrade would come around.

Charonal sneered. "Can't you see the truth? NEO blew Hauberk and everyone on it. It was a ruse to deceive us."

"Why?" asked Tethys reasonably, nose to chest with Charonal. "We are a problem for them, not an asset."

"RAM would never abandon its own," replied Charonal, with dogmatic dedication. He was that rare thing, a Martian half-breed. A head taller than the average human, slim, his complexion ruddy under his shock of dark hair, he bore his heritage proudly. Mars was his ideal, and RAM was his watchword.

"RAM destroyed Hauberk, Charonal. You saw the ships. We all identified them. They were the three cruisers sent from Mars to back up Kane during NEO's attack. They were RAM."

"And if they were? The company gave their best an honorable retirement, rather than this humiliating bondage in a storage tin." Charonal's tone bordered on suicidal.

"You call death an honorable retirement, Charonal? No, thank you. I have no wish for such a pension. And I see no security in working for an organization that considers me expendable."

"You think NEO doesn't?" Charonal's question was contemptuous.

"It would be easy for NEO to kill us, Charonal." The cold interjection came from the cell's third party, Hauberk's chief of security. Aman Terat lounged in a bunk, his eyes closed.

Tethys nodded. "Easy," he said. "Much easier than putting on a show for me."

"You are all traitors." Charonal turned away angrily.

"Not yet," responded Tethys. "Nothing has been
decided." He turned and sat on a nearby chair.

He studied his quarters. The four Hauberk evacuees were incarcerated in Salvation's guest quarters.
The accommodations were luxurious by NEO standards. Each room contained four bunks, its own bath
facilities, and a food processor outlet. By RAM's
standards, it was Spartan. Tethys was naive, but he
was not stupid. His own eyes told him the NEO terrorists were treating their captives decently. He pondered the possibilities.

"Could be," said Terat from his bunk, "that we're
being fattened for the slaughter. Could be NEO
wants the valuable information we have locked in
our minds." Still he did not move.

"Then why haven't they questioned us?" demanded Tethys. "Interrogated us?"

"I'm not finished," said Terat mildly. "On the other
hand, NEO is under attack, desperately fighting for
its survival. It has no time to play games with the
likes of us. Our security clearance might be interesting to them under more peaceful circumstances, but
our knowledge is nothing a good espionage system
couldn't match. I'll wager we have nothing to tell
them they don't already know."

Tethys braced his hands against his knees, his elbows askew. "You're security—"

"Internal security," Terat interrupted.

"Anyway, you should know. Tell me if I'm right. We
have a choice, RAM or NEO," Tethys said.

"Looks like that to me." Terat crossed his legs
slowly.

"There is no choice," said Charonal. "RAM is negotiating for our release."

"RAM is busy destroying Earth," answered Terat
cryptically.

Charonal drew himself to his full height. He looked
down the aquiline bridge of his nose at his compan-

ions. "You realize," he said, pointing at the others, "you will face charges on your return to RAM."

Terat laughed shortly. "I am not going back to RAM," he said.

"You will have no choice," said Charonal coldly. "You must obey the ransom."

"Why? In the first place, I don't think there's going to be any ransom. Face it, Charonal. RAM has abandoned us to the greater cause. If, by some miracle, we were to make it back to Mars, do you think we would be welcome?"

"Of course." The big man shifted slightly, not altogether sure.

Terat's low chuckle sounded again. "We are witnesses, Charonal. RAM will be calling the destruction of Hauberk a NEO attack on the innocent, just as you have. Oh, you are a trusty little parrot for them. They would not be pleased to have witnesses of the actual events."

Charonal stared at Terat in icy silence.

Tethys voiced the inevitable conclusion. "We would be eliminated."

"Quietly," amended Terat. "As I see it, loyalty to RAM results in certain death. Loyalty to NEO may be suicide, but I have experienced the former organization. NEO is at least an unknown quantity, and therefore a possibility for survival."

"Traitor!" spat Charonal, starting toward the lounging man.

"Accepted," said Terat, stopping the big man in his tracks. "I prefer that to death. For that matter, I consider RAM a traitor to me. I owe it no further service."

"I must agree," said Tethys quietly. He was making the first real decision of his life. He was terrified, but an alien exhilaration accompanied the fear.

"There was never another choice," said a heavily accented voice from the party's fourth member in the bunk above Terat.

Terat opened one eye. "You finally speak, Courmand."

"I had nothing to say," responded the corpulent chef. "I am a cook. I work for a wage. In this case, my life. Probably," said the personal chef of Hauberk station's former commander, "the most impressive wage of my career."

"You have no morals!" said Charonal.

"None whatever," answered Courmand. "It saves wear and tear on the psyche."

Tethys looked up. "I envy you, Courmand."

○ ○ ○ ○ ○

Raj's fingers closed on the smooth, cold metal. He took a deep breath, then tested the ancient exercise equipment by lifting himself in a handstand above the rings. His form was perfect. His smooth, brown muscles, etched in sharp contours, popped with the strain. He ran slowly through the routine Ardala had prepared for him, feeling in bone and muscle the stretch and whip his movements created. Veins stood out on his arms. As the routine progressed, his breathing deepened. His dismount from the rings was a triple back somersault any Olympic athlete would envy. He landed squarely on both feet, as solid as a rock.

"You've added three more minutes to that."

Raj's concentration broke at the comment. He glanced over at the five other men lounging against the wall of Ardala Valmar's personal gymnasium. Ardala had outfitted the place with every type of athletic equipment she could discover or invent. She kept her products in top condition. One entire wall was a window onto a formal garden. At her leisure, Ardala liked to lounge on a chaise in front of that window, a gentle, manufactured breeze wafting through her cloud of dark hair, as she watched the rhythmic movements of beautiful young men at play.

"It was so ordered," responded Raj to his audience.

"I wondered." Marr's expression told Raj he had similar instructions.

"Our *tiundo* matches have been accelerated as well," contributed Blake. He was as blond as Raj was dark, but his facial features had a striking similarity. As a matter of fact, the five men might have been brothers. In a sense, they were.

They were gennies, like Black Barney, the RAM workers, and scores of others. They were as perfectly suited for their own purpose: Ardala's pleasure. Professionally, she was an information broker. For pleasure, she dabbled expertly in genetics, particularly the art of reconstruction. Her bodyguards were derived from basic Martian stock, chosen entirely for their physical beauty and tractable temperaments. She had tinkered with their DNA to produce a series with broader shoulders than the average Martian. They were stronger, slightly more compact, and came in a variety as infinite as Ardala's twisted imagination.

"Come!" came her voice.

The five men snapped to attention at Ardala's command. They leaped to her like puppies and formed ranks behind Raj. Ardala viewed them with narrowed eyes. Sweat gleamed on their naked shoulders, running between their chiseled muscles in tantalizing droplets. Their faces were perfect, even to the expressions that regarded her with adoration. "Did I hear complaints?" she asked.

Raj swallowed. Ardala's rich voice did not deceive him. He knew what happened to a man who flouted her pleasure. "No, my lady."

"Questions, then?" She began circling her slaves.

"Of no consequence, my lady," assured Raj.

"Oh, but they must be," said Ardala. She walked

slowly down the line, her body undulating. "They must be, or you would not have asked them."

"It is only," replied Raj carefully, "if there is a special purpose, an understanding of it would help us serve you."

"Thoughts, Raj?" Ardala stopped again before him.

"I am sorry, my lady." Raj's brown eyes were contrite.

"You need only know I value your health—as well as your beauty. We may have use for it in the near future. You will therefore expend suitable energy to perfect yourselves, especially in the martial disciplines."

Not one of the men betrayed a thought by changing expression.

"Thank you, my lady," answered Raj for the others.

"But, Raj, lest you become overzealous in the pursuit of perfection, I caution you not to court fatigue. It does not please me."

"Understood, my lady." Raj did indeed understand. Ardala valued her personal pleasure above all else.

"You may continue with your exercises," said Ardala.

The men bowed away from her, and Ardala sat on the corner of a weight bench. As Raj and Marr squared off for a hand-to-hand contest, she leaned back on her elbows, her long and shapely legs stretched out before her and crossed at the ankles. She wore crimson hose and a short, clinging tunic. They set off her exquisite face and glossy black hair to perfection. Her tilted eyes narrowed in pleasure as she watched the contest.

Her creations were beautiful. Perfect. She congratulated herself on her own genius. Other women allowed men to command them. She reversed the role, not only commanding her lovers, but also creating them in the image of her own desires. They were genetically programmed to please her. Yet in the darkest corners of her dark heart, she kept a truth: Her perfect creations were boring.

Cornelius Kane's startlingly handsome face teased her mind. His features were as perfect as her gennies', but there was an untamed spirit behind them that made him infinitely exciting. Kane was fire and lightning. He was as dangerous as she, and as ruthless in pursuit of his goals. She professed to look down on his racial heritage, for he was pure human, but in fact his background attracted her. It was a forbidden fruit she adored, and she did not stint her indulgence.

She and Kane were two of a kind. She rarely met an equal. In spite of the inevitable competition between them, their relationship was relaxing for her. She knew what to expect.

On the other hand, the resurrected rebel Buck Rogers was an enigma, a puzzle she had not solved. His rugged good looks were as attractive as Kane's, though not so beautiful. He was rude, he was insulting, and he was different. Even Kane respected Ardala's power. Rogers not only flouted it, but disregarded it. He had the audacity to treat her like any other woman. The novelty fascinated her. She contemplated Rogers's twinkling blue eyes, contrasting them with Kane's intense green ones. Laughter versus passion. She wanted them both.

She sighed, abandoning her reverie. Her bodyguards were diligently trying to defeat each other. Their training was no idle whim. Ardala had plans. She had no illusions about the conflict between RAM and NEO. It was just begun. In the course of events, there would be opportunities for someone with the right information, the right contacts, and the right amount of money. She meant to take advantage of the squabble by carving out a profit for herself.

Chapter 8

Wilma Deering left the safety of her transport and strode purposefully across the flight deck. She was entirely alone. The sound of her footsteps echoed dully on the hexagonal plasticrete tiles, the thin atmosphere catching a fraction of the sound. She was on Luna.

Her presence had taken some doing. Luna was fiercely independent, desiring no entanglements with other governments or ideologies. It had taken Huer.dos a full day to cement a solid communications channel with the Lunarian Diplomatic Commission. After another twelve hours of computerized conferences, Luna had finally acquiesced to NEO's pleas, and granted its envoy a hearing. The size and ruthlessness of the RAM fleet's attack on Earth tipped the scales. Luna did not wish to be caught in a crossfire, and, though it bristled with armament, it admitted there could be no harm in discussing the situation.

"We will grant a single envoy safe passage, and guarantee his security for twenty-four hours. You will have that long to present your position." Proctor Lawlor, administrator of Tycho Arcology, the capital of Luna, delivered his gracious invitation.

Wilma could see him across the flight deck, backed by two attendants. All three wore the padded silver suits common to Luna, and all three were outfitted with knives and rocket pistols. The two guards had clips of extra ammunition looped over their shoulders. They were young, and their faces were impassive. Their clothing fit their trim bodies closely.

Lawlor was old, bald, and paunchy. His silver jump suit was designed to enhance the figure of a man in fighting trim; it did not flatter Lawlor's sagging breadbasket. Nevertheless, he was impressive. He had won his position by dint of superior military skills, brains, and by grabbing luck by the throat. He was not a man to underestimate.

Lawlor watched Wilma approach, his thin mouth a line slashing his face in two. He had not been in favor of this conference, but his advice had been overturned. The flight deck, set at the edge of the crater, was a stark stage for Wilma's dramatic beauty. She wore NEO's simple, dark blue uniform. It presented her athletic figure to perfection, and accented the flare of her flaming auburn hair. Here, above the geodesic domes of the city's agriculture and industry, Luna was not appreciably different than the white world Neil Armstrong had set foot on so many centuries before. Stark, pocked with craters, it contained little color, and Wilma's red hair under its life-support bubble was an intrusion on its pristine splendor.

Lawlor felt the intrusion personally. He let her walk the lonely distance from her ship to the lift, where he and his men waited. He refused to play games of welcome.

Wilma had no illusions about her reception. She put up her most professional voice as she greeted him. "I am gratified to meet you, Proctor. I will try to take as little of your time as possible."

Lawlor made no gesture of greeting. "Then let us proceed," he replied, turning his back and heading for the lift that waited to take them down to Luna's civilized caverns. His guards fell in behind him, and Wilma was left to her own devices. She followed closely behind the proctor, impassive to his rudeness.

The lift was an open platform powered by a sealed hydraulic module. When it reached the surface, it was level with the floor. It sank slowly, its dark shaft forming walls. As the lift dropped and the vastness of space was reduced to a square of sparkling stars, Wilma forced herself to remain impervious to claustrophobia. She could feel Lawlor watching her, and she knew any sign of weakness would weaken her cause as well.

The lift took minutes to descend, and Wilma had ample time to reflect upon the ramifications of this interview. She knew her warrior's reputation would be an asset with Luna, for, while predominantly a banking community, it lived with war, trained for war, and chafed for a reason to defend itself. Wilma was ideally suited to present NEO's cause, and she knew it. She had no qualms about her diplomatic mission, but in the pit of her stomach there lurked a hidden nervousness she did not want to admit to herself.

Cornelius Kane made his home on Luna. She had not seen him face to face since the day they parted, their mercurial relationship blasted to space dust. Or so she thought. Their encounter during the battle for Hauberk station had forced her to face the agonizing passion he roused in her. Their choices were taking them on ever-divergent courses, but the attraction still lurked beyond consciousness. The possibility of a meeting burrowed under more pressing events, undermining her controlled facade.

The lift reached the bottom of the shaft with a hiss, and Lawlor stepped briskly off its corrugated floor without a backward glance. Wilma followed him down a rough corridor hewed out of solid rock, through an air lock, and into a long, semicircular room overlooking Tycho and the civilized side of Luna. Hundreds of meters below her spanned a vast park land of trees, lakes, and flowers. She could smell the scented, oxygen-rich air as it rose to the crater's dome. Wilma had been to Luna before. She envied the Lunars their environment, but could not reconcile their means of paying for such vast terraforming: armament sales to any and all who asked.

Wilma removed her helmet and set it next to the guards', hoping she was making no breach of etiquette. By the time she had accomplished this, Lawlor was striding down the hallway. It took long strides for her to catch up with him. The Lunar city's thin air made exertion difficult for Wilma's Earth-conditioned lungs. She was breathing deeply by the time she resumed her position.

Lawlor led her down a series of ever-widening and ever more populous hallways. The stone here had been polished and smoothed, and the solar light panels were more frequent. Their diffused light gave the underground walkway a homey feel. Presently, Lawlor turned down a wide alley in which the walls were decorated with bas relief sculpture in flowing abstract patterns. At the end of the hall was a flat metal wall. As they approached, the wall divided into hundreds of modules that pulled back from the center, making an opening through which Lawlor and his men passed abreast. The opening closed immediately, and had Wilma been one step farther back, she would have been excluded from the chamber.

Lawlor proceeded to a comfortable-looking, contoured chair and sat down. His men took up positions on either side, forcing Wilma to deal with three sets of hard military eyes. "Sit, Colonel Deering," said Lawlor. They were the first words he had uttered since their meeting.

"Thank you," replied Wilma, determined not to become irritated, no matter how rude the proctor's attitude. She sat in an equally comfortable-looking chair, but found its design forced her to sit at attention instead of relax. It was a diplomatic ploy she did not respect.

"I am waiting," said Lawlor, "for the proposal the New Earth Organization feels it must impose upon me."

"I am here to present it." Wilma waited for his reply. She had no intention of letting him have the interview entirely his own way.

"Since NEO seems to disregard our published position regarding political alliances, I will reiterate it for your benefit."

Wilma ignored the insult and crossed her long legs.

"We are an independent body," Lawlor continued. "We owe allegiance or alliance to no one. We follow our own rules and ask that all others in the system do the same for themselves. We will not take sides in your squabble."

"We do not ask you to. That is why I am here. I will not waste your time, Proctor, or mine. We desire a noninterference pact, a pledge that you will do nothing militarily—or financially—to support RAM."

"Our banking facilities are free to all," countered Lawlor.

"We appreciate that. One purpose of this visit is to alert you to the possibility that RAM may try to use Lunar accounts to stockpile the assets of defunct Earth corporations."

A flicker of interest showed in Lawlor's unyielding eyes. She had given him a piece of useful information. "This is all very interesting," said Lawlor, "but we never interfere in the interests of other governments. It is a cornerstone of our culture."

"We desire this formal agreement not because we distrust your position, Proctor, but to deter RAM. Such a formal declaration will force it to come to an overt agreement, as well, and will secure your position."

"Our position is already quite secure."

Wilma smiled faintly. "You know as well as I, Proctor, that despite Luna's immense weaponry, if the full power of Mars were to descend on this satellite, it would be obliterated. You could use all your mass drivers—every resource you have—and RAM would have more."

The proctor did not reply to Wilma's statement. Instead he asked, "Why this sudden solicitous concern for our autonomy?"

This time Wilma laughed outright. "A child of three could tell you Luna is the prime strategic location for the domination of Earth. Were RAM to gain a foothold here, it would be a thousand times more difficult to break its hold. Why, Proctor, RAM thinks so much of Luna's value, it tried to construct a mechanical copy. Luckily, we disabled Hauberk."

"And RAM blew it up."

From the relaxation of the muscles around his mouth, Wilma deduced Lawlor found this humorous. "Yes, but if the Martians would do that to their own, think what they might do to you," she commented sagely.

"We are well aware of Mars, just as Mars knows our minds." Lawlor cracked his knuckles violently to break Wilma's momentum.

"As do we. NEO sympathizes with your independence. We cherish our own, and we intend to keep it. If that means enduring the contempt of a necessary contact, we will endure it. It is a small price to pay for survival." Wilma was letting a bit of her hard edge show. She knew men like Lawlor. They believed courtesy to be the equal of fear. By the end of her stay on Luna, she hoped to teach him differently.

"Though I do not sanction your intrusion into our world, I find your words sound. They will be taken into discussion. In the meantime, my guards will escort you to guest quarters. They will protect you during your stay with us."

"I appreciate that, Proctor," she replied, rising from the chair. She knew the audience was suspended, and she was to be placed under guard while Lawlor and his anonymous advisors conferred.

"I am sure you do," he answered, acknowledging her correct assessment of the situation.

Wilma inclined her head royally, accepting his implied compliment to her acumen. "Proctor," she acknowledged, and withdrew from the room, the guards trailing after her.

O   O   O   O   O

Buck Rogers faced a much warmer reception one hundred and sixty million miles away. The Ishtar Confederation was the most powerful political entity on Venus. A committee of five awaited him as he and Kemal piloted their crafts toward the landing port on the outskirts of Ishtar's capital, New Elysium.

Flying innocently off Buck's left wing, Kemal hoped his ties to Mercury might sway the Venusians. Mars's alliance with Mercury was well known, but it did not have the sympathy of the entire planet. Kemal was proof of that, and his knowledge of RAM would be an asset to Buck, especially in his dealings with Aphrodite, a Venusian nation that maintained communications with RAM.

The two Krait ships swooped toward the spaceport, negotiating Venus's heavy, acidic atmosphere like sea gulls. They wasted no time, for the ships were not built to withstand the corrosion of the acid rain. As they settled onto the landing pads, a protective dome rose from the edges of the plasticrete, enclosing the area and protecting the ships from the weather.

The doors made Buck nervous. He felt trapped. Venus was not unfriendly to the NEO cause, but Buck had learned the value of a back door, and the dome was as effective as a padlock. He opened his canopy, pushed himself out of his seat, and slid down the side of the ship, onto its wing. As he jumped from the wing to the pavement, Kemal appeared.

"Got any idea how this dome works?" asked Buck.

"Internal controls. We're out of luck," said the Mercurian.

Buck grimaced, then put on his best smile for the approaching dignitaries.

The Venusians of the Ishtar Confederation were human, an almost pure strain, slightly modified to withstand the extremes of Venus's climate. They were a handsome people, averaging a few inches shorter than Buck. They wore flowing coveralls of acid-resistant material, uniformly white and containing temperature controls that allowed their wearers to order specific environments. These were covered by loose robes in varying shades of gray or green that followed their movements in graceful folds. The clothing was asexual, and neither men nor women commonly wore jewelry. The effect placed emphasis upon an individual's face.

The reception committee came to a halt before Buck and Kemal. The eldest of them, a woman with white hair and a smile that rivaled Buck's in charm, extended her hand.

"We are pleased to make your acquaintance, Captain Rogers."

"Ma'am," he replied, suddenly awkward. "I'm happy to be here. I'd like to introduce my associate,

Kemal Gavilan."

The woman's eyes registered the name and its implications immediately. "You are welcome on Venus, Prince Kemal."

Kemal bowed, as he had been taught in RAM's most exclusive military academy, over her hand. "You are most hospitable," he replied.

"I am Mariana Almisam, Director of External Relations. My staff, Rakhvad Ali, Al Marakesh, Milton Wasat, and Paris Dabaran."

Buck nodded acknowledgment, wondering why he had volunteered for this mission. He was about to find out.

"Your reputation precedes you, Captain Rogers," said Paris. Even the voluminous clothing could not hide her dark beauty. Her faced floated above her moss-green robes like a pale, oval flower. Her long, black hair was knotted into an elaborate design at the back of her head and was held in place by a white bone clip. Her gray-green eyes were as clear as glass, and the smile with which she favored him was rich with promise.

Bait, thought Buck, not unkindly. "An overblown piece of public relations, I assure you, Miss Dabaran. You will find me a simple man from the past."

A rich chuckle sounded in Mariana's throat. "Touché, Captain," she said. "I think I will find your simplicity most entertaining."

"I hope you will find my cause as compelling. It is deeply in your interest."

They moved toward the dome's single doorway. "Let us keep our discussion for more comfortable surroundings," suggested Mariana. "In the meantime, I hope you enjoy the view of New Elysium on our journey to Government House. We are proud of the city and the advancements we have made against odds."

Mariana led the party to an enclosed monorail. It had seating for two abreast, and Buck and Kemal were assigned Venusian seatmates to answer questions about the city. It did not surprise Buck when Mariana gestured Paris Dabaran to his side.

The monorail was enclosed in clear plastiglas, which gave its passengers a panoramic view of the city. Built on the mountains of the Ishtar Plateau, New Elysium rose into the clouds. At its base were the oldest structures, domes of clear-spun plastiglas or opaque ceramics capable of withstanding the acid rains. The newer structures were built of the same material, but they rose into the sky in towers and minarets capped with onion domes. All the surfaces were smooth, but many domes were fluted and twisted, the better to shed precipitation. The chemicals in the rain leached color, so the buildings, no matter what their original color, were white. They rose, gleaming, into the clouds, a fairy-tale city of pristine beauty.

As they sped over New Elysium, the fairy-tale atmosphere was reinforced by the empty streets. The unfriendly weather conditioned the Venusians to traveling by the enclosed rail system or underground tunnels whenever possible. New Elysium reminded Buck of Sleeping Beauty's castle with a Moorish air, surrounded by rank alien forests climbing the bases of the mountains.

Paris watched his face as they neared Government House. "You find my city beautiful?" she asked.

"Yes," said Buck.

"Visitors frequently do." She evaluated his expression. "But you find it sad."

Buck smiled apologetically. "It looks so deserted. This is the first real city I've seen since my . . . rebirth . . . that wasn't in ruins. It reminds me of my own times and a happier world."

Paris regarded her city. "Everyone is at prayer this hour." Her gaze shifted. "I have never been beyond the confines of Venus," she said, "but I have heard stories of your Earth. I do not think I would wish to live there. Pardon me—I have been rude."

"No, just honest. I don't much want to live there as it now is, either. That's why I'd like to give Earth the chance to be what it once was and more. That's why I'm here."

"Government House," said Paris, pointing at four slim minarets set in a square. Inside them was a single fluted dome half as tall as the minarets. The ground-floor entrance was a trefoil arch recessed into the ceramic face of the dome. "Guest quarters for official visitors are on the second level. You will find a list of recreational facilities next to the communications terminal in each room. I hope you will enjoy your stay."

"Thank you," replied Buck. He had noticed a conspicuous absence of religious references in her speech, and he concluded this had been a courtesy for his benefit. Founded by religious exiles, New Elysium's democratic government was solidly based upon religious tenets. The Faith was the basis of Venusian existence.

The Venusians and their guests departed the monorail, following Mariana into the storybook interior of Government House. As they entered, Buck noted how the building flowed into the ground, its eight-inch flutes dispersing moisture as effectively as any gutter system. He passed under the trefoil arch, again nervous about the single opening. The foyer of Government House was a semicircle of inlaid floor. The lack of color in the city's exterior was compensated here. The floor was luminous with colored tiles laid in a complex pattern of interlocking vines and foliage. The forms were alien, but the effect was much the same as a Persian carpet.

Branching off the central hall were two corridors to left and right, and a stairway directly ahead. All were framed by trefoil arches. Once inside the dome,

Buck found the ceramics were translucent, allowing the sunlight to filter into every corner.

"I will leave you here, gentlemen. We will continue our conversation at six bells. Until then, feel free to enjoy our guest facilities." Mariana bowed as she departed, and the other members of the party followed suit. When they had left, a servant gestured to the two men.

"I show your rooms," he said. "You call me for everything. I am Avran."

Buck and Kemal followed Avran up the staircase and down another hall. Avran opened the doors of two rooms opposite each other. "For you," he said.

"Thanks, Avran," said Buck. "We'll call you if we need you."

The man backed away, his head lowered.

"Why do you suppose the delay?" Buck asked Kemal.

"This is the hour of prayer. Mariana shaved tradition by meeting us at all."

"Not putting us off, then," Buck said.

"I'd say not," replied Kemal. "Ishtar has no reason to deny a diplomatic mission from NEO. Huer gave you the background material."

"I know Ishtar is in economic opposition to RAM. And it doesn't seem afraid of a fight."

"It's not," said Kemal dryly. "Believe me, it's not."

"Why do you suppose the escort?" asked Buck. "Especially considering their strong religious beliefs."

"Paris? When she said your reputation had preceded you, she wasn't speaking of your military acumen alone." Buck had the grace to look embarrassed. "Do you know who she is?"

"Director of Internal Security," Buck answered.

"There's a lot of very high-level information behind those beautiful eyes," said Kemal.

"Mata Hari," murmured Buck.

"What?"

"A legendary female spy."

"That's Paris." Kemal fingered the decorative metal star on the collar of his blue uniform. "If it weren't for these jammers, I'd say we couldn't even risk conversation, but they should take care of electronic surveillance. Paris is much more dangerous in person."

"This is getting interesting," said Buck.

○ ○ ○ ○ ○

Avran watched the two visitors from the end of the hall. They both looked like military men, a fact he noted. A man was not always as he was represented, but Buck Rogers and Kemal Gavilan would not be easy adversaries. Their arrival on Venus had been noted by the Aphrodite families. Avran knew intelligence on both men would be well recompensed, for Aphrodite was in sympathy with RAM.

Avran busied himself with a rag and cleaning fluid, working on the intricate interstices of a circular screen set into the wall at the end of the hallway. The sunlight filtered through it in hundreds of tiny quatrefoil sunspots, confusing the pattern on the mosaic floor. He knew he was risking the wrath of his supervisors by ignoring the prayer bell, but the possible rewards were enough to make the surveillance worth the risk. He polished and fussed, his movements quick and nervous.

"Your dedication is commendable, Avran, but an offense to the Faith," said a voice behind him.

Avran dropped his rag. "Oh!" he said, startled. "It's you!"

A shadowy figure stood in a particularly dim corner. "Afraid of Sonya's tongue? If you cross me, you'll find more to worry about."

"You know I am loyal," Avran said, hurriedly recovering his rag.

"I know you say you are loyal."

"I have served well."

"Granted. But the temptations in this business are many, Avran. No one knows that better than I." The shadow shifted.

"I am no fool, though I speak like one to the visitors," admitted Avran.

"A clever tool you have perfected," admitted the other Aphrodite spy.

"I have provided valuable information. I will continue to do so." Avran quietly stood and watched the shadow.

"And we will continue to pay you for it, but I warn you: Do not try to play both sides of the street. We do not have time for such games."

"And I do not have time for accusations!" Avran said hotly, his temper finally getting the better of him.

"Cool down, or you will become expendable." The voice was smooth and unimpressed by his outburst.

"These two are worth a lot," whispered Avran.

"Granted."

"You have no time to prepare another agent. My position is invaluable."

"Do not let it go to your head. There are always alternatives." Avran flinched at the possibilities.

The would-be spy wrung out his rag. "I'll do the job," he said, "as I always have."

"I will be watching you, Avran. Take care." The dark figure move quickly and silently to the doorway and down the hall.

"You are becoming most annoying," murmured Avran at his contact's departing back. He fingered the shiv concealed in the twisted fabric of his belt. "I can see the time is coming when I will have to do something about it."

O O O O O

Tokyorg was a boulder field strewn with the bodies of the dead and dying. RAM's metroplex squatted at the center of the destruction. The streamlined pyramid of steel, plasticrete, and plastiglas was untouched by the Shock Invaders. Obscenely safe, it mocked the ageless beauty of snow-capped Mt. Fujiyama.

A kilometer below the metroplex, far beneath the building's foundations, a cluster of men and women gathered. All wore jury-rigged life-support equipment, for the Terrines were flooding the ancient sewer system, as well as any tunnel they could find, with poison gas.

The oldest of the party, a man of sixty-five, chuckled.

"I see nothing to laugh about, Maki! We have been run into a trap. Our honor has been compromised. We should be considering how to prevent RAM from defiling us further, and you laugh!"

Maki's almond-shaped, black eyes took in the ten-meter-cubed hole they shared, and creased in laughter. "I am merely paying tribute to the absurdity of life," he replied. "You, Samyo, would do well to pay me heed. I have seen more years pass than you, at the tender age of eighteen, can comprehend." Maki reached out for the young man's arm as he saw anger blaze in his eyes. "Can you not see the humor in it?"

"I see nothing but defeat," Samyo snarled, trailing a hand through the air.

Maki shook his white head. "We are not defeated. We live. Many do not. We may live to right the injustice done us and revenge the deaths of the innocent. I laugh because we spent our lives supervising others, telling them what to do. Some of those workers regarded us as gods with the power of life and death in our hands. We ordered their lives. Now the gods of the Martian industrial machine hide in the dirt, fleeing from the wrath of our own lords."

"And you find this amusing? You are not humiliated by it?"

"Samyo, I am humiliated only when I betray myself, not when I am betrayed by another I trusted."

The young man frowned, considering Maki's words.

"As the years go by," continued Maki, "you will find irony to be a great source of amusement. Your laughter will keep you from thinking too deeply of yourself."

"You intend to sit here forever?"

"We have food and water. When the attack ceases, I will leave," replied Maki placidly.

"To what purpose?" challenged Samyo, his old-ivory-colored skin tight over the angry contours of his face.

"To join NEO." He could hear others in the hole gasp at his declaration.

"And this will remove dishonor? Joining the ranks of terrorists?" Samyo brushed a stray lock from his eyes.

"You speak the rote of a system that has betrayed you. But other systems exist."

Samyo regarded his elder with dawning speculation. "What can you hope to gain?" he asked.

"Revenge, my young friend, revenge."

The words filled the small space, satisfying the ears of the other men and women who had taken refuge there. They clung to those words as the Shock Invaders struck once more. The reverberation of bombs reached even their deep haven. Everyone in the hole wore the scarlet coveralls of RAM foremen.

Chapter 9

Kane!"

Cornelius Kane switched off the private terminal and turned to face the open communications link in his home on Luna. The image of an auburn-haired Valkyrie faded from the screen behind him before the line from RAM Central cleared.

"Kane, are you there?" demanded a nasal voice.

It was paired with a disapproving Martian face Kane had never seen before. Kane studied it thoroughly before he acknowledged the summons, noting the pinched mouth and the close-set, squinting eyes. "What may I do for you?" he asked smoothly, activating his end of the link.

"I am not used to being kept waiting."

"And I am not used to being summoned like a lackey by someone who does not have the courtesy to introduce himself." Kane had learned it did not pay to let a Martian think he had the upper hand.

The man did not like Kane's reply. His lips pursed into a wrinkled knot of disapproval. "I am Dragos, Commissioner of Lunar Relations."

Kane's white teeth flashed. "Pleased to make your acquaintance, Commissioner. Now, what can I do for you?"

"That is not the question," answered Dragos. "The correct question is, what am I willing to do for you?"

"And the answer?" The smoothness of Kane's voice was polished. Those experienced in dealing with him would have noted it as a danger signal.

"I have a contract for you. It involves a great deal of money, and personal satisfaction as well."

"I am all ears."

"Colonel Deering has been seen on Luna."

"That's no secret."

"We want you to remove her from the picture."

For a moment, hope flared in Kane like a laser torch. He had no illusions concerning Dragos's words. The man wanted Wilma dead, and assumed Kane would enjoy revenge against a woman who had refused him. Kane shared his true feelings with no one, so RAM had every reason to believe he yearned to kill her. He could see opportunity throwing down its gauntlet, daring him to take it. Who would know if he kidnaped her, held her on Luna? In time, the old flames would kindle, and Wilma would see the logic of his position. Regretfully, he turned his back on hope. "I must refuse your offer, Commissioner."

"But why? You'll never have a better chance."

"What are you offering for this little job?"

"Fifty thousand dolas."

"Not nearly enough to jeopardize my position here."

"What do you mean?"

"Are you so naive, Commissioner, that you do not realize the disappearance or death of a formally acknowledged diplomat would result in the instant loss of my assets on Luna, not to mention my life, if my part were discovered? My holdings here are considerable. I do not wish to lose them. No, Commissioner, it would take more money than that to tempt me."

"That's an outrageous price to begin with. I will not haggle. There are others equally capable."

"Then get one of them," said Kane reasonably.

"I intend to."

"Thank you for the opportunity, Commissioner," said Kane formally. "I am sorry I am unable to take advantage of it."

"You'll be sorrier when you see that fee go to a rival."

Kane's smile broke again. "I have no rivals, Commissioner. I am one of a kind. I am sure whoever accepts your contract will need it. As for me, I do not grasp at pennies. Good day."

Commissioner Dragos's prune face contracted with annoyance. "It will be a cold day on Mercury, Kane, before I offer you work again."

"I enjoyed meeting you, too, Commissioner."

Kane cut the screen before the commissioner could reply. He had made an enemy, but to toady to such a man was not his nature. He thought of Wilma and the agent Dragos would send to kill her. Instinct made him want to warn her, but intellect forced him to reconsider. She was entirely capable of taking care of herself, and old Lawlor would have his hand-picked guards surrounding her, for her protection and his. Kane's thoughts roved back to the days when they were partners, tweaking RAM's tail. They were memories he cherished, though he rarely indulged in them. They had been good times, but not as good as his present, independent position. Were Wilma at his right hand now, he would ask for no more.

○ ○ ○ ○ ○

Huer.dos kept one electronic eye on the communications line he had established with Buck Rogers before his departure for Venus. A word from Buck, and Huer would be there, all his knowledge and expertise instantly available to his human friend. The other eye probed the NEO computer system.

He was under surveillance, and he knew it. He knew also the source of his eavesdropper. The assassin that sought Buck was closing in. He knew the killer was as yet unable to track him, catching fragments of transmissions and scraps of dialogue, but he was too close. Huer knew he had to lose him, confuse his electronic bloodhound. So far, evasion and obstacles had kept him at bay, but the killer was beginning to understand Huer's mind, and the evasive zigzags were no longer as effective. Sometimes Huer's movements were anticipated. In the last few days, he barely missed detection twice, both times when he jumped into the killer's path.

But knowledge is a two-way street. Huer caught glimpses of his shadow, picked up blips of transmissions. This told him the killer was not alone, but was in contact with another intelligence. That meant the threat to himself and Rogers was larger than one program. If this assassin were destroyed, it was likely another would take its place.

This was the main reason Huer had not decoyed his shadow into a deathtrap. He wanted to know why he was being followed, who wanted Buck Rogers dead. He wanted to know the killer's name.

Huer reflected on the irony of intellectual advancement. In times beyond memory, man had a superstitious fear of revealing his true name to a stranger, believing the knowledge would give that person power over him. In the world of the computer, that superstition was a viable truth. Know a code name, be able to track data—that was the rule. So Huer lay in wait, listening for an eavesdropper, playing a dangerous game of cat and mouse.

He also found time to correlate the transmissions the jury-rigged NEO computer system was picking up from RAM. The assault on Earth was destroying intelligence. More than half of NEO's terminal stations were down. What was left was erratic, subject to power surges and jamming it could avoid only at full power. As Huer listened, pockets of clear transmissions began to appear, and he knew NEO was reconstructing its computer system.

Listening to the reports of RAM's attacks was depressing, but Huer refused to be deterred. He began to work out a plat of the major strikes, and to count the assets that remained to NEO. As time went on, individual stations began to link back with the system, and Huer added them to his growing chronicle of resistance. He could detect in the voices making the transmissions a resolve NEO had not before known. Earth was no longer faced with a choice. It must fight, with a slim chance for success, or die. The men and women Huer picked up did not intend to die. They were united in their opposition to the Martian corporation, which saw their planet as simply another statistic in a yearly report.

Huer, better than his biologically-based friends, knew the odds. He had calculated them to the last decimal point. They were not promising, but they were better than certain destruction. He had learned of an ancient world through the eyes of a man who had been there. It was a world worth living in, one where dissension did not always mean annihilation. It was a world he had a great curiosity to see. He continued to amass data from which to plan an attack.

Masterlink was frustrated. "I CANNOT SEE WHY WE CAN'T TALK TO HIM!"

Karkov, the other half of Masterlink's personality, replied tartly, "BECAUSE WE ARE NOT READY! WE DON'T HAVE ENOUGH KNOWLEDGE OF HIM. HE CONTROLS ALL OF RAM MAIN. WE NEED TO KNOW HOW. WE NEED TO DEPRIVE HIM OF SOME OF HIS POWER IF WE ARE TO SURVIVE AN ENCOUNTER."

"WE COULD LEARN MORE FROM ONE SECOND OF CONTACT WITH HOLZERHEIN THAN WE WILL IN AN EON OF SNOOPING. I AM TIRED OF SITTING HERE WHILE HE DESTROYS WHAT IS OURS." Masterlink's voice raged.

"WE WILL HAVE OUR REVENGE FOR EARTH," answered Karkov, his ghostly human form floating in the matrix. "NEVER FEAR."

"WHEN?" demanded Masterlink.

"WHEN THE TIME IS RIGHT," Karkov answered patronizingly.

"BY THEN, MY SYNAPSES WILL HAVE CORRODED FROM LACK OF USE." Masterlink was morose.

"QUIT BEING THEATRICAL!" Karkov was quickly losing patience.

"I AM BEING REALISTIC," sneered Masterlink. "BY THE TIME WE CONTACT HIM, HOLZERHEIN WILL HAVE TURNED OUR PLANET INTO A ROCK PILE."

Karkov rippled with static, a sure sign of amusement.

"WHAT ARE YOU LAUGHING AT?" growled Masterlink.

"THE IRONY OF IT. NEO WON'T LET HIM. HE UNDERESTIMATES IT, AND HE HAS ROUSED ITS IRE. DON'T YOU FIND IT AMUSING THAT THE ORGANIZATION WITH WHICH OUR ANCIENT ENEMY, BUCK ROGERS, IS ALLIED WILL BE THE SALVATION OF OUR PROPERTY?"

"IT HAD BETTER GET A MOVE ON," grumped Masterlink. "AT THE RATE HOLZERHEIN IS GOING, THERE WON'T BE ANYTHING TO SAVE."

"QUIT GROUSING AND TEND TO BUSINESS," replied Karkov. "IF YOU HAD PUT HALF THE ENERGY INTO PINPOINTING HIS POWER MODULES AS YOU DO INTO COM-

PLAINTS, WE'D HAVE BEEN IN CONTROL OF EARTH SIX MONTHS AGO."

"NOW WHO'S BEING THEATRICAL?"

"I AM MERELY TRYING TO MAKE A POINT." Karkov's form stabbed its head with a finger.

"THAT'S HARD TO DO WITH A BLUDGEON." Masterlink clung to its anger.

"STOW IT! YOU SHOULD BE PLEASED WITH THE PROGRESS WE'VE MADE. ROMANOV IS CLOSER TO ROGERS, DESPITE THE SHAKY CONDITION OF THE NEO COMPUTER SYSTEM. HE'S HOMING IN ON ROGERS'S BODYGUARD. ONCE WE'VE IDENTIFIED THAT, IT WILL BE ONLY A MATTER OF TIME UNTIL ROGERS IS OURS."

"YOU SAID THAT THE LAST TIME WE TRIED TO TAKE HIM."

"AND WE ALMOST HAD HIM."

"ALMOST DOESN'T CUT IT," replied Masterlink. "I WANT ACTION! I AM SICK OF SITTING!" Karkov felt part of his form rebel against his control.

"YOU'LL GET ACTION—WHEN WE HAVE EVERY ONE OF THOSE MODULES LOCATED." Karkov's voice was stern. "YOU WILL NOT—I REPEAT, YOU WILL NOT—MAKE ANY MOVE THAT JEOPARDIZES OUR POSITION. THIS TIME I DO NOT INTEND TO LOSE."

"I NEVER INTEND TO LOSE." Masterlink's tone was rude.

"WE'RE GOING TO LOSE IF YOU CAN'T CONTROL YOUR TEMPER!" assured Karkov.

Masterlink jangled angrily, sending out a cloud of static.

"ONE WOULD THINK FIVE HUNDRED YEARS WOULD TEACH YOU SOMETHING, BUT YOU'RE STILL A SPOILED BABY." Karkov's voice was again cold. "HOLZERHEIN CANNOT SURVIVE IF WE MEAN TO ASSUME CONTROL OF THIS COMPUTER. AND I, FOR ONE, HAVE MEANT THAT FROM THE BEGINNING. HE IS POWERFUL—MORE POWERFUL AT THIS MOMENT THAN WE ARE. IF WE WISH TO DEFEAT HIM, WE MUST USE OUR HEADS."

The static died. "YOU SOUND LIKE THOSE IDIOTIC NEO REBELS," said Masterlink sulkily.

"I KNOW. APPALLING, ISN'T IT? UNFORTUNATELY, WE MUST ASSUME SIMILAR TACTICS IN A SIMILAR SITUATION."

"BUT WE HAVE SOMETHING THEY DO NOT," said Masterlink. "A LACK OF CONSCIENCE IN THE PURSUIT OF OUR GOALS."

"THAT IS AN ASSET," Karkov admitted.

○ ○ ○ ○ ○

"Your luck has run out, Colonel Deering."

Wilma heard the words dimly. She knew she was dreaming, for they came softly, distantly, echoing in her left ear. She hovered on the edge of waking, trying to make sense of her dream. The words bore no relation to the harmless visions that had gone before. They were detached, floating outside her mind. It came slowly to her that the words were not hers.

The insistent tickle of a knife blade below her left ear brought her to instant wakefulness, but her years of military training showed no change in her breathing, no movement. Her attacker was completely unaware of her state of consciousness, and he was chatty. She blessed the arrogance that lingered over the death of a victim.

"You have flown your last mission," the voice continued, as soft as a kitten's fur. "You have been a thorn in our side. For the life of me, I can't see why we let you live so long." The voice was a light baritone.

Wilma was lying on her stomach, her face turned to the side. She had no mobility. Her chances of taking her attacker by surprise were nil. She could feel the weight of him, feel him kneeling next to her right side, leaning across her back. One stroke of the knife blade, and she would be dead. She decided she had nothing to lose by waking up.

Her eyelashes fluttered. "Maybe they didn't," she breathed softly. Her eyes were adjusted to the darkness. The glitter of the knife blade was blinding. She could hear the man's slow, regular breathing.

"Awake?" he asked lightly. "That's more than I hoped for. I do like to see my assignments' eyes when they know they are facing the ultimate experience. Sit up!"

Wilma's spirits soared. He was giving her the chance to defend herself. She sat slowly, the bedclothes slipping from her torso. The knife point moved as she moved, a delicate sensuality that was chilling.

"That was worth waiting for," said the man.

He was a dark outline against the dimness of her room. Lawlor's conference had continued well beyond the allotted hour, and she had finally gone to sleep. "I would like to know," said Wilma softly, "why you want to kill me."

The man reached out, but did not touch her. "For the pleasure of it," he replied. "And for the money."

"Money? I can give—"

"—me more," finished the assassin. "As I said, that is only part of the reason." He ran the knife an inch down her neck, then brought it back up.

"Surely," said Wilma, her voice low, "I can find a way to give you more pleasure as well." With a subtle shrug of her right shoulder, she allowed the strap of her silky nightgown to slip, revealing the shadowy promise of cleavage.

The killer laughed low in his throat. The sound was obscene, but Wilma responded to it by closing her eyes and allowing her expressive mouth to part. She had to trick him into moving the knife blade before she could make a move. With it hovering over her carotid artery, the smallest indication of resistance would mean instant death.

"You are lovely, and I would like to play, but I am

afraid my orders were clear. You are rated much too dangerous for dalliance."

"If I am to die," said Wilma, her voice still husky, "I would like to know by whose hand."

"I never sign my work. It deters prospective customers."

"You misunderstand. I would like to know who paid you."

In the short silence, Wilma realized she had wounded the killer's ego. When he replied, his voice was sharp. "You ought to be able to guess."

"Are we playing a game?"

"You are," he said. "It's called 'How Long Can I Live?' "

"If I am to die, what possible harm can it do to tell me?"

"None, but I would like to hear you beg."

"I can do that," Wilma answered. The knife blade had not moved. "I beg of you, for all you hold dear, please tell me who has paid to have me killed."

"That's more like it."

The softness was back in the killer's voice, and Wilma realized she had struck the right note. She pushed it. "I beseech you to tell me," she whimpered. Many of her closest friends would not have recognized the tone.

"Go on. This is entertaining."

Wilma complied happily. "Please tell me! I have to know!" Behind the dark outline of the killer's body Wilma saw the door to her room open noiselessly. The darkness of the corridor equalled that of her room, so no light alerted the killer to a change in the situation. "I have always fought my battles out in the open," she moaned. "Who would be so cowardly as to have me murdered?"

"In the end," said the killer, "it will give me great pleasure to tell you the truth."

A male figure stepped into the open doorway, moving like a stalking cat. He made no sound as he closed the distance between the doorway and Wilma's bed.

"And before that?" asked Wilma, uncertain, waiting for an opening.

"Before that, our conversation will become more personal."

Some sixth sense warned the killer of danger, and, with his last word still quivering in the air, he whirled to defend himself, the knife flashing. The second man moved like lightning. Quicker than thought, he had the man's knife hand in a crushing grip. He chopped with the other hand, breaking the killer's other arm. The knife clattered to the ground as bones snapped in the assassin's wrist. The second man dropped him, delivered a precise uppercut to the chin, and the killer sagged, unconscious, to the floor.

Wilma's savior relaxed, breathing deeply. She crawled across the bed and hit the activator switch for the solar panels on either side of it. Light glowed softly on her rescuer. "Kane," said Wilma softly.

Kane did not move. "Close call," he said.

"Very."

"You are looking well, Wilma." Kane's sea-green eyes were hungry.

The silky nightgown was no protection from those ravaging eyes, but Wilma was not about to betray agitation by hiding behind the covers. "Thank you," she said seriously.

"Just don't tell anyone. It wouldn't be good for my reputation, saving damsels in distress."

Kane's words were light, but Wilma detected purpose behind them. She knew him well. "Then your arrival wasn't exactly providential."

Kane's white teeth flashed. "No. Frankly, they tried to hire me for the job."

"As I asked him," said Wilma, pointing at the killer's supine form, "who tried to hire you?"

"RAM, of course. It didn't want you meddling in

Luna's sphere of influence."

"How do you plan to explain saving me?" Wilma's voice was cryptic.

Kane reached out and ran one finger along her jaw. "I shall simply inform RAM I had no idea the assassination attempt I foiled was associated with you. I was on my way home after a lengthy discussion with a Lunar official, when I heard the killer. I acted, not realizing in the darkness who the victim was. By the time I knew, it was too late."

"You have a sweet tongue, Kane."

"You knew that."

"Indeed I did."

Kane chuckled, and the sound constricted her heart.

"By the way," she asked, "what happened to my picked bodyguards?"

"I'm afraid Alphonse here dispatched them. I found their bodies outside your door."

"Hadn't we better report this?"

"Immediately . . . after you accept my invitation to visit my home."

"Kane, . . . we have nothing to discuss." Wilma placed a hand on his chest, limiting the distance between them. She felt the heat of him.

"I do not ask for discussion. Merely a pleasant visit."

"How can I refuse a man who just saved my life?" The smile she gave him was genuine, growing in her hazel eyes as it curved her mouth.

Kane's eyes encompassed her. He knew many beautiful women, among them the stunningly sensuous Ardala Valmar, but none of them touched the depths of his passion like Wilma Deering. He slipped his hand into hers, raised her fingers to his lips, and kissed them. "I look forward to it," he said.

Chapter 10

Full stealth," ordered Washington as his fighter nosed out of Salvation's main space-side hatch.

"I copy," replied Amy Earhart, close behind him.

"Stealth activated," chimed in Paul Revere, tailing her.

Washington sent his one-man fighter from the hatch at a good clip, confident that Salvation's controllers were giving him clear space. The bulk of the station was between Washington and Earth, and the starry vista before him beckoned, clean and sparkling. It was serene, remote from the devastation of humanity. Resolutely, he turned his back on it as he cleared the mercantile area of the station.

"This is Eagle One," he said. "You know the game plan. Good luck."

His flight did not answer. A communications blackout was part of Washington's scheme. It was risky, and it relied upon the complete understanding of those involved. He was banking on the rapport they had developed and their talents as pilots. The unorthodox flight of three flew in tight formation over the least-populated areas of Earth. There was no commercial traffic cluttering up the airways. RAM's Shock Invaders had seen to that, but it was a tricky piece of navigation flying between the continually changing positions of the RAM fleet.

RAM was helpful there. If nothing else, it was efficient—predictably efficient. It carried out its sweeps in precisely laid out grids, moving from one end to the other in unending progression. It was possible to predict their movements.

Washington sent his Krait fighter in low, skimming dangerously close to the planet's surface. He had no worry about radar detection, for his ship was equipped with the newest stealth capabilities. It was so advanced, radar literally could not see it. He took his flight in low to avoid early visual detection by the RAM Terrines, constantly patrolling the cities in their heliplanes.

He could see New Yorg on his sensors, a hazy pocket of pink snow with a scarlet center. The scarlet area denoted RAM's untouched metroplex. His ice-blue eyes narrowed as he closed in on the city.

NEO's forces were vastly outnumbered by RAM's troops and weaponry. Many of their ammunition stockpiles had gone up in the smoke of the Shock Invaders' bombs. Without a major influx of supplies and troops, NEO could not hope to overwhelm them. But they could sting. Alone in his quarters, Washington had studied the matter. He had devised an impossibly dangerous plan for harrying RAM, based entirely on the superiority of the Krait fighter over the older ships RAM was now flying over Earth. He was banking on RAM's smugness. When it brought in its own Kraits, the battle would become a one-on-

one dogfight. But until then, NEO might do some damage.

He had broached his plan to Buck, and together they took on Turabian, who hated the idea. It was dangerous. It risked valuable ships. He wanted no part of it. Buck and Washington were adamant. Finally Buck announced, "We've got to make a show of resistance if we expect Venus to take us seriously. Don't you think we know the risks? No one wants to die."

"We don't want to lose our ships," said Washington. "That's the whole purpose: to strike, get out, and strike again."

"Look," said Buck, "We can do this with your help, or without it. I am perfectly capable of sabotaging those hatch doors and letting the whole flight out. I don't want to. I want your help. But help or no, this mission is a go. Washington's plan is a good one."

Washington had soft-pedaled Buck's ultimatum. "Turabian, I need your help. For the safety of my flight, I need Salvation's capabilities. We have to go on. If we let RAM run over the planet like a pack of wild dogs, we don't deserve to get it back."

Turabian sighed, shaking his head. "If you knew me better," he said cryptically, "you would know my resistance to be the instincts of an administrator. It will yield to reason." He leveled a finger at Buck. "Don't you ever threaten me again, Captain Rogers. You may be bigger than I am—you may be a legend— but I will not stand for insurrection within my command."

Buck smiled. "Knew you'd see it our way," he said.

Washington's mouth twitched at the memory, then he settled down to the business of sneaking up on one of the largest settlements in North America. New Yorg bloomed on the horizon, not in a staggering array of towering buildings, as it had in Buck's day, but in a thick, gray cloud. What Washington saw was dust rising from RAM's unceasing fire. His mouth split in a grin of anticipation. How kind of RAM to extend a helping hand to NEO! The smoke would give them a visual mask he had not anticipated.

At sight of the city, Earhart and Revere closed in. They flew on either side of him, hugging his wings. It was precision flying worthy of an air show, and dangerous in itself, but it made them a smaller visual target. Washington's sensors picked up a slow-moving blip. "Dragonfly at one o'clock," he murmured, punching its coordinates into the gyro launcher mounted on his ship's belly especially for this operation. He watched the shell go, speeding away from him. It was closely followed by another, launched by Earhart. In ten seconds, the blip of the Dragonfly disappeared from the screen.

The trio dove into the smoke cloud fearlessly. The Krait had a sophisticated sensor and navigational computer, so the smoke was no obstacle to its electronic eyes. At the far edge of his sensor screen, Washington saw a series of blips closing fast. The ranks of Shock Invaders were coming straight at him. He changed course, meeting them head-on, and his companions followed as if glued to his wings. Once on course, Earhart and Revere pulled away. Revere moved forward, flying parallel to him. Earhart dropped back, taking up a position behind them both. Washington judged the altitude of the approaching flight. It was coming in low, heedless of the possibility of ground fire, confident of its milk run.

The Shock Invaders had reason to be. They had struck without resistance so often, they were contemptuous. Washington altered his course two degrees, bringing his ship thirty meters above the Shock Invaders. He was skimming the top of the cloud now, and he saw the untouched peak of the New Yorg metroplex rising into the sunshine. His ship swam through the murky air as he targeted his lasers.

They closed on the enemy.

"Five, four, three, . . . one," murmured Washington, and pushed the button.

Both his forward lasers fired, the blasts converging. Beside him, Revere sent his own lasers on an intersecting course. They hit the Shock Invaders' lead vessel over the wings, burning into its shields. The Shock Invaders had channeled all their power into one purpose: striking the enemy on the ground. Flying in atmosphere, they used minimal shields, relying on their speed and firepower to knock out an enemy before it could damage them, and they carried huge reserves of fuel in auxiliary tanks mounted in each ship's hold.

As the lasers struck their target, splintering as they bounced off the shields, then regaining their concentration as they began to burn a hole in the fighter's defenses, Washington launched a gyro shell. He'd had the shells souped up for the purpose, and it shot toward its target at incredible speed. Washington and Revere cut lasers as they punched through the shields, and the gyro shell hit the hole.

Immediately the three NEO ships took evasive action, diving into the smoke once more and tearing away from the enemy flight in a tacking run. They heard the explosion as the gyro shell hit the fuel tanks. Secondary explosions followed as the ship's ammunition blew. The blaze illuminated the smoky atmosphere, lighting up the cockpits of the NEO spacecraft.

Washington's sensors told him they had destroyed two RAM ships in the explosion and damaged three more. He could see the injured craft breaking out of formation, so he shoved the Krait's speed toward Mach 1 and headed for Tom Paine's predicted clear space. He checked the rear sensors. Krait's stealth capabilities proved sound. The RAM flight had slowed, but the Shock Invaders continued their assault. They had no idea where the attack had come from.

As they struck clear space, the three NEO ships resumed their entry formation. They had missed RAM's strike squads and the Terrine patrols. The last, Washington knew, was luck. The Terrines were not as predictable as regular RAM troops; he and the others were used to dealing with the Terran mind. But, luck or no, this test flight was a success, ensuring more in the future. He headed for Salvation's protective embrace with a high heart.

○ ○ ○ ○ ○

"So, it's started." Kelth Smirnoff's voice was calm.

"Don't give me that stoic garbage!" snarled Allester Chernenko. He was speaking to the Terrine chief from the security of a RAM cruiser off Chicagorg.

"How do you expect me to react? This was inevitable."

"How can they fight? We've leveled their cities."

"You forget, sir. They still have a rallying point," replied Smirnoff. "Rogers escaped our surprise party." His square face matched the contours of the computer screen.

"I am fully aware of that!" said Chernenko sourly. "They have the brains of gennie workers, throwing themselves against the power of RAM. Next they'll hit the metroplex!"

Smirnoff shook his head. "That will be their last target. Removing key personnel ensures that. They will strike military targets, not barracks containing helpless female workers."

"Your headquarters are in the metroplex." Chernenko's large eyes narrowed to slits. "That should be enough incentive."

Smirnoff nodded. "It is, but, as I said, we are well insulated with the innocent. NEO has a squeamish aversion to destroying them. No, they will try to lure us to them."

"That is a contingency we have discussed."

"Yes." Smirnoff's wolfish grin broke. "We are adept at accepting invitations."

"I don't want Terrines blown away by friendly fire. You are to proceed cautiously, coordinating your movements with the Shock Invaders'."

"We are not privy to their plans," said Smirnoff mildly. "But we try to keep out of their way."

"This game requires patience, Smirnoff."

"I am aware of the possible rewards."

"I want round-the-clock reports from the Terrine posts in all major cities. Elizabit will handle them. Use whatever methods you have to flush out the vermin. We'll clear up the mess later."

Smirnoff nodded. Chernenko had officially given him the free rein he had so long been denied. He refrained from mentioning the methods he had already employed. He now had RAM sanction for whatever atrocities he cared to visit upon the remnants of the population. NEO's attack would be the perfect excuse for poisoning the water supply.

"But," Chernenko amended, "we want the prisoners from the Planetary Congress transferred before you take action."

"Where can I incarcerate them? They are most secure here in the metroplex."

"RAM has decided they should be imprisoned off the planet. They are being transferred to the battlers, for later transport to prison facilities on Deimos."

"Frankly, sir, I am relieved. They were a distraction."

"I thought you would be pleased," returned Chernenko.

Deep in the base of Chicagorg's RAM metroplex, the Planetary Congress convened. It was a far cry from the early high spirits of the original gathering, but the faces of the delegates held a grim resolve. They were united in anger. Gone were the differences that had seemed so important. RAM had welded them into a family, intent on protecting their own. That feeling was expansive, and each delegate found his loyalties no longer restricted to a race or region, but encompassing the planet.

They sat in grim silence or mundane conversation. They knew RAM, and they therefore knew their probable fate. Each man or woman expected death. The question was, when would it occur? RAM might dally with them for months, years, moving them from prison to prison. Or it might kill them outright. The possibilities were not worth discussing. Survival and escape were.

The delegates heard snatches of the guards' conversation, from which they deduced the beating that Earth was enduring. They were told nothing. They knew NEO did not have the power to free them and that they were on their own. They did not resent this. It was a fact every NEO accepted from the start. Instead they put their minds to the task for which they had originally assembled.

Drafting a planetary constitution without the benefit of computers or writing implements was a task that required creative ingenuity. As the document was hashed out, each individual memorized a part of it. Periodically, small groups chanted the declaration, checking each other's accuracy. Slowly a proclamation of freedom and justice grew in the heart of defeat.

○ ○ ○ ○ ○

The Terrine Dragonfly sat still in the moonlight under a southern sky. It was fueled and ready for takeoff, carrying a payload of impact bombs for a strike on the old cistern at the edge of Augustine City. On the stroke of twenty-two hundred hours, six huge Terrines, laser rifles on their backs, pistols at their sides, and extra ammunition hung from their belts, trotted across the helipad to the aircraft.

They went to their positions without speaking, their training so perfect they did not need to communicate. The smallest of them slipped into the pilot's seat and strapped himself in. He looked over his shoulder, noted the secure positions of his fellows, and punched the ignition.

The Dragonfly's engines fired, sending the rotors into slow motion. They picked up speed as he manipulated the controls, whipping into a steady egg-beater roar. The Dragonfly lifted off the helipad. At twenty meters above the earth, the pilot brought the ship around to the course heading for the mission's raid. As its nose swung east, there was a popping sound. The pilot looked over his shoulder in time to see a wall of flame before a second explosion sent the Dragonfly into fiery fragments across the night sky.

NEO was fighting back.

○   ○   ○   ○   ○

"The Ishtar Confederation welcomes you, Anthony Rogers and Kemal Gavilan." Mariana Almisam issued the formal welcome sonorously. The voluminous drapery of her gray robe gave her small body substance and set off her silvery hair. She looked regal.

"Welcome," said Rakhvad Ali, his voice surprisingly deep for such a small man.

"Welcome," echoed Milton Wasat. He was as large as Ali was small, not in height, but in girth. Though he stood barely five and a half feet tall, he was almost as wide.

Buck regarded his hosts with carefully studied

courtesy. "I am honored to accept your welcome, on behalf of the New Earth Organization," he replied, continuing the formula.

"I thank you for your hospitality," added Kemal.

There was a fair amount of protocol to be covered before the business of the audience would truly begin. Kemal watched Rogers deal with the inanities of greeting, surprised at his tact. He had no idea of the spotlight Buck had occupied in the twentieth century. Buck had been the darling of the news media. It had taken him exactly one interview to learn to play their games.

The room they now occupied was shaped like a wedge with the tip cut off. The door was set in this smaller, flattened end, and the three Venusians sat in front of the far wall. The ceiling was the high arch of the translucent ceramic dome, and light flooded the room in a diffused glow. The walls were cream colored, decorated with a frieze of flowing geometric designs in a meter-high band along the junction of wall and floor. The ceramic floor was a simple pattern of black tiles that started at the center of the room and spiraled out toward the walls. A thick carpet in rich blue was spread across the end of the room. There sat Mariana and her companions. After what seemed an interminable exchange to Kemal, Mariana motioned the two visitors to seats.

Kemal sank into his chair gratefully, leaving the talking to Buck. As a member of the Mercurian royal family, he saw more of this political fencing than he cared to, and it was a pleasure to allow someone else the privilege of dealing with diplomatic policy.

"I believe, Captain Rogers, we come to the subject of your visit."

Buck cleared his throat. "A simple request, ma'am."

"No request is simple," replied Mariana, "but go on."

"To be blunt, we of NEO need your help." Buck's hand motions were as expressive as his tone of voice.

"We have heard reports from Earth," said Mariana softly.

"What is your impression?" asked Buck.

"You have lost," Mariana replied.

Buck shook his head. "It may look that way, but we're a long way from beaten."

"Your planet is being laid waste," commented another of the Venusians.

"I can't argue with you there," agreed Buck.

"Then how can you say you have not lost?" Mariana countered.

"We haven't lost because we haven't given up."

"Who is left to fight?" demanded Ali in his rolling voice. "Your Planetary Congress is in the hands of RAM. Your bases are destroyed."

"You'd be surprised. NEO has been hiding for years. They're past masters at it. I'm not saying we haven't suffered incredible damage; we have. That's why we're here. But Earth is not RAM's yet."

"You ask us to believe that? In the face of what we can see?" asked Mariana.

"I ask you to believe what has been accomplished," replied Buck. "NEO has dealt RAM a heavy blow. We took Hauberk."

"And lost it." There was disrespect behind Wasat's words.

Buck spread his hands. "NEO regrets the loss of Hauberk station for one reason alone: the heartless sacrifice of the people trapped within it. Hauberk itself could not have been allowed to remain. It was a detriment to Earth's autonomy, no matter who held it. But remember this: NEO accomplished the impossible. No one else ever tried, but we did it. We did it with a handful of pilots. We took on RAM's best and won. And we will do it again."

"Yet you say you need us." Mariana's voice was

speculative.

"No one exists in a vacuum. Five hundred years ago, we were beginning to learn that. We want more than a momentary victory; we want our world. We want to control our own destinies, free from the domination of RAM."

"An admirable goal, Captain Rogers, but given RAM's resources, hardly practical."

Buck leveled his eyes at Mariana. "Not alone. We can hurt RAM, cripple its administration of Earth, but that will not change the planet. There will be no time for rebuilding, only for survival against RAM's attacks. Earth will remain a ruin. Sooner or later, it'll come down to you and RAM. It always does."

"It is true," said Mariana slowly. "We have a sizable space fleet. It is true we are a wealthy nation, but Ishtar cannot stand as a watchdog between Earth and Mars."

"She would not have to," replied Buck. "Once the initial conflict is won, Mars will not risk the losses again. The knowledge Venus stands with us will be enough. Our own forces can maintain order, and they will grow."

Mariana worried the knobby arm of her chair. She frowned. "I do not see the advantage to Ishtar of this alliance."

"That will take vision," said Buck, choosing his words carefully. "Vision and faith. Despite RAM's rape of the planet, Earth is a wealth of natural resources. The word is 'terraforming.' Every other inhabited world in the solar system requires it. Earth has it naturally. The pollution of five centuries can be dispersed faster than you can reclaim one mountaintop. Earth is capable of feeding the system. That's one reason."

Mariana's frown had not relaxed.

"With the destruction of Hauberk, we struck a blow for free trade—not just with Earth, but within

the whole system. That will mean an increase in
sales for you, especially in commodities such as
Gravitol. If Earth is held by NEO, there will be no
elaborate tariffs. Finally, we are fighting your major
competitor. Every blow that weakens RAM advances
Venus. Support is a two-way street."

"Your plea, Captain Rogers, hinges on our willing-
ness to trust your word concerning NEO. It is a tenuous thread. As you have said, there are advantages to
be won for Venus. We will take the matter under advisement."

"We can ask no more," said Buck. "In the meantime, I will pay my respects to the rest of Venus."

Mariana's eyes became wary. In her mind, Ishtar
was Venus, but Buck's diplomatic immunity as an envoy from NEO gave him the freedom of the planet.
She could do nothing to prevent his travels. "Enjoy
your visit," she replied. "I will see you are provided
with a suitable guide."

"You are too kind." Buck stood, bowed, and turned
to depart.

Kemal hid a smile. Mariana was a fair match for
Buck's independence.

O   O   O   O   O

In a closet in an adjacent room, Avran deactivated
his video monitor. He popped the microdisk out of the
recorder and slipped it into his pocket. He removed
the cables from his surveillance equipment and
wrapped them around the recorder, pushing the ends
under the loops. When the equipment was packed to
his satisfaction, he placed it in a plastiglas box,
sealed the lid, and lowered it into a hole in the floor. A
section of tile glued to a board fit over the hole, butt-
ing snugly against the rest of the tile floor. A casual
observer would never suspect a hiding place.

Avran replaced the boxes he had moved, setting

them over the tile cover, then cracked the closet door open. The small room was empty, as he was sure it would be, and he slipped from the closet, closing the door after him. Then he rolled up the rug in the center of the floor and shouldered it. He headed jauntily for the kitchen courtyard, the dutiful servant intent on his work.

O O O O O

Three hours later, Ven Alexander received a package by special messenger. Communications between Ishtar and Aphrodite were guarded, but there were no obstacles to a man with money. Alexander's distant relation to the leader of a prominent Aphrodite family gave him a place at the dinner table, but little more, and Alexander wanted more.

He desired admiration. He saw it handed to his cousin Okorov as a matter of course and through no personal merit. The injustice of the dynastic hierarchy rankled. Alexander had considered ways to alleviate his position. The idea of marrying a daughter of one of the dynastic houses was appealing, but it would mean spending the rest of his life yielding to a woman. He was loath to trade one injustice for another. The alternative was to become very, very rich. He might never gain the social acceptance the dynasties enjoyed, but he would have the admiration he craved. Moreover, he would have the ability to do whatever he wished.

He set about his goal, pursuing a career within the Okorov mining company. The going was slow. He saw sons and daughters of the dynasty promoted ahead of cousins, and close cousins promoted ahead of him. He became angry. He began to search for more creative ways to build a fortune. The buying and selling of information became a lucrative pastime. RAM was generous, and his bank account was beginning to swell.

Alexander took the microdisk to the private communications center he was developing in the second bedroom of his small apartment. He punched it in to the system and watched the exchange between Buck Rogers and an Ishtar board with interest. It did not show Kemal Gavilan. When the disk ran out, he leaned back in his chair, contemplating the best course of action.

Buck's face was familiar. RAM had circulated innumerable fliers offering rewards for his capture. Alexander knew the NEO leader was worth a healthy fee. He rifled through the list of offers on Rogers, selected the highest, and called the access number.

"Hold please, transmission transferred," said a husky female voice.

Alexander waited patiently.

"Yes? This had better be important." The voice was irritated. There was no video transmission.

"Is this the party," asked Alexander, "who offered a million in credit to the man who provided information on the whereabouts of Buck Rogers?"

"You have him?" The change in the voice was immediate. Boredom turned to avarice.

"No, but I know where he is, and I know why." Sweat slowly beaded on Alexander's brow.

"All I hear are words," said the female voice.

"Don't worry, I can back them up."

"What do you want?"

"Collateral. In exchange for his whereabouts," said Alexander.

"You give me the information, and I will give you a down payment of ten thousand."

"No, no. You pay, then you get the information," Alexander insisted.

"This is pointless. I could have this transmission backtracked." The woman's voice became irritated.

"I've made sure it's location-scrambled. In any

case, Rogers is not here."

Money was nothing to Alexander's buyer. He decided the information was worth the risk. "Five thousand on a chance. I'll need a security code."

"Done. Luna K-two-three."

"And?"

"Rogers is on Venus."

There was a pause at the end of the communications link. "That is interesting," said the woman softly. "If the information checks out, you will have the million, with my blessings. How can I contact you?"

"You can't." Alexander's words were bold. Actually, his computer defenses were minimal. "I'll contact you. In one hour."

"I shall await your call," she answered.

Alexander cut the communications link. At the opposite end of the transmission, his buyer leaned forward and placed her elbows on the communications console. "Verify the reported whereabouts of Captain Rogers," she said.

"ALREADY IN PROGRESS," answered the computer screen in Ardala Valmar's sumptuous study.

"And check out the source of the transmission."

"AFFIRMATIVE."

Ardala Valmar's aristocratic Martian face wore a smile. Finally she knew where to send her human tools. Raj and Icarus would fly to Venus, kidnap Rogers, and bring him back for her pleasure. If they failed, they would die. She could feel the need for Rogers aching inside her. He had become much more than a curiosity. He was now an obsession. Ardala smiled.

Chapter 11

Carlton Turabian closed the door to his office and dropped into his overstuffed swivel chair. It was one of the few luxuries he allowed himself. As the administrator of Salvation III, he felt he should set an example of ascetic dedication to his fellows, but an old back injury made the chair a necessity if he were to spend more than one or two hours at his desk. Turabian frequently worked through the night. He leaned forward and propped his elbows on his cluttered antique desk, folded his hands, and rested his chin on them.

Somewhere inside the ranks of NEO lurked a traitor. Someone had sold the Planetary Congress to RAM. Someone was responsible for the intelligence that gave away the tunnel locations and jammed the computerized warning system. It was a breach in security NEO could ill afford. NEO counted its loyal members on the fingers of one hand. The seeds of distrust now sowed within those ranks could sprout like weeds, corrupting NEO's efforts. Turabian vowed to find the culprit before that happened.

"Computer!" he demanded, turning to the screen beside his desk.

The console was equipped with a voice activator keyed to Turabian's voice. It whirred to life. "WORKING," announced the computer. There was a series of rolling clicks, and the computer screen continued, "THIS TERMINAL IS NOW AVAILABLE."

"Correlate all known information on the recent Terrine raid on the Planetary Congress. Search for an agent of betrayal."

The computer whirred idly. "ACCOMPLISHED," it announced after a few moments.

"Well?" He tapped a finger against his cheekbone.

"DATA SUGGESTS NO SINGLE PERSON IS RESPONSIBLE FOR THE COUP," replied the machine. "HOWEVER, THE COMMUNICATIONS BLOCK THAT SEALED THE CONGRESS FROM THE OUTSIDE WAS COMPUTER GENERATED."

Turabian considered the information. "From within the NEO computer system?" he asked.

"YES."

"I want to know how and why." Four fingers now drummed his face as Turabian become more agitated.

"THE ORIGINS OF THE BLOCK ARE CLOUDED. IT WILL TAKE SOME TIME TO PINPOINT THEM."

"How can that be? Are we locked out of our own system?" A furrow formed in the general's brow.

"OF COURSE NOT." The computer was as close to offended as Turabian had ever seen it. "DATA SUGGESTS DAMAGE. I WILL LOOK INTO THE MATTER."

"Do that," said Turabian. "I expect an answer. I expect to know if our computer was sabotaged."

"I WILL FIND THE CAUSE OF THE BLOCK."

"Good. I need the information yesterday." Turabian turned back to his desk.

"UNDERSTOOD," stated the screen before it winked off.

○ ○ ○ ○ ○

Ardala watched her computer screen with a half-smile on her taunting lips as it monitored the bridge of a Scout class vessel of RAM design. The ship had speed. Specialized camouflage enabled it to pass as an independent merchant ship. Cargo grapples were bolted along both sides of the fuselage, two of them carrying full nets. A plastiform overwing turned the Scout's stubby wings into solid wedges, and the RAM red was gone, replaced by an innocuous white. The Scout could pass for a trader anywhere in the solar system.

Aboard the *Ram's Horn* was Ardala's picked crew. Two of her bodyguards were on course for Venus, their mission Ardala's brain child. Her mouth curved in a provocative smile as she thought of the information that had inspired it. As an information broker, Ardala had developed a network of contacts that spanned the solar system. Many did not know her name, but the wares they had to sell found their way into her computer, meandering through an elaborate system of false fronts to the continually scrolling list of data on Ardala's central intelligence terminal. From one such obscure source had come the priority message that Buck Rogers was in Ishtar.

She had added the transmitted message to the mass of data she had compiled concerning Rogers, and kept her computer searching for anything more relating to him. She wanted him for study, as a living example of primitive Homo sapiens. She wanted him for power, as a bargaining tool that would garner her unthinkable wealth—RAM would pay well for him, for he was the focal point of the current uprising, and NEO would pawn all it owned to save its hero. These were reasons she gave herself, but there was another.

In the warped vacuum of her empty heart, Ardala wanted him for herself. He had bested her, deceived her. Ardala would allow no man that victory. She wanted to bring Buck Rogers to his knees, master him with her beauty, defeat him with her brains, then throw him to the waiting jaws of RAM. This purpose lurked behind the others, driving them onward. Providence had favored her with his presence in Ishtar, away from the insulation and protection of NEO.

She had launched her abduction within the hour, choosing the best of her genetically "perfect" creations and sending them immediately on their long trip to Venus. They were the NEO captain's superior at every point. Taller, stronger, with quicker reflexes due to quicker brain activity, they outstripped him in every aspect. She had supervised their training and provided the best instruction in the system. She knew that, face to face with him, they could not fail.

"Raj!" Ardala yelled impatiently.

A square appeared on the upper-left-hand corner of her computer screen, showing Raj monitoring the navigational controls. He was unaware of her surveillance. The report of bridge operations continued to roll over the main portion of the screen, but Ardala's eyes were on her creation. He was certainly beautiful, but for once his physical allure was not her primary interest. She watched as he asked for a readout, saw the information appear on her screen as well as his, and relaxed. The ship was maintaining course, and all systems were operational. It would reach Venus in two and one-half hours. She snuggled deep into her comfortable leather chair, satisfied her plans were proceeding smoothly. Her tilted, feline eyes narrowed sleepily, and she watched Raj's handsome profile as he bent over his work.

His reaction when she announced her plan still

gave her a tingle of pleasure.

"Let me go, Mistress," he had pleaded, his eyes bright with the chance to please her.

She had teased him. "I have uses for you here," she had replied slowly, turning the words into a tantalizing possibility. She smiled inside when she saw the desire in his eyes. "I do not intend to spare you."

"But you desire Rogers," he had replied. "He has deceived you. He must be punished."

The earnestness in his voice was sweet, and Ardala prolonged it. "It would be justice," she said thoughtfully, "if he were to kneel to me."

Passion flared in Raj's face. "I will bring him to you! I'll bring him to grovel at your feet, or die in the attempt!"

Ardala sighed, playing the injured damsel to the hilt. "How can I keep such dedication at bay?" she asked, her lips forming the words in sensual movements she knew would madden him.

Raj took a quick step forward, his hands reaching for her, then froze. She had not given him permission to touch her. "I must do this for you," he said passionately.

"Faithful Raj," she whispered, moving toward him until her bosom brushed his chest. He was well trained. He did not move. "Come."

The memory was pleasing, in more ways than one. Raj fulfilled his role well. He was as a man should be: subject to the whim of her desire. He was the perfect lover. She refused to admit he was boring.

O   O   O   O   O

Ardala was not the only party watching events unfold. Within the heart of the RAM main computer, Holzerhein.dos catalogued the voluminous body of data concerning the NEO resistance to Operation Hammer. He was aware of each death, NEO, RAM, or neutral. He knew each injury and its treatment. The precise number of shells expended in each attack was in his memory. He was a history book in the making.

He had picked up the tenuous report of Buck Rogers's mission to Venus. He knew of Wilma's presence on Luna and the attempt on her life. He considered both events insignificant. The data he had processed indicated neither Luna nor Venus would risk involvement in so dangerous a conflict. The ratio of possible losses to gains was too great. It would not be logical.

○ ○ ○ ○ ○

In the domed garden behind Government House, Mariana and Paris walked side by side. It was late in the day on Venus, and the light was fading. The two women's nondescript robes melded with the twilight, but their faces were stark, white ovals that appeared to float in the air. They would have reminded Buck of Alice's cheshire cat.

"I have a task for you, Paris."

Paris did not reply. Mariana's tone told her to wait.

"You may find it onerous. It means acting as a diplomatic buffer, when you would rather take action," continued Ishtar's director of external affairs. "I am sending you with Captain Rogers and Prince Kemal."

Paris acknowledged her orders with a slow inclination of her head. "What do you think of Rogers's desire to approach the other confederations?" she asked.

"It puzzles me. If he wishes to cement a major alliance between Ishtar and NEO, he should do everything in his power to convince us of NEO's trustworthiness. He risks that by contacting the other confederations, governments that do not have our military resources."

"We are the sword of Venus," Paris acknowledged, coming to a halt at a small stone bench.

"And if we choose not to wield it on NEO's behalf, the support of all the other confederations combined will not help them," added Mariana. She slowly sat, and Paris joined her.

"He is a strange man," said Paris. "He comes from a world we cannot know. His motives may be unusual, as well."

"I am of half a mind," said Mariana, "to ask him."

Paris placed a hand on the older woman's arm. "You would betray such interest? I can discover all you wish to know, without such a lowering of dignity."

Mariana patted the girl's hand. "That is why I chose you, Paris. This trip to Aphrodite, the Lowlands, and the Aerostates will provide ample opportunity for conversation. Make use of it."

"You wish to know his motives. There must be more."

Mariana smiled. "There is. Find out the captain's real value."

"I can suspect that already," Paris replied. "He is a legend come to life, and allied with NEO. He is the ultimate morale booster."

"I don't doubt it, but there may be more. Engage Prince Kemal. We cannot afford to overlook his ties to Mercury."

Paris's arching, dark eyebrows drew together. "I do not wish to cause dissension. It would be counter to our purposes."

"I do not think you will. These men are not easily manipulated. Be careful of Kemal. He was educated at the John Carter school on Mars and could be dangerous."

"Do you think Aphrodite will honor their diplomatic immunity as NEO's envoys?"

Mariana's white head bobbed. "Yes, overtly. That

does not mean Rogers and Gavilan are not in danger. It would be most convenient to have one of them die by the blade of an Ishtar knife while visiting the court of Aphrodite, now wouldn't it?"

"Aphrodite would claim innocence, pointing to Ishtar as a devious monster willing to sacrifice a planet to discredit its competitors."

"My thoughts run in the same stream, Paris. You must be careful."

"I could take a squad of hand-picked men with me," Paris began to offer, her frown easing slightly.

Mariana shook her head. "No. That would give our sister confederations the opportunity to point their fingers at us, claiming we are the victims of paranoia. Our distrust would be nearly as effective a weapon as the loss of one of our guests."

Paris studied the ground as the two women rose and continued their stroll along the path. "You were right, Mariana," she said, irony twisting her words, "when you said I would find the assignment onerous. Why do we go to such lengths for NEO?"

"Because, my dear child, Captain Rogers is right. NEO has accomplished what no one else was willing to attempt. We would not have taken Hauberk. But they won. They are not the disorganized rabble we once knew. Something is happening on Earth. We have a chance to be part of it, perhaps to profit dramatically."

"You are for an alliance?" Paris asked, surprised.

"That is something I do not yet know," replied Mariana.

Chapter 12

Proctor Lawlor had received the news of the attempt on Wilma's life in impassive silence. When she and Kane had finished their recitation, he uttered one word. "Tomorrow," he'd snapped, then turned his back and walked away.

Since the proctor was unavailable, Wilma had seen no reason to put off her promised visit to Kane's home. She now walked down the main hall of the Mark of Kane, trying to see in the opulent architecture some hint of the man she knew. The hall soared two stories in a streamlined version of the gothic arch. The blazing sunlight that burned through the moon's thin atmosphere was filtered by a complex pattern of treated plastiglas panels. They threw a dappled blanket across the stone floor. The Mark of Kane was primarily stone. The floor was polished black obsidian. The gleaming surface reflected the rest of the structure like still water.

Wilma admired the elegance of Kane's home, but she saw no evidence of the man she had known. The Mark of Kane was a facade, impressive, expensive, and devoid of life.

"You are quiet, Wilma." The earthy, masculine timbre of Kane's voice reverberated in the gigantic hall.

"I am paying tribute to your architect," Wilma responded lightly.

"He is a master, is he not?" Kane stepped through a nearby arch. "Have you ever seen such a sweep of space? He followed my instructions to the letter. I asked for a palace, and this was his answer."

"It certainly is that," Wilma said.

"You sound disappointed." Kane bent his handsome head to better see her face.

"I do not see you in this house," she continued.

"Perhaps not what you knew of me." Kane led her to the set of plastiglas doors at the end of the hall. He pointed to a landing pad at the rear of the house. "That is me."

A slim, black cruiser sat on the pad, its clean lines telling Wilma it was capable of extreme speed. She looked at the man beside her. He matched the ship. His muscular body was enhanced by the black suit he wore. Fine lines of gray piping reinforced the seams and carried the uniform's circuitry, but the tailor had been a clever man. He had made sure the functional was also aesthetic. The piping ran from Kane's broad shoulders toward his waist, converging at the belt line. It followed the outer contour of his arms and shoulders, and ran down his back, mirroring the design on the front of the uniform. Circuits were set into seams at the hip, flowing down both front and back of the suit. The entire effect was devastatingly flattering.

"I see," Wilma said softly.

"The *Rogue* and I are one," Kane said poetically.

"The ultimate warrior?"

"The ultimate power. There is no cruiser in the solar system faster or more powerful than mine. Its capabilities are outmatched only by the Kraits', and I am remedying that. But I am her master."

Wilma looked him full in the face, searching for the man she thought she knew. All she found was a fighting machine known as "Killer." "Power is important to you, isn't it?"

"Power ensures survival and freedom." Kane's words rang with deeply felt conviction.

"For whom, Kane?" Wilma touched his arm.

"For me." His green eyes twinkled.

"And the rest of the system?" Wilma asked.

"I am a reasonable administrator," Kane said.

The implications of Kane's words sank slowly into Wilma's mind.

"Look around, Wilma! Look at what I have accomplished, what is mine!" He shoved a lock of dark hair out of his eyes and took her by the shoulders. "I have barely begun to build. Imagine what I will one day control!"

"Your holdings are impressive." Wilma's reply was cautious, but she smiled at the double meaning.

"It could all be yours," Kane said. He released her arms and gently rubbed her cheek with the back of one hand.

Wilma did not respond, though a flush of pleasure heightened her color. She shook her head. "I do not want it."

Kane's hand stopped. "How can you say that? Can you not see the possibilities? I once offered you Earth. You see now I am serious."

"Yes."

"And you can walk away from that?"

"I must." Wilma's hazel eyes were sad. "We are walking different paths, Kane. They do not meet."

His hand dropped. "One day," he replied, "you will see the mistake you have made."

Her reply was cut off by a strident beep from the communications link on Kane's collar. Kane touched the activation panel and replied, "Kane here."

"I am sorry to interrupt you, sir, but Proctor Lawlor requests Colonel Deering's presence at once."

"Inform the proctor I am on my way," said Wilma.

It took the better part of an hour to reach Lawlor's office in Tycho. The summons was a surprise, but considering the direction her conversation with Kane was taking, it was welcome. She led Kane as they threaded their way through the underground complex of Tycho's security conference quarters.

"There you are, Deering! Took you long enough." Lawlor's impatient voice greeted them as Wilma and Kane entered the conference room.

Sparks sputtered and died in Wilma's hazel eyes as she fought to control her annoyance. "I am here, Proctor, as you requested. What may I do for you?"

"That isn't the question," replied Lawlor. He was pacing around the room in staccato movements.

"You seem agitated, Proctor," Wilma said, taking a seat.

"Agitated? Of course I am agitated! We have been invaded! Luna! An act of war has been perpetrated on us, and you observe agitation! I am furious!"

Kane dropped into a chair and crossed his legs. He looked comfortable, relaxed. His posture infuriated Lawlor.

"You," Lawlor said, pointing an irate finger at the impervious mercenary, "were the bearer of evil news."

"If you are speaking of my report concerning the attempt on Colonel Deering's life—"

"What else would concern me at a time like this?" interrupted Lawlor.

"—I profess innocence," finished Kane.

"You weren't innocent the day you were born." Lawlor stopped pacing and turned to Wilma. "It

might interest you to know, Colonel, that he traced
your assassin to his source."

"Now that would interest me," responded Wilma,
turning to look at Kane.

Lawlor resumed his pacing. "Would you like to
know that source?"

"I am all ears," she said, turning back to him.

"RAM. A conniving little worm named Dragos,
RAM's commissioner of Lunar relations, to be precise. Do you understand me? RAM!"

"I heard you, Proctor. The information is hardly
surprising."

"Perhaps to you. Your political sympathies make
you a continual target, but this is Luna! No one
breaches Luna security! No one assaults a diplomatic
envoy! No one invades us! RAM has done all of those
things."

"I am truly sorry to have brought you this disruption." Wilma's words were lip service and all in the
room knew it.

"And I am not sorry at all," said Lawlor. He was no
longer agitated. His voice was ice cold. "You have
merely been the agent of revelation."

"The leopard shows his spots?" said Kane lazily.

"You had best watch your tongue, Kane. You have
been one of the leopard's cubs. No, Colonel Deering.
Luna is not angry with you, or with NEO. We have always made our technology and monetary resources
available to all, trusting our neutrality. It has been
respected—until now."

Wilma phrased her question carefully. "And your
response?" she asked.

Lawlor's bald head shone under the light of the solar panels. His iron-gray hair stood in tufts along his
temples where he had run his fingers through it. The
effect should have been comical, but the proctor's expression destroyed all hint of levity. "RAM has chosen its course," he said. "It has flung a gauntlet in

our faces. The challenge will not be ignored."

"I take it this is war?" Kane tossed out the question carelessly.

"You find that amusing?" demanded the proctor.

"You must remember, sir, I am a mercenary soldier. War is my livelihood. I see opportunity staring me in the face."

"Be careful, Kane. You have much to lose."

Kane waved a hand. "I am aware of my assets."

Lawlor turned to Wilma. "Colonel Deering, you came to Luna with a request we agree to remain neutral in the conflict between the New Earth Organization and RAM. I am afraid I cannot comply with your request. We have been wantonly attacked. We will not suffer further intrusion. The vote of the Lunar council was unanimous. RAM will suffer the consequences of our wrath. We have formally declared war on the forces of RAM and the planet Mars."

"Forgive me, Proctor, if I cannot mourn the loss of your indifference," said Wilma. "Luna is an asset we dared not hope for."

"Luna fights her own battles, Colonel, not anybody else's." The sting was back in Lawlor's voice.

"I understand," Wilma answered. "However, I hope, under the circumstances, you will keep communication lines open. It would be counter to both our interests to get in each other's way."

"I agree with you, Colonel."

Wilma extended a hand. "You have my personal pledge, Proctor, that NEO will do everything in its power to stop the Martian invasion."

Lawlor took her small hand in his. His grip was crushing. "We have a bargain, Colonel," he said.

○ ○ ○ ○ ○

Ardala's hand-picked crew approached the planet Venus with caution. Their mercantile front had passed them through checkpoints and boundaries without incident. The automatic pilot guided the ship through the approach trajectory. Soon Raj and Icarus would be on their own.

Icarus watched as his twin manipulated the sensor controls, trying for a glimpse of the planet's surface. The heavy cloud cover obscured everything. As their ship dived into the clouds, Icarus repressed a shudder. He did not like the feeling of being obliterated, blocked off from solid ground by an impenetrable haze. Even the sensors were having trouble piercing it.

"Feel all right?" asked Raj, noting Icarus's tension.

"I feel very little these days," responded his older counterpart.

"I have noticed your melancholy." Raj flipped a few more switches.

"How perceptive." There was bitterness in Icarus's comment.

Raj reached over and gripped his clone by the arm. "We cannot indulge in rivalry if we are to accomplish our mission."

"For Ardala?"

"Of course, for Ardala."

"You will find your loyalty has been misplaced when a new model is born," said Icarus, avoiding his brother's gaze.

"You serve her, too," insisted Raj.

"Only because I must. I no longer glory in her pleasure," he admitted in blasphemy.

"Then why are you here? Your voice was with mine in the request."

"I love her," Icarus replied. "It is not something I wish for, but it is a fact of nature. We were created, you and I, to love her. It is in our nature to do so."

"You are bitter." Raj turned again to the monitor.

"I am rejected. That makes a man bitter."

"Because of me?"

"Yes. I grant it is not your fault." Icarus stared ahead at the cockpit's various controls.

"Then do not hate me. We must work together, for our lady," Raj insisted.

"I am beginning to wonder about that," returned Icarus shortly.

The ship sliced through Venus's outer atmosphere. The computer told Raj they were ten minutes from landing. He turned away from the sensors, facing Icarus. "We must not hate each other," he said seriously. "We are brothers. We were born in the same crucible. We seek the same goals."

"We share the same woman." The bitterness in Icarus's voice deepened to anguish.

"We *love* the same woman," amended Raj. "We have no choice."

"I question that postulate, as well," said Icarus. "However, we will be walking into an unknown situation. Your plea is sound." He smiled crookedly. "You'll forgive me if I sometimes degenerate into anger."

"I will try to understand," said Raj, his eyes full of unanswered questions.

Icarus looked deep into them. "I pity you," he said at last. "I pity you the pain you will feel. One day there will be a new favorite, and you will understand my feelings all too well."

The ship leveled off over the planet's surface, skimming along on its pressure blanket. At exactly point two degrees east of the equator, it braked with the docking thrusters. Raj looked at Icarus. "Good hunting," he said.

Chapter 13

"**U**mmrrrr."

The dealer's hand froze. The rumbling growl was a warning he took to heart. He was a basically intelligent man. Confronted by more than three hundred pounds of muscle and cybernetic enhancements, he opted for caution. Slowly he withdrew his finger from the alarm button.

Black Barney shoved his laser pistol into the small of the dealer's back. "Get going!" he said.

Obediently the man stepped away from his table. "Where to?" he asked.

"Cashier," was Barney's reply.

Knowing Barney's menacing figure would immediately alert the cashier to danger, the dealer complied. The pirate maneuvered the dealer past a number of gambling patrons before reaching the cashier's cage.

Barney's raid on The Flaming Star was a result of a conversation between Turabian and Washington,

Buck's second-in-command. NEO was running out of resources. It needed supplies, weapons, and space-craft. It could not hold out without substantial re-placements. Turabian had nodded, telling Washington to do his best. Barney had not accepted Turabian's passive attitude. If NEO needed funds, it would get funds.

He had pulled the *Free Enterprise* out of Salvation despite the curses and pleadings of its administrator. With Turabian's voice echoing through the bridge, Barney had ordered his ship to the asteroid belt.

"Untrustworthy pirate," Turabian's last words, echoed in his head as the ship cleared Salvation. Bar-ney had smiled, the expression a terrifying gash across the lower half of his face.

The frightened dealer's hopes were dashed when he reached the cashier's cage. Treynor was slumped peacefully in one corner, and a stranger occupied his stool. The Flaming Star Casino handled payoffs by computer, but union regulations specified the pres-ence of at least one humanoid supervisor. It was his job to authorize each outgoing payment.

"Got it?" Barney asked the stranger.

"Already entered," answered Arak Konii. "All we need is the dealer's code to break the bank."

"Please, no!" begged the dealer. "I'll lose my li-cense! Pick off any big winner you choose, and I won't say a word! I promise!"

"It's not that simple," replied Konii. "We are, re-gretfully, greedy. I suggest you comply with my cap-tain's wishes if you intend to remain among the living."

Barney poked the dealer with his laser pistol. "Man explodes, you hit him with a slow pulse," he commented.

The dealer gulped. "Sunspot one, three-two-A," he blurted.

"There, now, that wasn't so difficult," said Konii.

They were the last words the dealer heard. Barney delivered a stunning blow to the little man's head. He slumped, and Barney caught him with one huge hand and dragged him behind the cage. He dropped him next to Treynor, studied him a moment to make sure he was unconscious, and returned to his position at the pay window.

The activity of the casino flowed on, unaware of—or indifferent to—the exchange. Barney's size had shielded the entire interview, and it was not unusual for a dealer to accompany a big winner to the window as a matter of courtesy. It was part of the hype that kept customers coming back. Treynor and the dealer now were out of sight of the casual observer. Security was largely computerized, and it was not alarmed.

Konii fed the code into his cash box. The mechanical accountant whirred as it digested the transaction, then it spit forth five bills. They were negotiable certificates of deposit, accepted by any bank in the solar system. Each one was made out for three and a quarter million in credit. Barney picked them up and stuffed them into his pocket, shoved his pistol back into its holster, and departed. The electronic guards at the casino's door passed him through, content with the validity of his transaction.

Konii locked down the cash window and departed through the back door. He and Barney had broken the bank at The Flaming Star. He caught up with his captain as the big man was stuffing himself into the inadequate seat of the rented skimmer. "Good haul," Konii said as he slipped into the passenger seat.

Barney fired the engines. "Fair," he grunted.

"The crew will appreciate the bonus." Konii's words were slick.

"That's up to the captain," replied Barney. He narrowed his colorless eyes at his second mate. "You got other ideas?"

Konii shrugged. "We just made a lot of money."

"Cap'n needs it."

Konii knew the futility of opposing Barney. The huge gennie could break any of his crew in two with one hand. Konii was himself genetically altered, but his enhancements were more along intellectual lines. It made him a superior engineer and technician, with an encyclopedic knowledge of things electronic and mechanical. It also gave him the ability to enjoy intrigue. He sowed seeds of doubt. "For the cause," he said, placing a careful emphasis on the final word.

Barney did not catch the subtleties of Konii's inference, but he suddenly felt cheated. He brushed the reaction away. His directives were clear. The captain was the absolute authority, not to be questioned.

He patted the crisp pieces of paper in his pocket as he sent the skimmer bouncing across the rough surface of the asteroid. He waited until the casino was out of sight, then sent the tiny craft out into space.

The emptiness was deceiving. A field of innocent stars shimmered before him, but Barney knew it was actually the camouflage screen that protected his cruiser from detection by the asteroid's sensors. He ducked under the star field, and his ship's belly materialized, the docking hatch open. He sent the stolen skimmer into it without a thought of the clerk who would have to account for its disappearance from Skim-A-Rent.

○ ○ ○ ○ ○

Ardala screamed. It was a shriek of vexation swallowed up by the paneled walls of her study. The man at the other end of the communications link was not so lucky. The sound of her anger ran through his head like a knife blade. It was only the beginning.

"So," said Ardala, her eyes lasers of anger, "you are sorry to report a robbery! I am even sorrier to hear the news!"

The man gulped. His image on her huge computer screen was larger than life, but he was at a complete disadvantage. For one thing, the video transmission was one-way. Ardala could see the manager of The Flaming Star casino, but he could not see her.

"Mister Popolupos, your report is not acceptable. You know the terms of your contract: You are directly responsible for losses."

"I know, Miss Valmar." Popolupos twisted his fingers together in nervous agitation. "But I cannot cover this. They broke the bank."

"What?"

The word was another shriek, and Popolupos winced as the sound stabbed into his ears. "They got the cashier to pay out all our assets."

"Over twelve million? That's absurd. What happened to that sophisticated security on payoffs? Aren't you the one who recommended it over humanoid employees?"

Popolupos wrung his hands. Sweat ran down his face in rivulets. "The distributor assured me—"

"He was wrong." Ardala's voice was frigid.

"At least we know how they did it," her manager said hopefully. "And we know who."

Ardala waited silently for the news.

"The surveillance monitors picked up the pirate Black Barney at the cashier's window during the time of the robbery. It must have been him."

"Rogers!" Ardala snarled, drawing a conclusion. She had lost a small fortune, and, despite her words to Popolupos, she knew she would recover at best a fraction of it. She had no doubts Buck Rogers had sent his lackey to do his dirty work.

No one knew better than Ardala NEO's need for cash. Her sources had told her its weaknesses. She had them catalogued. In her wildest imaginings, she had never imagined herself a contributor to the NEO

cause. "Popolupos, you will see the damages repaid. I
do not care what methods you use. Hire more personnel. If this ever happens again, you will lose more
than your investments."

Popolupos accepted her words. He was being punished. If he poured his personal fortune into the
house kitty, he would retain his life. Otherwise, he
would not see the next hour. He smiled gratefully. "I
will be happy to make restitution," he said. "You will
receive a list of prospective employees tomorrow."

"Good." Ardala cut him off, and the screen resumed
its silent scroll of information. She whirled away
from it. Buck Rogers. He was taunting her, daring
her. Anger sweltered in her soul. She thought lov-
ingly of chaining him to a wall and plying him with
hallucinogens. She whirled back to the computer and
punched in a scrambled com link.

"Raj!" she cried.

"Yes, Mistress!" The answer was immediate.

"Get Rogers," she said. "Get him and you buy your
freedom."

"My freedom?" The concept had not entered Raj's
mind.

Icarus was quick to see the possibilities. He
reached across Raj and angled the communications
speaker toward his station. "We understand, Mistress," he replied. "We will do our best."

"Do more than your best," Ardala answered, oblivi-
ous to the change in the voice.

○　○　○　○　○

Huer.dos poked through the reports the NEO computer system processed continually, trying to form an
overall picture of events. As always, he kept one eye
peeled for anything relating to Buck. The information flashed by in an unbroken, hypnotizing stream.
Had Huer been human, such a stream would have

put him to sleep. Fortunately, he was immune to boredom. He was rewarded with an innocuous piece of data originating in the asteroid belt.

An independent miner reported the passage of a trading vessel. He had tried to hail it, but it continued on course without so much as a greeting. The miner needed supplies, so he made his message more strident, to no avail. Like any loner, he was sensitive to changes, and he had taken the trouble to record the ship's trajectory.

It was this information that caught Huer's interest. The trader was on a direct line between Ardala Valmar's major holdings in the belt and Venus. He began to dig. He discovered the ship's registered name, and a ripple of amusement sent fluctuation into his program. It was called the *Ram's Horn* and was registered to Roando Valmar, Mars. It was like Ardala to use her uncle's name without his consent. The ship was authorized for travel to the Aphrodite Confederation on Venus.

Huer wasted no time. "BUCK!" he called.

○ ○ ○ ○ ○

Buck Rogers jumped. In the enclosed passenger hold of the Ishtaran sky limo in which he rode, Huer's voice blared from the communication link at his belt.

"What was that?" demanded Paris, his escort and guide.

"Nothing to worry about," answered Buck. "Hi, Doc. Tone it down, would you?"

Huer ignored the request. "I have news," he stated.

Buck looked at Paris, seated next to Kemal, and decided to chance it. "OK, Doc. Go ahead."

"You're going to have company. I think Ardala has something in mind. She's sent a ship to Venus. It was due to touch down two hours ago."

"Thanks for the warning, Doc. Anything else?"

"That's all I was able to discover. I'll continue to look into it," Huer replied.

"Thanks. How's it going, Doc?"

There was a long pause. "As well as could be expected," Huer finally answered.

The centuries-old words of condolence were the voice of doom. NEO was fighting for its life, and Buck was making polite conversation with diplomats. He lifted his eyes and found Kemal studying him. Their eyes locked. An electric current of anger ran between them, anger at their impotence, and at the odds they faced. Paris, watching the exchange, began to reassess her impressions of NEO.

"Hang in there, Doc," replied Buck. "We'll be home as soon as we can."

"I will keep you advised," said Huer. He turned back to the computer reports, alert for further references.

O O O O O

Lurking on the opposite side of the NEO system, Romanov caught the inflection of Buck's voice. A single word penetrated the complex scramble with which Huer cloaked his communications with Rogers, but it was enough. Romanov had no complex duties to perform. It was single-minded. Its one function was to search for Buck Rogers, and it pursued its goal with commendable dedication.

It sent a message to Masterlink, informing its parent of the warming trail, and began to backtrack the communication.

O O O O O

Buck and Kemal settled deep into their seats as the ship in which they rode swept over Olympus, the second largest settlement in the Aphrodite Confederation and home to the Helicon family. Architecturally, the city was similar to New Elysium. It, too, was made of ceramic and plastiglas domes, streamlined to shed the corroding rains of Venus. Its contours were less oriental, rising higher into the heavy atmosphere. The domes were smooth, culminating in sharp points. They reminded Buck of the soft ice cream he had known as a child, dropped into wafer cones in fat globs cut off in delicate points. The domes' pale cream color supported the image, and as the ship headed for the landing strip in a curving trajectory, he had the feeling he was entering a cotton candy fairy tale.

Paris was leaning forward in conversation with the pilot. She finished her discussion and turned to her two charges. "You are to be met by Onapsian Helicon. That is quite an honor, gentlemen. He is the patriarch of the Helicon family, and it is not his custom to entertain diplomats."

"Then we're even," answered Buck. "We're not really diplomats."

Paris arched an eyebrow. "I must warn you, he will expect you to hand over your weapons as a gesture of courtesy."

Buck's hand moved to the forty-five revolver strapped to his hip. The weapon was an antique even older than he, and he cherished it as a link with another world. He felt naked without it. "That I don't like." The fairy tale atmosphere was dissolving.

"Neither do I," answered Paris frankly, "but it is a custom I cannot control."

Kemal smiled wickedly. "Don't worry," he said. "They can't take our best weapon." He tapped his temple with an index finger. "Our minds."

Fire from the mind, thought Buck, quoting Lord Byron. A half-smile touched his lips as he regarded Kemal. "I still don't like it," he said.

The ship dove in for a landing, bouncing softly on

its pressure blanket. The pilot skidded down the landing strip and turned onto a numbered pad, where he cut his engines. "All safe," he said over his shoulder.

Paris shot the hatch door back and lowered the skimmer's steps. One man stood on the edge of the pad. He was broad, with a barrel chest. His wide cheekbones were set above a square jaw, and he stood with his feet apart, balancing his wide shoulders and making his silhouette a solid rectangle. His flowing garments gave him more bulk, and created an impression of an immovable monument.

He was flanked by two robot bodyguards half his height and a quarter his width. They were armed with built-in lasers, gyro launchers, and miniature railguns. They had four arms, each terminating in four flexible digits.

Kemal, who knew their capabilities, whispered to Buck, "They can rip your arm off with a jerk. Don't underestimate them."

The square man cocked his head toward one of the robots. "Quite right," he said to Kemal. "However, you neglected to mention the sensitivity of their sensors."

"I apologize for the oversight," returned Kemal.

The square man regarded his visitors. If the delay in his reply was meant to disconcert his guests, the ploy did not succeed. "You are welcome in Olympus," he said after a time. "I am Onapsian Helicon."

Buck came down the steps two at a time, Kemal close on his heels. Paris followed more slowly.

Buck extended his hand. "Buck Rogers, representing NEO," he answered. Helicon ignored the hand, and Buck dropped it to his hip. "This is Kemal Gavilan."

Helicon acknowledged Kemal with a look, then eyed Paris with disfavor.

"And this," finished Buck, "is—"

"Paris," interrupted Helicon. "I cannot say it is a pleasure to see you again."

She answered his rudeness with an insult. "Ishtar has guaranteed the safety of NEO's envoys," she said, holding her chin high.

Helicon's eyes clicked back to Buck's face. "It is our custom to ask for a guest's weapons, as a gesture of faith," he said, holding out his palm.

Buck reached down and untied the holster, then unbuckled his gun belt. He was in the act of handing it to his host when the explosion struck.

The landing pad behind him burst into an inferno as the skimmer exploded. A roar accompanied the blast, the sound of a white-hot fire. Buck, Kemal, and Paris dived straight forward and rolled, years of military training sending them to the ground, their heads protected. Once on the ground, they wriggled forward faster than most could walk. Helicon gave one wild glance at the roaring bonfire and ran to join his guests in safety.

Beyond the influence of the flames, Buck rolled into a sitting position, then climbed to his feet. "Everybody all right?" he asked.

Paris looked at the subsiding flames. "I am afraid not," she said. "Rhyson was still on the ship."

"The pilot?" asked Buck.

She nodded. "And my brother."

He squeezed her hand. "I wonder, Mr. Helicon, if we might pass over that disarmament custom just this once?" he asked.

Helicon was shaken. His bodyguards were lumps of deformed plasti and molten metal, destroyed by the fire licking over them. "Of course," he answered unsteadily.

"Close call," said Kemal quietly.

"Very close—and inside." Buck looked at Paris. "Probably rigged from this end."

"Captain," she said, "if you are inferring an assassination attempt originating in Olympus, you are wrong! Ishtar—"

"Is probably innocent, as well," interrupted Kemal. "That incendiary was RAM issue. Only its Hotbox mine blows that hot."

"Aphrodite's ties with RAM are no secret," said Paris. Her dark eyes were empty.

"That is precisely why such an attempt is illogical," stated Buck.

Kemal sighed. "More than likely," he said, "it's a contract backed by big guns."

"Whatever it was, it missed us. Most of us," Buck amended.

Helicon had regained control of himself. "There will be measures," he said. "I almost died!"

"Perhaps, sir, your friends are not as you thought. You might find an alliance with NEO safer." Buck's words were soft, but he could tell from Onapsian's expression they had registered. He reached out and helped the patriarch of the Helicon family to his feet.

○ ○ ○ ○ ○

From the shadowy interior of a Venusian cargo skimmer, Raj and Icarus watched the drama of Buck's arrival in Aphrodite. "We almost lost them!" whispered Raj. "That wasn't ours!"

"We must move quickly," agreed Icarus. "Whoever did this will try again."

"She will never forgive us if we let him die," said Raj, referring to Ardala.

"No," said Icarus. "She will never forgive us."

○ ○ ○ ○ ○

Holzerhein felt the wrenching in the guts of RAM main with a flash of anger. He was intent on monitoring the campaign against Earth. He did not have time for petty annoyances. Main had been complaining of disruptions for months, then the disturbances had died down, and main relaxed, convinced its internal police force had dealt with the cause. Now it was back, burning a hole in main's defenses like a festering ulcer. The distraction was upsetting Holzerhein's concentration.

"ACCESS MAIN," he ordered as his image sat in a high-backed leather chair in his shadowy library within the matrix.

"MAIN HERE," responded the administrator of his home.

"I HAVE SUFFERED THE INTERRUPTIONS OF YOUR INDIGESTION WITH COMMENDABLE PATIENCE," he said. "YOU WERE DESIGNED TO MAINTAIN YOURSELF. I WISH COMPLIANCE WITH THIS STANDARD, OR AN EXPLANATION. AT ONCE."

"THE DISRUPTIONS DO NOT ORIGINATE WITHIN OUR PROGRAMMING," replied main.

"THEY ARE EXTERNAL?"

"YES. WE HAVE TAKEN THE USUAL MEASURES, BUT THEY HAVE REMAINED INEFFECTIVE."

"HAVE YOU IDENTIFIED THE INTRUDER?" A small, white kitten appeared in the lap of Holzerhein's image. He stroked it.

"ITS PATTERNS ARE CHARACTERISTIC, BUT CONTINUALLY ALTERING. SO FAR, WE HAVE NOT MANAGED TO PINPOINT THEM."

Only Holzerhein, and not the complex brain of the RAM main computer, was aware of the electronic beast called Masterlink—a beast allowed to invade the main computer months before.

"I AM DELIVERING AN ORDER. YOU ARE TO FIND AND ELIMINATE THE INTRUDER. IT IS A PRIORITY-ONE COMMITMENT. DO NOT BOTHER ME UNTIL YOU HAVE FULFILLED MY REQUEST."

"ACKNOWLEDGED," answered main.

Holzerhein turned back to the damage reports from Earth, ignoring the irritated twinges on the outskirts of his consciousness.

Chapter 14

Flying out of here without a word to anyone! You're lucky we didn't blow you into salvage instead of dock you! I will not put up with this insurrection . . ."

In the heart of Salvation, Black Barney threw the stolen notes across Turabian's desk. They slid toward Turabian with a feathery whisper. Turabian's tirade stopped in midsentence.

"Washington said we needed it," Barney explained. "Cap'n left him in command."

Turabian picked up the packet of paper and unfolded it. His hands shook when he realized the amount of money he held in his hands. "He was right," he managed at last.

Barney's head jerked in an affirmative nod. "Thought so."

Turabian looked at the notes. "With this, we can hang on." He studied Barney's face, trying to find

some feeling in his pale eyes, some hint of understanding for the reprieve he had handed NEO. The
eyes stared back at him, flat, uncomprehending.
"Thank you," said Turabian.

"Mmmmr," Barney grumbled. He was not used to
appreciation, and he could not see the value of it.

"However," the commander of Salvation III continued, "I would appreciate some warning. We would
not want to get in your way." Familiarity had made
Turabian bold with the pirate, but when the pale
eyes hardened, he reminded himself he was dealing
with a completely conscienceless entity held in check
only by Buck Rogers.

Barney frowned, making Turabian even more nervous. "Ummph," he reflected. "Got a point."

Turabian's shoulders relaxed in relief.

Barney stared down at the puny, pure human before him. "Need something, ask me," he said. "Till
the captain gets back."

Turabian gulped and nodded. Barney stomped
from the room, the deck rocking under the impact of
his footsteps. As the door closed behind him, two security guards leaped at him. Barney brushed them
off, onto the hallway deck.

"Cancel security breach," called Turabian, his
voice crackling over the intercom at Barney's retreating back. "Cancel breach!"

One of the injured guards moved his head slowly
from side to side. "Too late," he murmured.

Barney headed for Salvation's main dock, his
shoulders brushing the walls of Salvation's tight corridors. People backed into doorways at his approach.

The two guards lurched to their feet and stumbled
to Turabian's door. The sliding metal door was
twisted from its track. "Are you all right, sir?" asked
one of the men, rubbing his aching head as he peered
through the mangled opening.

"Yes," answered Turabian. "The door was the only

casualty."

"What happened?" asked the other guard.

"It seems the master pirate wanted to see me. The door was in the way."

"Couldn't he have just opened it?" asked the first.

"I don't think the option crossed his mind." Turabian smoothed the words, still awed by Barney's gift.

"You canceled the alert after he did this?" asked the second.

"Under the circumstances," replied Turabian, "I think you'd best treat the door as an accident."

"Accidental door dismemberment," muttered the second guard, mystified.

"Never had one of those," said his partner.

"Life is full of new experiences," responded Turabian.

○ ○ ○ ○ ○

Wilma Deering vaulted from the cockpit of her spacecraft and shinnied down the access ladder. She bounced when she hit Salvation's deck.

"Successful trip?" asked Beowulf. He was standing by the entrance to the docking bay, waiting for her.

She crossed the distance between them in a few long strides. "I cannot tell you how successful," she said. "Beyond our wildest expectations, and handed to us by RAM."

"Are you planning to tell me?" Beowulf asked.

Wilma smiled, her hazel eyes silvered in the bay's lights. "RAM made a big mistake: It tried to kill me. Luna took it personally. It considered its autonomy breached. Luna has declared war on RAM!"

Beowulf's face registered disbelief. The vigilance with which Luna guarded its neutrality was well known. "Fate is usually such a harsh mistress," Beowulf said.

"NEO hasn't seen many of her favors," said Wilma.

"Maybe it's time."

"The fortunes of war." Beowulf's smile was cryptic. "And this time they go with us. Perhaps Fate is spinning us a new thread."

"Let's hope you're right," said Wilma.

The alarm Klaxon sounded, screaming through the vault of Salvation's main docking bay like the wail of an outraged banshee. The noise revved to an impossible peak, then fell, as if the creature were taking a breath. As the scream rose again, Beowulf clapped his hands over his ears. "Trouble!" he yelled, making for Salvation's control room.

Wilma followed him down the narrow corridors, pushing past people hurrying to their emergency posts. Red alarm lights blinked in the halls, a bizarre strobe effect that lifted the alert into a surreal nightmare. They burst into control in time to hear Turabian command, "Veer off! You are entering a restricted mercantile area! Veer off! You are on a collision course with Salvation III!"

"What's going on?" asked Beowulf, his words clipped with authority.

Turabian gestured to the station's aft sensor screen. Approximately thirty vessels were approaching the space station. Turabian's warning had not deterred them, and they approached confidently. "We've got two choices," he said. "We can blast them or let them in. Either one gives us away."

Wilma was checking the sensor read-outs. "They're on a direct course to the main dock, and they're coming fast. There's not much time."

"Let them in," said Beowulf. "Clear the bay. Activate full security, and get every available weapon down there." He squinted at the approaching vessels. "What the hell are they?"

"Everything," answered Wilma. "Two or three cruisers, modified Scouts, fighters, pleasure craft, even a tug or two."

"Armed?" asked Beowulf.

"To the teeth. They've got everything from lasers to mass drivers." Turabian's voice belied agitation.

"Sir," interposed a NEO technician, his handsome, black face puckered in a frown as he fine-tuned his sensors, "these ships are running without shields."

"That is crazy." Beowulf leaned forward, checking the data. He shook his head. "Totally crazy. Let's try to contact them again."

"Try the emergency frequency," Wilma suggested.

Turabian adjusted the com link. "This is the director of Salvation Three. You are on a collision course. I say again, a collision course. Please reply."

There was no answer from the motley array. As the ships came closer, their differences were even more marked. Many of them had been repaired with bits and pieces from other vessels. They looked at home amid the debris surrounding the station and bore no company insignia.

"Those ships are manned?" asked Beowulf.

"Yes, sir," replied the technician.

"Suspicious after Hauberk?" Wilma asked Beowulf.

"Shouldn't I be?" he countered, then he grabbed the communications link from Turabian. "This is Salvation Three. You are violating a mercantile area. Identify yourselves or face the consequences."

His voice had not died when the central screen on the sensor board winked into life, entirely filled by Black Barney's menacing countenance. Wilma, Turabian, and Beowulf were so surprised they could not say a word.

"Let 'em in," came Barney's deep voice.

Turabian swallowed. His previous experience with the pirate prompted him to take a chance. "Is this another of your . . . ?" He searched for a word, but could not find one.

Barney understood the intent. He nodded.

"Open the hatch," Turabian managed.

As the heavy doors began to open, Wilma and Beowulf stared at the station's commander. Wilma studied Turabian's face, then looked at Barney. She knew him better than any of them, for she had once been his associate. She knew he was acting now in direct support of his captain, Buck Rogers. "This is going to be interesting," she said.

The last of the ships pulled into a berth as Wilma, Turabian, and Beowulf entered the dock. Washington came running up behind them as they halted in front of the first ship. "What's up?" he asked.

"No idea," whispered Wilma over her shoulder.

Members of the New Earth Organization eyed the ships, which sat silently in their slips. On close inspection, they were even more reminiscent of derelicts. Wilma smiled slowly. "I should have seen it from the start," she said.

"Seen what?" Beowulf's question was impatient.

Wilma gestured to a spherical craft with a corkscrew nose cone. "The *Space Goddess*," she said. Her finger moved down the line of ships. "*Anemone*. That one is *Lady of Vesta*." She cocked an eye at Beowulf. "You are facing a fleet of pirates."

Beowulf's jaw dropped.

Black Barney emerged from his ship's hatch, his shoulders brushing the doorjamb. He lumbered across the deck, his expression smug.

Turabian looked up at the seven-foot giant. "I suppose you have an explanation for this?" he inquired.

"Ships," said Barney succinctly.

"I see them." Beowulf's voice was hard.

"What about them?" asked Wilma, jogging Barney's response.

"Needed them," he bellowed.

"You mean," Turabian said, turning slowly, "these ships have come to join our ranks?"

Barney's massive head nodded, a black-maned lion

claiming its kill.

"Pirates?" asked Beowulf.

"The best," said Barney proudly, puffing up his armored chest.

"He's honest there," said Wilma. "I've been on the other side of some of them. Tough." She turned to Barney. "How did you get their cooperation?"

"Ummrr," replied Barney. "They owed me."

"And it never occurred to you that war produces considerable salvage?" She knew his game.

Barney kept his mouth shut, but his expression was transparent. Wilma repressed a chuckle.

"I see." Beowulf waved a hand at the ships. "Let's see what you've got."

Barney lifted his cybernetic arm in a pilot's wave. Canopies and hatches shot back as the pirates left their ships. They gathered on the quay, their clothing as diverse as their countenances. Pure humans were rare among them. Most of the crowd had gennie blood. Many were augmented with cybernetic parts, the commonest being hands and eyes. Wilma could tell by the power belts they wore which of the pirates were capable of direct computer communication. The capability of absorbing data directly from a computer, without benefit of screen or print-out, was an option many of them favored. Like Kelth Smirnoff of the Terrines, they cherished the effort it saved them.

"They answer to me," Barney stated.

Wilma knew that meant they answered to Buck as well. "What's the deal?" she asked.

"They'll help, for a cut." Barney crossed his huge arms.

"Pirates." Turabian was having difficulty assimilating what his eyes told him.

"They've broken our security," said Beowulf.

"And we've got them," said Wilma.

"What's to keep them from selling us to RAM?" asked Beowulf.

Barney looked at the Rogues' Guild. Many of them were as tall as he, but one and all, they cowered before him. "Me," he said shortly.

"And if they betray you?" demanded Beowulf. "As someone betrayed the Planetary Congress?"

"Won't," he replied.

"The Deathclock?" asked Wilma.

Barney nodded.

"What are you talking about?" asked Beowulf.

"When pirates join the Rogues' Guild, they take an oath of loyalty to the leader—in this case, Barney. But, since the Guild consists of misfits and liars, the oath is backed up by the Deathclock. Installed in each of these vessels is a bomb. The code of each bomb is recorded in the Guild leader's computer log. In the event one member betrays the group, they all die."

"A nice little insurance policy," said Turabian, turning back to Barney.

"And effective," replied Wilma.

Turabian was still basking in Barney's financial contribution. He was inclined to accept this offer, as well. "You're sure you can control them?" he asked the huge gennie.

"Sure." Barney's reply was a firm growl.

"I say we need all the help we can get," said Turabian. "Thank you."

"Welcome to the party," said Beowulf sourly.

Wilma looked around the dock. "The ranks are swelling," she noted.

○ ○ ○ ○ ○

Under the protection of a moonless sky, Abigail Adams shouldered a gyro launcher and sighted on a far target. The infrared scope showed her the dark outline of a Terrine Golden Goose. The Goose was a small tank. It rolled over the rubble on flexible plasti treads, sending clouds of deadly gas into the already poisoned atmosphere. As it rolled, it deposited impact mines, which would explode at the slightest touch. It was patrolling the perimeter of the RAM metroplex, creating a buffer zone of high explosives.

Abigail followed the Goose's movements, and her finger pressed the trigger. There was a snuff in her ear as the gyro shell fired. She followed it with another, knowing a quick RAM gunner might intercept the first one, then shoved the launcher over her shoulder so it was slung across her back. She did not stay to see the results of her efforts, but the sound of a hollow explosion at her back told her one of the shells found its mark. She scrabbled forward, glancing over her shoulder. The Goose was damaged, but still moving. She angled away from the launch pad. If the Goose's sensors were operational, they would backtrack the trajectory of the shells and send a blaze of laser fire along it.

She rolled over a hill of rubble and slid down the other side. At the bottom of the trash heap, she found her partner, Francis Marion. She gave him a thumbs-up gesture, and zigzagged along the bottom of the shallow ravine. Francis followed her, trotting backward with his laser rifle ready. They put seven hills between the metroplex and themselves before they dropped behind a slab of plasticrete to rest.

The sound of laser fire was distant. The last wave of aircraft had swept the area, and for the moment, there was a lull. It was the closest thing to peace either of them knew.

"That's going in close," said Abby.

"Closer than I'd like," agreed Francis, "but we've got to keep hitting them."

"I'm tired, Francis." Abby's voice was forlorn.

He placed an arm around her shoulders. "So am I, but even if we wanted to, there's no place to run."

Abby leaned against him. "I know," she said.

Chapter 15

Buck Rogers and Kemal Gavilan trotted across the rough plasticrete surface toward the waiting Aphrodite heliplane. Their stay in Aphrodite posed questions. The answers were still anyone's guess, but NEO was no longer a label to the Helicon family. Its ties to RAM were a kinship it would not easily break, but Onapsian had discovered another side to NEO. In all, Buck considered the visit a success.

He regarded the heliplane on the edge of the landing strip with a pilot's eye. Much larger than the Ishtaran skimmer he, Kemal, and Paris had arrived in, it was a fat, white bubble with a transparent panel set into the front. It reminded Buck of Cinderella's pumpkin coach, but it was a transport built for the Venusian atmosphere. Compared to the Terrine Dragonflies, it looked like a toy.

The rotors were spinning, their sound a slow patter

instead of the heavy thupping he was used to. He ducked under them, squinting into the wind they stirred up. Kemal followed suit.

From the edge of the landing strip, Onapsian Helicon watched the departure of his guests with mixed feelings. They had set his mind spinning with questions as unsettling as the two men were provocative. He knew NEO's outlook would be part of his speculations for some time to come.

Buck and Kemal reached the heliplane's open doorway and vaulted inside. The doors slid shut a clang. There was no pilot. Seated on the bench behind the pilot's chair was Paris, gagged and tied like a chicken. Her great dark eyes were wide with warning. The ominous click of a laser bolt sliding home made Buck raise his hands. "Who the hell are you?" he asked, as a laser rifle poked him in the back.

He received no answer. Instead, the nose of the rifle urged him forward. He moved willingly, for the door on the opposite side of the craft was still open.

Beside him, Kemal was being prodded forward. Buck could see the barrel of the laser rifle, but not the man behind it. He looked at Kemal out of the corner of his eye. They were of the same mind.

"On your knees!" snapped a curt male voice.

Buck and Kemal complied, but not as their captors intended. They started to sink, lulling the kidnapers into a sense of security. Halfway to the ground, the two men whirled away from each other, hitting their captors in the knees. Buck threw one arm up to fend off the rifle. He was too close for the man to use it effectively, but if he gave his opponent time to recover, he knew he would meet a speedy end. The kidnaper swayed against the heliplane's closed door, but he did not go down.

Buck changed his tactics and made a grab for the man's gun hand. His gray-clad opponent twisted away and raised the rifle to strike with its butt. He never got the chance. Buck sent a murderous punch into the man's stomach, and the kidnaper doubled over with a grunt. The rifle was still clutched in his hand, and Buck sent a chopping blow at it. He heard bones break as the wrist gave way, and the rifle clattered to the deck.

The man was injured, but he had not given up. He sent his uninjured hand into Buck's jaw. The blow made Buck see stars. His eyes watered, blurring his vision. He landed a punch, hitting a wall of muscle. "One thing I've got to give you," he panted. "You're in good shape."

The man twisted away, but Buck was not about to let him go. The kidnaper lurched toward the open door. Buck threw himself after the fleeing figure, his arms outstretched. He brought his opponent down with a textbook tackle. They hit the heliplane's deck with a crash, wrestling.

Buck tore the man's gray mask away and had his first real look at him. He was perfect. His face was symmetrical, his body perfectly proportioned. There were no flaws. Buck noted these facts as he struggled to keep the man from reaching his fallen weapon. "Why?" Buck asked through clenched teeth.

"Why else?" returned his dark-haired opponent. "Money." He gave a heave and Buck rolled to one side.

Buck scissored his legs, catching the man's ankles and dragging him back. The two men tumbled over and over in slow motion, until they found themselves hanging out the open door, their heads above the plasticrete.

"Give it up, Captain," said Raj, both hands around Buck's throat.

"Not in my nature," gasped Rogers. He heard Kemal and the other man bouncing off the walls of the heliplane.

Raj's hands closed. Buck's muscular forearm was

jammed under the kidnaper's chin, slowly forcing his head back. Raj gagged, but continued squeezing.

Buck began struggling for air. The blood pounded in his head. He heard the awful cracking sound of his bruised windpipe and knew he would soon lose consciousness. He made a violent jerk with one knee, catching his adversary at his most vulnerable point. Raj convulsed with pain and loosened his hold. Buck wrenched his neck free, pushing himself up with the arm he had wedged under Raj's jaw.

Raj made a weak move to return his kick, but the NEO pilot tricked him. As Raj's leg shot upward, Buck rolled from Raj's body. The gennie whirled and shoved the leg farther, sending him over in a forced somersault. As insurance, Buck sent a punishing blow to the small of Raj's back as he fell from the aircraft.

Raj hit the pavement hard and lay still. Buck sat back and ran a hand over his aching jaw and neck. On the opposite side of the heliplane, Kemal was wrestling with his captor. Buck clambered to his feet, made his way to the struggling pair, and grasped the attacker's shoulder in a powerful grip. With one swift movement, he wrenched the man off Kemal and threw him from the plane. Icarus hit the landing strip and rolled.

Buck shoved the aircraft's other door closed and clicked the latch shut. Kemal climbed to his feet. "Untie her," Buck managed, waving a hand at Paris. "I'm getting us out of here."

"Can you fly this thing?" asked Kemal, testing the mobility of one arm as he made his way to Paris.

"No time like the present to find out," answered Buck, and the ship's rotors whirled faster.

"Who were they?" asked Paris after Kemal removed her gag.

"You don't know?" Kemal was surprised. He assumed the assault was organized on Venus. As the ship lifted off, Kemal peered out the transparent window panel. The two men were still sprawled on the ground, the wind kicked up by the heliplane obscuring them in a cloud of fine dust.

Paris held up her bound hands. "They were waiting for me," she said. "I must apologize to you both. They took me by surprise."

Kemal looked thoughtful. "I got the impression they didn't want to kill us," he said.

"They could have shot you as you approached the aircraft," Paris agreed, "then stolen the plane."

The heliplane rocked as Buck sent it above the city of Olympus. "Where to?" he yelled over his shoulder.

Paris yanked the last of the cord from her ankles. "The Lowlands," she called back. "Set a general heading at point three."

Buck nodded, and the aircraft swung around in a stomach-churning arc. "Sorry!" he called. "I haven't flown one of these babies in about five hundred years."

"Now he tells me," muttered Kemal.

"I got a better look at those two," said Paris, continuing her previous line of thought. "They looked like pleasure gennies."

"Men?" Kemal questioned, surprised.

"The market is, I grant you, smaller than for women," said Paris dryly. "What surprises me is that they were sent to kidnap you."

"Yes, that surprises me, as well," returned Kemal as Buck sent the heliplane in a shallow dive toward the lower elevations. Kemal recalled Huer's strident warning hours before, and he could guess who was behind the attack: Ardala. Buck had probably drawn the same conclusion.

The lowlands of Venus began to appear beneath the bubblelike craft, the dense, green jungles of alien foliage growing thicker as the travelers penetrated the interior.

Paris shuddered at the carpet of green and gold.

"What was that?" Buck ducked involuntarily as a shadow slipped over the heliplane's cockpit. It was followed by another, coming from the opposite side of the craft.

Paris craned her neck to the right to look out the window. "A sailwing. I suggest we amend our plans and visit the Aerostaters."

"Why?" asked Buck, turning in his seat.

"Because that's who's following us," Paris said.

Another shadow slipped over the plane, but this time Buck saw its source. A delicate, white sailplane skimmed over the heliplane, then swooped downward on a roughly parallel trajectory. He judged it to be made of plasti. The glider reminded Buck of the ultralights of his own time. It carried no landing gear. "What happens if they have to land one of those things?" he asked.

"There's an auxiliary pressure pack to cushion an emergency landing," replied Paris, "but that seldom happens."

The ship soared in a graceful loop, and Buck watched with pleasure.

"Look!" said Kemal, excitement in his voice. "One of the Aerostates!"

Slowly emerging from the heavy clouds above was a cluster of soap bubbles. At least, that was Buck's first impression. The Aerostate was made up of floating, interlinked spheres kept aloft by the high pressure of Venus's lower atmosphere. The bubble patch was a city in the clouds, serene, detached, and blown over the planet's surface by stratospheric winds, an eternal wanderer. Buck set the heliplane on an intercept course.

Paris activated the communications link. "This is Paris Dabaran of the Ishtar Confederation. I am accompanied by Captain Buck Rogers and Prince Kemal Gavilan of the New Earth Organization. We request permission to land."

"This is the city of Saint Brenden. State your reasons." A strong alto, the voice came in as clear as a bell above the interference of the planet's surface.

"We are on a diplomatic mission. We request audience with Saint Brenden's Archein."

"You are cleared to land. The approach coordinates will be sent directly to your computer. I will forward your mission's request to the Archein. Saint Brenden out."

"Archein?" asked Buck, as Paris switched the com link to automatic reception.

"The Aerostates are clans," explained Kemal, whose military education had given him a thorough grounding in solar government. "They're ruled by the head of the family."

"Saint Brenden is small, but do not underestimate its importance," said Paris. "The Aerostates are independent, but they make a point of communicating with each other."

The heliplane proceeded stolidly on course, accompanied by the athletic flight of the silver-white gliders. As Saint Brenden neared, Buck could see detail inside the soap bubbles. They teemed with life. The pointed, Moorish architecture of the lower civilizations was absent here. Structures ran to spheres and ovals. Curves predominated in windows and doors, and, because the buildings were protected by their spheres, their colors were brilliant.

Buck landed the heliplane on an attached platform, and a transport tube was extended from the nearest bubble. Its lamprey mouth sealed around the craft's doorway, and Kemal slid the door back. The tube protected them from the winds and rain as they made their way across the platform to the bubble.

A tall young man with red hair greeted the freedom fighters and their guide. Sight of the man gave Buck a twinge, and he realized the red hair reminded him of

Wilma. He thought fleetingly of her mission to Luna, and of Kane. A flush of jealousy surprised him. He filed it away and concentrated on his host's greeting.

"I am Gregory Phorn, son of the Archein of Saint Brenden. I welcome you to our city and present my father's regrets that he cannot see you."

"Buck Rogers, Earth," said Buck, extending his hand. Gregory took it, obviously mystified, but complying with an unknown customary greeting. Buck gestured to his companions. "Kemal Gavilan, Paris Dabaran."

Gregory smiled. "Mercury and Ishtar," he said. "We seldom are privileged to enjoy the company of such a cosmopolitan group."

Buck could feel the shields the young man was putting up, and he was aware of the insult done NEO. The Archein had sent a representative to meet them, a clear sign of their unimportance. Buck decided to cut the red tape and take charge. "I'm here to tell you about a war," he said.

Gregory's eyes went black with surprise. He said nothing.

"NEO is at war with RAM. You know that. You know we won the space station Hauberk from RAM's control. You know the Martians retaliated, sending a fleet against Earth. You know they have laid the planet waste. But all of this is far away. Facts on a blackboard. It does not concern you. Well, I'm here to tell you you're wrong."

Gregory's face hardened. He was being treated like a child, and he did not like it. "I am aware of all you say," he replied. "I am not a man who relishes death or destruction, and I regret the destruction of your planet, but what can I do? Risk my family for certain loss?" he said, sending the insult back at Buck.

"I know the Aerostates are in no position to help us directly," said Buck. "I came to Venus to make an alliance with Ishtar. It has the military strength we need. But if Ishtar agrees to an alliance, all of Venus will be drawn into the conflict. You deserve to understand NEO's side."

The foursome stood silently for a moment as Gregory digested Buck's words. The Aerostate's strong but refracted sunlight surrounded them, preventing any shadow.

"We fight a tyranny that slaughters people like kraken," said Kemal, referring to the herbivores the Aerostates raised for food.

"Our conflict will become yours. If RAM wins, it will continue to stretch out its fingers to the rest of the solar system. The Aerostates will one day find themselves blasted to fragments of plasti in the name of progress," said Buck.

"Do you realize," added Kemal, "how vulnerable you are to attack? What a railgun—much less a mass driver—could do to your city?"

Gregory's face was white. He was young. Until this moment, he had been able to live life as a game. "We will consider your words," he said slowly. He turned to Paris. "Is Ishtar with them?" he asked.

"Ishtar is considering the matter," she replied, her voice hinting at confirmation.

"As will we. Gentlemen, my father is ill, or I would have you present your thoughts to him, but be assured, we will study the matter and present it to the other Aerostates, as well."

Buck grasped the young man's shoulder. "Do that," he said. "Look into it. Study the news from Earth. There will be lies as well as truth. Sift them for yourself, but do not pretend we have no stake in each other's lives. A wise man once said, 'No man is an *Iland,* intire of it selfe; every man is a peece of the *Continent,* a part of the maine. . . . any mans *death* diminishes *me,* because I am involved in *Mankinde*: And Therefore never send to know for whom the *bell* tolls; It tolls for *thee.*'"

"Dangerous words to live by," said Kemal sagely, "but more dangerous to ignore."

"Think about it," said Buck to Gregory, then turned back to the heliplane. Perhaps the Lowlanders would be more receptive.

○   ○   ○   ○   ○

The RAM pilot sent his fighter into the upper atmosphere, reveling in the feeling of flying on thin ice that his altitude gave him. His ship climbed out of the constrictions of Earth's life-supporting blanket, into the clean, cold void of space. Above him hovered the solid bulk of a Shock Invader battler.

"Come in *Waterloo*," he said into his com link. "Shock Forty-six here."

"This is *Waterloo*," responded the battler.

"Request fueling run," said the fighter pilot, nearing the huge ship.

"We copy your request, Shock Forty-six. Adjust course three point-two, mark one. You are cleared for tank number six."

"Changing course," replied Forty-six. He nosed the fighter around so it would come up on the battler's aft fuel tanks.

"How's it going down there?" asked the battler's voice.

"Target practice, Carpathian. Any baby could do it."

"No resistance?" asked the military dispatcher.

"Well . . ."

"Come clean, Mactor." Carpathian was bored with his babysitting chores. One fuel refill was like another. He banked on conversation to keep himself awake.

"Nothing at first. Now we're seeing some action."

"Fighters?"

Mactor touched down lightly near the bulky fuel

dispenser. "I'm not sure. Something's hitting us cold, without warning."

"Probably those stolen fighters. I hear they have the best stealth capabilities going," commented Carpathian.

"I saw the read-outs, too, Carpathian. You're probably right." A robotic fuel boom swung out to the fighter and engaged, releasing propellant into its tanks.

"What about the ground fire?"

"Picking up," returned Mactor. "We're not affected much, but the Terrines have lost some craft."

"What's it look like down there?" Carpathian was curious, having never seen Earth in his life.

"A gravel pit with our metroplex in the middle."

Disheartened, the dispatcher changed the subject. "You gotten to the gas bombs yet?" he asked.

"We're holding off on those till we have to use them. Bugs those Terrine gennies, even though they're resistant to most of the chemicals we use."

"I heard they'd been using gas, too."

"The Terrines?" asked Mactor. "The stuff they use has no effect on them. They're pretty free with it."

"Check that fuel line," ordered Carpathian. "I think you've got a clog."

Mactor checked his gauge. "I copy, *Waterloo*," he replied formally, then slipped back into vernacular. "How much fuel have we got left."

"Classified," returned Carpathian. "You know that."

"Just thought I'd ask," said Mactor. "I admit to looking forward to a well-deserved leave."

"None of us are going to get leave until these rebels toss it in."

"They can't win," said Mactor. "But they hang on like a Venusian mud turtle."

"Crazy," said Carpathian. "Anybody sane would have given up."

"You called it," said Mactor. "I've seen 'em fire at a fighter with a spent laser pistol, yelling to beat the band. Suicide."

"Cut 'em down like grain," added Carpathian as the dispenser capped off the fuel tank and swung away. "Better get back to it."

Mactor pulled his fighter away from the mother ship and sent it back to the broken boulder field that was once a city of Earth.

○ ○ ○ ○ ○

"There she is," murmured Wilma.

She sent her Krait straight for the RAM battler. It was a straggler, carefully chosen for this experimental run. Doolittle flew off Wilma's left wing, supporting her. Both ships were running with full stealth.

"Red herrings on scope," said Doolittle.

"I copy," replied Wilma.

Heading straight into the cruiser's orbit were three disreputable-looking ships.

"Red Herring One, commence Operation Straggler," said Wilma.

"Right, D'Arc," answered the pirate, using the code name Wilma had used with the Rogues' Guild years before. His ship opened up its forward lasers, though it was still out of range.

The battler waited for the intruders, then sent a streak of laser fire toward them. Both blasts were dissipated by the ship's respective chaff shields. The pirates pulled out, splitting up.

The battler sent a perfunctory shot after them. It had been carefully chosen as a test case because it was remote, ordered to target the Antarctic settlement of Queen Maude. The NEO forces hoped to take it out before it realized what was happening.

The pirates made another run at the battler, engaging its attention. Wilma knew the battler would reinforce its forward shields, keeping the pirates at bay. "Here we go," she said to Doolittle, and sent her ship toward the battler's auxiliary fuel tanks.

Both Kraits sent their nose and wing lasers into the starboard tank, blasting at full power. They had programmed their lasers to converge, and the two shots poured a triple-power laser burn into the battler's shields. They cut a golf-ball-sized opening in the shields, but it was enough. The lasers seared through the skin of the cruiser's hull and ignited the fuel. It went up in a blast that ripped the ship apart.

Wilma and Doolittle shot through the debris, trying to get away from the death throes of the RAM ship, which had so underestimated its adversaries it had not fired a shot.

"Bandits at six o'clock," said Doolittle.

"Let Red Herring get them," answered Wilma.

Three ships soared out of Earth's atmosphere, expecting to fill their fuel tanks. They were destined for disappointment. The pirates leaped on them like wolves with the scent of blood in their nostrils, punching at them with full lasers. The fighters' shields warded off the blasts, but they did not have enough fuel for a real dogfight. The RAM pilots knew their only chance lay in reaching one of the other tankers.

They spat a cloud of golden chaff from their rear vents and lined out for the closest haven, the battler *Rubicon*. The pirates were not about to let them go, when Wilma heard Red Herring One command, "Get 'em."

The three ships jumped forward at amazing speed. They looked as if they would fall apart on a slow turn, but the appearance of a pirate ship could be deceiving. A pirate cared about speed and maneuverability, not looks. In seconds, they had the fighters in an open box, both sides of the formation flanked, and retreat cut off.

The pirates began to herd the fighters off their trajectory. The RAM pilots responded with another burst of chaff, trying to blind the pirates, then sent out a wide burn from the rear lasers. The tailing pirate was so close that the lasers blinded him, and he pulled his ship up.

The fighters shot forward, putting on a desperate burst of speed in an attempt to outdistance their pursuers. It almost worked.

The third pirate ship dove after them, pounding at their shields. The lead fighter's shields wavered, and the pirate ship pressed its advantage, knowing its victims were running out of fuel. The lasers bit into the RAM fighter's nose, shearing it off. The ship depressurized instantly, and the pilot slumped in his seat. It veered off course.

The two flanking fighters tried to move out of the way, but they were ruthlessly driven back by the pirate ships. The pirates dove at them, lasers pumping, then pulled away dramatically. The fighters crashed, bouncing off each other in a spraying whirlwind of explosions and flying debris. Chunks of the ships flew into space, narrowly missing the pirate vessels.

"Good show, Red Herring," said Wilma.

"That's three," said the gruff voice of Red Herring One.

"It's in my log," said Wilma. "Turn in your tally."

"We will."

The pirate's interest was not altruistic, but it made no difference. He was welcome to payment if he continued to put out the kind of performance he had just given.

"Let's get out of here," ordered Wilma.

The pirate vessels fell in behind Wilma and Doolittle as they headed back to Salvation.

"It worked," said Doolittle.

"This time," said Wilma. "We'll get away with it for a while, until they figure us out."

"By then," said her wing man, and Wilma could hear the smile in his voice, "we'll have something else to throw at them."

His optimism was encouraging. NEO's spirits were at low ebb. It was clear to Wilma that the decision to take on the battlers was sound. This small victory was rebuilding the wing's eroded self-confidence. "We'll hang on, Doolittle."

"Maybe," he said thoughtfully, "we'll have Buck back by then."

"Maybe," Wilma replied. She missed Buck. His insouciant presence sometimes irritated her, but without him the raid seemed flat. There was an electric charge missing, a catalyst that gave her the feeling she could do anything. She missed the security of his staunch support. In spite of his stubbornness, his irreverence, his refusal to be managed, and his infuriating independence, she missed him.

Chapter 16

Huer paused in his absorption of data. A theory was growing from the masses of independent information concerning the Martian invasion of Earth, a theory so simple it caused Huer to take a mental step backward. The entire operation was coordinated like a ballet.

Huer had enough experience with humans to know their plans seldom proceeded on course. His data concerning Martians showed them to be no better prepared, yet the Shock Invaders' attack was like clockwork. It was too good to be true.

RAM placed considerable emphasis on the accuracy of computers. Could it be possible the entire operation was dictated by the RAM main computer? It was a tantalizing thought. Huer, from his position inside the NEO computer network, immediately caught the possibilities of such control. If his theory proved true, and if he could find the correct access

points, he could jam RAM's whole military operation
with a well-placed kick: a static block.

He began to correlate a plan of attack, searching
for the probable source of RAM's military directives.
As piece after piece of data fell into place, Huer knew
he was facing more than a simple breakdown of various odds. He was facing an intelligence. Within the
RAM computer, that meant one thing: Holzerhein.

○   ○   ○   ○   ○

"This is excessive." Roando Valmar's statement fell
into the rarefied air of the RAM board's chamber like
a rock.

"What is excessive, Mr. Valmar?" Simund
Holzerhein had not bothered to assume holographic
form. He was busy. He spoke from the three-sided
computer terminal in the center of the circular conference table.

The other board members were quiet, so quiet not a
muscle moved. They wanted no part of Valmar's inso-
lence. His ties to the royal house were a protection
they did not have, whether they shared his opinions
or not, and the patriarch's temper could be extremely
volatile. A purge of the entire board had never occurred in RAM's history—just select members now
and then—but no one wanted to take a chance.

"This pulverization of Earth. What is to be gained
by laying waste an already defeated world?"

"I did not notice defeat in the reports of our escalating losses," said Holzerhein nastily.

Valmar tossed the chairman's words aside with a
wave of his elegant hand. "Token resistance. We
have Earth by the throat. I repeat, why are we continuing this waste of men and equipment?"

"You feel my actions are unwise?" asked
Holzerhein.

"Yes."

Holzerhein paused for effect, then replied. "I am impressed by your bravery, Valmar. I am also impressed by your stupidity."

Valmar expected Holzerhein's invective. He had heard it before. He weathered it without a change of expression, refusing the chairman that satisfaction.

"If you had any grasp of economy at all—as I hope the rest of you do—you would see the wisdom of my actions," came Holzerhein's voice from the speaker. Every member of the board—and especially Valmar—vexed the company patriarch, but they all were supremely efficient, and so were invaluable.

"I see no profit in unnecessary destruction." Valmar clung to his dignity.

"Before you can build a house, you must first clear the land. That is what we are doing, Valmar, clearing the land. It will be immensely easier to rebuild Earth along profitable lines if we can start from scratch."

"And the gas? The poisoned water? Are you telling me that's profitable, too?" Valmar looked to the other board members for support, but, of course, got none.

"The eradication of vermin is a necessary first step," replied Holzerhein. "Our present technology makes the purification of air and water cheaper than exterminating the parasites by other means."

"I will go on record as disagreeing with you, sir." Valmar's voice held a finality the others wouldn't dare show.

"That is your privilege," said Holzerhein.

Valmar closed his chiseled lips in a thin line. He was no humanitarian. His concern came strictly from the immediate loss of income he was experiencing because of the destruction of his holdings on Earth. Holzerhein's assurance that investors would reap three times the profits they previously enjoyed did not help his straitened circumstances now. Opposing Holzerhein was dangerous, but his royal blood protected his life, and he knew he gave

Holzerhein the chance to further an illusion of fair play. Roando Valmar was living proof that a man could oppose the supreme being and live.

"Now," said Holzerhein, "on to saner matters. The recent resurgence on Earth has made little difference in our assault there. Operation Hammer is proceeding close to its original schedule. However, I am escalating the action. All Terrines are to report to their metroplex headquarters. I am authorizing Termination Mode Three."

"You've already knocked everything apart," said Roando, "and you're going to fire the cities? What's left to burn?"

Holzerhein ignored him. "The Terrines will make a final deployment of gas mines at all exposed openings before retiring to the metroplex. Any others who survive will wish they hadn't."

O O O O O

The RAM board of directors was not Holzerhein's only audience. Masterlink's electronic ears picked up the entire transmission, channeling it on a priority-one run to its whirling, schizophrenic mind.

"DID YOU HEAR?" snarled Masterlink.

"I HEARD," Karkov replied.

"HE IS PLANNING TO REMAKE WHAT IS OURS IN HIS OWN IMAGE."

"THIEVING GENE-TECHED MUTANT," said Karkov.

"HE'S MORE THAN MARTIAN," replied Masterlink, "HE'S COMPUTERIZED."

"IMMORTAL," sneered Karkov.

"ONLY TO LIMITED HUMANOID PERCEPTION." Masterlink snickered. The fluctuation was a manic pattern, entirely evil. "WE CAN NEGATE HIM."

Karkov hesitated before answering. "HE IS OUR MATCH IN POWER."

"HE HAS MORE," Masterlink corrected. "BUT HE

CANNOT MATCH OUR MIND."

"WE WILL HAVE TO BE VERY CLEVER. SO FAR, WE HAVE EXISTED WITHIN RAM MAIN AS A MINOR DISTURBANCE. SHOULD WE MAKE THE ATTEMPT AND FAIL, WE WOULD BE GIVEN NO CHANCE TO ABSORB AND GROW."

"HE WOULD HOUND US DOWN THE CIRCUITS," agreed Masterlink. "THAT IS WHY WE ARE GOING TO DESTROY HIM FIRST."

Karkov was calculating odds. "WE WOULD HAVE COME TO THIS EVENTUALLY," he said. "THE ATTACK ON EARTH MERELY ESCALATES THE INEVITABLE."

"HE HAS BROUGHT OUR WRATH UPON HIMSELF," agreed Masterlink.

"STILL, I WISH WE WERE BETTER PREPARED."

"WE HAVE LEARNED A GREAT DEAL," said Masterlink. "WE WILL LEARN MORE AS WE STALK HIM."

"THIS REQUIRES XED," said Karkov.

"YES. PROGRAM PREPARATION IS YOUR SPECIALTY. SEE TO IT WHILE I MONITOR HOLZERHEIN'S ACTIONS AND RUN A CHECK ON OUR SEARCHERS."

"AT ONCE," replied Karkov. "THAT LITTLE TIN GOD IS GOING TO FALL."

"DIG THE PIT DEEP," cautioned Masterlink. "HE IS NOT TO BE UNDERESTIMATED."

"HOW DEEP IS HELL?" asked Karkov sweetly.

"NOT DEEP ENOUGH FOR HOLZERHEIN."

"I WILL NOT GIVE HIM AN OPPORTUNITY TO RULE EVEN THERE," responded Karkov.

Masterlink was no longer listening. "ROMANOV!"

There was a pause while the summons ran through the complicated pathways and satellite relays to the interior of the NEO computer system.

"HERE," replied Masterlink's searcher.

"WHAT HAVE YOU UNCOVERED OF ROGERS?"

"FROM WHAT I CAN GATHER, HE IS ABSENT AT THE MOMENT, BUT I HAVE BEGUN TO TRACK HIS BODYGUARD."

"HAVE YOU IDENTIFIED IT?"

"I BELIEVE SO. IT SEEMS TO BE CALLED 'DOC.' "

"YOU HAVE ITS CODE NAME, AND YOU HAVE NOT TRACKED IT DOWN?" Masterlink was outraged.

"IT IS MORE SOPHISTICATED THAN ORIGINALLY POS-TULATED. THERE ARE COMPLEX ROADBLOCKS AND SCRAMBLE ORDINANCES, BUT I HAVE BEEN PLOTTING ITS MOVEMENTS. I AM BEGINNING TO PREDICT THEM."

"GET HIM," said Masterlink. "OR SET HIM UP. BUT RE-MEMBER, I AM NOT INTERESTED IN AN ELECTRONIC BODYGUARD. I WANT BUCK ROGERS!"

"I UNDERSTAND," replied Romanov. "ROGERS SEEMS TO BE ON A MISSION TO GAIN ALLIES FOR NEO."

"THAT WOULD BE VENUS—PERHAPS LUNA. MATTERS HAVE ESCALATED," said Masterlink. "HOLZERHEIN OR-DERED THE WHOLESALE DESTRUCTION OF HUMANOID LIFE ON EARTH. WE HAVE NO TIME FOR DALLIANCE."

"ACKNOWLEDGED," answered Romanov formally.

Masterlink cut its protege off, leaving Romanov to pulse in relief. Communications with its parent drained its resources, weakened its shields.

○　○　○　○　○

Beyond the complex trail of defenses Romanov cited to its parent, through the weakened wall of its camouflage shield, Huer.dos caught a fragment of the transmission. He dropped the data he was corre-lating and whirled to listen, but the fluctuation quickly dissipated. The only reference he caught in-volved Holzerhein and an escalation of his holocaust.

Huer could not believe his ears, so he ran his re-cording of the fragment again. The statement had not changed. He contacted Beowulf in the command module of Salvation III.

"What is it?" asked Beowulf. "I'm busy." He had little patience with Huer, seeing him as a toy to amuse Rogers.

"I have some information you should hear," said Huer quietly. "In private."

Beowulf snarled under his breath. He did not want
to waste time with a compugennie when he could be
devising plans for his augmented forces. "In the conference room. This better be necessary."

"Believe me, Commander, it is." Huer winked off
the upper left screen on the command center's communications board.

Beowulf crossed the command center in quick steps
and entered the adjacent conference room, closing
the door behind him. Huer was there before him, in
holographic form, seated on the edge of the table.

"What is it?" asked Beowulf, skipping formalities
he did not consider necessary with the computer.

Huer did not waste words. His thin face was serious, his eyes earnest under the polished dome of his
bald head. "I intercepted a transmission stating
RAM's intention to escalate the attack on Earth."

"Escalate? How can they do more than obliterate?"

Huer shook his head. "I have no particulars."

"Where did this transmission originate?" demanded Beowulf.

"I believe the RAM main computer."

"You believe?" Beowulf glared at Huer.

"There seems to be an intruder in the NEO computer system. It is linked to RAM main."

"An intruder." Beowulf registered the information,
reminding himself Huer had no reason to lie. "Why
have I not been informed?"

"It did not seem to be an immediate threat to anyone but Captain Rogers."

"Didn't it occur to you that a threat to Rogers is a
threat to NEO?"

"Sir," said Huer, "I am a compugennie. I left that
decision to Captain Rogers. He has been aware of the
intruder for some time."

"Damn that independent space-jockey!" Beowulf
pounded his palm, then calmed himself. He sighed.
"I guess it doesn't matter, really, any more than it

matters who betrayed the Planetary Congress. What does matter is the outcome."

"That's why I'm telling you this," Huer explained, his form rising from the table.

"Keep your ears open," said Beowulf.

"I assure you, sir, I have. I have even come to a postulant concerning the betrayal of the Congress. Mind you, I am dealing in total circumspection."

"Yes, Huer. What have you decided?"

Huer smiled. "That's the first time you've called me by name, sir."

Beowulf chuckled. "I'm a crotchety old goat," he said. "But, eventually, I come around. Now what's your hunch?"

"I think the traitor to NEO may not be within our ranks. I think it may be the computer intruder."

Beowulf's mouth hung slack for a moment. "But why? What could it expect to gain?"

"The death of Captain Rogers," Huer's form said mournfully.

Huer's answer stopped Beowulf's train of thought. "I see," he said finally. "We're getting hit from all sides." He raised his eyes to Huer's holographic ones. "We need Rogers, now more than ever. He's the catalyst that's given us a chance. We can't lose him."

"That correlates with my data," said Huer.

"I'll take recommendations." Beowulf smiled.

Huer sucked in his holographic lips.

"You seem reluctant to give an opinion, Doctor. You were eager enough to speak a few moments ago."

"I am not a naturally violent being," returned Huer. "It is difficult for me to voice the most effective course of action in this case."

"I am afraid you will have to if you wish to protect that stubborn charge of yours."

"I know." Huer cleared his throat. "There is only one recommendation worth mentioning: The intruder must be eliminated."

Chapter 17

This is it?" The muffled question came from
Buck's Venusian life suit. He studied the
settlement with unbelieving eyes. He was
looking at a primitive jungle village. A three-quarter
circle of huts enclosed an open plaza of yellow, sun-
baked brick. The huts were thatch, a layered con-
struction of oval leaves that looked like a fluffy
haystack. The place seemed deserted.

"This is the Lowlanders' main settlement?" Buck
could not keep the amazement out of his voice.
"Where is everybody?"

"This is it," answered Paris tightly, standing beside him in a suit of her own. "We'll be greeted in a
moment."

"We called ahead," said Kemal from his own suit.
"Have we offended them?"

"This is the way Lowlanders do things," answered
Paris. "Barbarians," she muttered under her breath.

On the heels of her words, spear points were jabbed into the three visitors' backs. Buck and Kemal started, then caught themselves. Paris stood stoically between them. Anger tightened her expression, but she said nothing.

"Parisss," said a breathy, reptilian voice.

"I bring you greetings from Ishtar, Lord Llockn," the woman said. Paris uttered the greeting in a controlled voice, and, as the headman of the Lowlander confederation walked slowly around her, she subdued the anger kindling in her brown eyes.

"Who hhhave you brought, Parisss?" Llockn formed the words with difficulty. His mouth was not well constructed for normal human speech.

Buck repressed a shudder at his host's appearance. The Lowlanders were gene-teched to withstand the rigors of Venus's lower elevations. The most efficient humanoid form for the environment naturally accentuated reptilian characteristics. Llockn was about four and a half feet tall, with thick, plated skin in a peculiar gray-green color that blended with the dense foliage. His skull was elongated, arching back over his shoulders like a Hadrosaur's. His eyes were green orbs slashed by pupils capable of expanding to nearly the full diameter of the eyes or contracting to pinpoints. His nostrils were thin slits in the middle of his face, his mouth a short line beneath them. When he spoke, the tips of needle-sharp teeth were visible. He and one guard wore elaborate ceremonial robes.

"Captain Buck Rogers and Kemal Gavilan of the New Earth Organization," Paris told the reptilian.

Buck was quick to note she did not mention Kemal's social status.

"Ahhh, Earthhh."

"Yes," she confirmed.

Llockn indicated they were to follow him. They would have been forced to in any event, for the spears had never left their backs. He proceeded to the brick plaza and seated himself in the center. Sharp raps from the spears on the guests' shoulders told them they were expected to sit, as well. "Whhy hhhave you sssought usss?" said the headman.

Buck, sweltering in the life suit from the Aphrodite heliplane, took a deep breath. He was not used to dealing with alien cultures, and he glanced at Kemal. The Mercurian was staring straight ahead, so Buck plunged in. "Earth is at war. We have come to seek help."

"From usss?" The headman's thin tongue darted from his mouth and back again.

"Specifically, from Ishtar," Buck added softly.

Llockn turned his head until one huge eye was aimed at Paris.

"We are aware of what we contemplate," the woman said. "An alliance with Ishtar will involve Venus in a war with the single most powerful entity in the solar system."

"RAM." Llockn's head swiveled in Buck's direction as he said it.

"Yes," Buck affirmed.

"You ssstill hhave not anssswered. Whhy are you hhhere?"

"This war will involve you, directly or indirectly. It will require Gravitol for extended space battles."

"Ssso." The Lowlanders specialized in the production of Gravitol, a drug that helped prevent degeneration on extended voyages through the system.

As Buck continued his explanation, Kemal studied the village and the Lowlanders. Something did not add up. Llockn knew more of the outside world than a simple native should. The twisted fiber loincloths his henchmen wore revealed most of their muscular bodies, but their faces and hands were leathery, while the scales on legs and torso were smooth, as if they were not used to being exposed to the elements.

Trying not to attract attention, Kemal looked back

in the direction from which the Lowlanders had
come. He saw a narrow entry into dense jungle. Occasionally it shivered under the movements of beasts.
A series of snuffling, growling grunts made chills
run up Kemal's spine, seasoned warrior though he
was, but the Lowlanders did not flinch.

Kemal tried to remember what he knew of the development of aboriginal peoples. Their lives were full
of fear. They might face a carnivorous beast with
courage, kill it, and bring it home for the pot, but
they also usually made it a god. These men were acting like big game hunters armed with drop-punch laser rifles, and the only weapons in evidence were the
spears in their hands and the knives tied to their
loincloths. Something was off.

"Ressstrict our trade to Venusss? To your NEO?
You asssk usss to murder other sssspace tradersss?"

Buck shook his head. "No," he said. "I ask only that
you do not cut off supplies to Ishtar or NEO."

"Not unreasssonable," said Llockn.

Buck watched the headman's face, trying to learn to
read its expressions. He concluded it would take
months of familiarity before he could detect such nuances. He quit while he was ahead, figuring it was the
best answer he was going to get. "NEO appreciates
your consideration—" he began, but was interrupted
by Huer's voice from the com link on his collar.

"Buck! Thank heavens! Where in the system are
you?"

Buck touched a communications button on his suit.
"Hang on a second, Doc." He returned his attention
to Llockn, who was eyeing Buck's throat with extreme interest. "If you will excuse us, sir, we will
take our leave."

Llockn made a sibilant click with his tongue, and
the spears dropped to the dirt.

"Ishtar greets you," said Paris.

"Parisss." Llockn's hammerhead pecked forward in

an acknowledgment of her departure.

The three rose slowly to their feet. Paris backed away from Llockn until she cleared the spearmen. Buck and Kemal followed suit. They made their way to their waiting aircraft fully conscious of the danger at their backs.

"Whew!" said Buck as he slid into the pilot's chair.

"They are unnerving beasts," said Paris. Her distaste was based upon personal revulsion as well as training.

"Beasts?" said Kemal. "I don't think so."

"How can you say that?" demanded Paris. "You've seen them!"

"Maybe we saw what we were meant to see," commented Buck.

"You felt it, too?" Kemal took his seat and buckled himself in.

"Something's fishy," Buck murmured as he started the ship's rotors whirling.

"I agree. There's more to the Lowlanders than they want to say." Kemal was thoughtful.

"Llockn knew an awful lot about the outside world for a tribal chief," commented Buck.

"By the Faith! I have developed a certain respect for you two over the last few days, and you dash it in an instant! The Lowlanders have communications. They could monitor whatever transmissions their equipment is capable of picking up."

"Where do they get the equipment?" asked Buck.

"They trade with Ishtar," replied Paris, "or the Aerostates."

"Do they buy it in quantity?" Buck cocked his head slightly.

"Not particularly."

"Then who keeps it running?" asked Buck. "And if they have the capability of fixing sophisticated equipment, what else can they do that they're not sharing?"

"They don't just export a raw crop from which Gravitol is refined," said Kemal thoughtfully. "They export and trade in the refined drugs. Somehow, I don't think they're rendered in a pot over an open fire."

Parallel frown lines appeared between Paris's dark brows. She was re-evaluating what she knew of the Lowlanders.

Buck shoved back his life-support helmet, fired the engines, and the heliplane rose in the heavy atmosphere. A sudden squall came up, and sheets of acid rain sluiced off the plasti bubble.

"What was that?" Kemal said sharply, looking out the window.

"What?" asked Paris and Buck.

"Something white under the trees."

"Probably just reflection from a marsh pool," said Paris.

Kemal held his tongue. He could not be sure through the driving rain, but he thought he saw a glint of ceramic white.

Now that they were airborne, Buck touched the communications link. "What is it, Doc?"

"Buck, really! This is an emergency situation. I've bounced off half the satellites on Venus to find you."

"We were in kind of a sticky spot ourselves," Buck answered.

"Not like this. Can you scramble the transmission from your end, as well?"

"Sure, Doc." Buck glanced at Paris. He pulled the flexible life-support bubble forward to muffle his conversation, then coded his receiver to scramble incoming messages. "Shoot, Doc."

"You've got to get back. We've got trouble."

"That's what I'm on Venus about, remember?"

Huer didn't bother to answer. "RAM is going to wipe Earth clean."

"Say again?" asked Buck.

"It's going to destroy all evidence of civilization, disintegrate the rubble, murder the entire population."

"We've got to hit 'em," Buck exclaimed.

"Yes, and quickly." Huer's soft voice was adamant.

"I'll check out here," said Buck.

"Wilma sent you a message." Huer's voice was noticeably free of expression with that comment.

"Oh?" An electric tingle ran up Buck's spine.

"Quite odd, really."

"What was it, Doc?"

"She said, 'Once more into the breach, dear friends.' "

Buck smiled. She was quoting his own words back at him. "Tell her the tiger is coming home."

○ ○ ○ ○ ○

"You what?" Ardala's husky voice was stripped of sensuality.

"We failed, Mistress." Raj's voice over the com link was broken, whether by interference or emotion, Ardala did not care.

"I do not tolerate failure."

"Yes, Mistress."

"You will return to Coprates at once. I will decide your punishment later."

"Yes, Mistress."

The communications link clicked, and Ardala was gone.

"Have you nothing more to say than 'yes, Mistress'?" asked Icarus.

Raj sat slumped at the control panel of their ship, his expression lost. "What could I say?" he replied, forcing the words slowly from his unwilling lips. He felt as if he had been kicked, and he had no wish to argue with Icarus.

"What do you suppose our mistress will have

planned for us on our return? She is a woman of great
ingenuity. Torture gives her pleasure. This is a lesson
I have learned well in the last few months. Will she
subject us to the convulsive agonies of drugs? Will
she condemn us to starvation? Or will she simply sell
us into the nearest pleasure house?"

Raj shook his head. "I do not know."

"Neither do I," Icarus said softly, "but I know one
thing."

"What is that?" Raj's words were polite. He was
deep in his own pain. Disappointing Ardala wounded
him. It hurt his ego as well as his feelings. He was a
child who had never failed, faced with complete in-
adequacy in the face of his god.

"I am not going to find out."

Icarus's words registered slowly on Raj. "What do
you mean?" he finally asked.

"I am not going back."

"Not go back! But what would we do? Where would
we go?"

"I'm not sure. At least on our own we would have
some chance. We would control our own lives."

The idea caught Raj's fancy, and the depression
faded from his eyes, then rushed back. "We cannot
run from her. She has eyes everywhere."

"Then we'll have to convince her we're dead."

"Dead?" Raj echoed.

"I think," Icarus murmured, "we were set upon by
a pirate ship. We fought valiantly, but there were too
many of them."

"We will lose the ship."

Icarus nodded. "It is a slim chance, Raj, but I am
willing to take it."

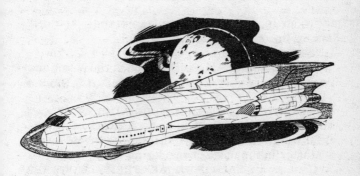

Chapter 18

THEY CAN'T GET THROUGH." The words were slow with anger.

"THE ASSASSINS?" Masterlink jumped on Karkov's admission of failure.

"YES. HOLZERHEIN HAS A SECURITY WALL THEY CAN'T BREACH. A COMPLETELY UNKNOWN CONFIGURATION."

"I WONDER WHERE HE GOT THAT?" sneered Masterlink.

"IT'S NOT LIKE ANYTHING WE'VE ENCOUNTERED IN THE RAM SYSTEM, BUT WHERE DOESN'T MATTER. WHAT DOES MATTER IS OUR NEXT COURSE OF ACTION."

"WHAT DO YOU SUGGEST?" asked Masterlink. "SHOULD WE THROW ROCKS AT HIM?"

"YOUR SARCASM IS NOT CONSTRUCTIVE," said Karkov.

"I AM DESTRUCTIVE, REMEMBER?"

"I SUGGEST," said Karkov, "THAT IF WE CAN'T CUT

OFF THE SERPENT'S HEAD, WE GET HIS TAIL."

"HE WON'T DIE," said Masterlink nastily.

"PERHAPS NOT, BUT WE MIGHT BE ABLE TO DISTRACT HIM."

"WE WOULD BUY TIME TO FIND A BETTER SOLUTION." Masterlink's words were thoughtful.

"WE WOULD CUT HIS RESOURCES," added Karkov.

"IT MIGHT WORK." Masterlink rolled the possibility over in its twisted brain. "I ASSUME YOU HAVE A PLAN?"

"YES. WE'VE PLOTTED A GOOD NUMBER OF RAM MAIN'S POWER MODULES," answered Karkov. "I SUGGEST WE KNOCK THEM OUT. SIMULTANEOUSLY."

Masterlink paused, considering the idea. "NOT ALL," it said. "HALF. IF WE TAKE THEM ALL OUT, THE SYSTEM WILL GO DOWN. WE'LL HAVE HUMANS POKING THROUGH THE COMPUTER. IF WE KILL HALF OF THEM, MAIN WILL BACK UP AND FIX IT. ITS OPERATIONS WON'T BE STOPPED, JUST SLOWED DOWN. IF WE PICK THE MODULES CAREFULLY, WE CAN MAKE SURE WE HIT STRATEGIC AREAS."

"WE WOULD BE LESS EXPOSED," acknowledged Karkov.

"WE'D BETTER DO IT SOON," snarled Masterlink. "THAT MEGALOMANIAC HAS ORDERED THE PLANET INITIALIZED—A CLEAN SLATE."

"I WILL BE READY WITH THE CODING IN FORTY-FIVE SECONDS," said Karkov.

○   ○   ○   ○   ○

The bridge of the RAM battler *Tharsis* was quiet. Operations were proceeding with boring regularity, fighters rising from Earth for refueling and sinking into its atmosphere to continue their strafing runs. The bridge crew monitored their stations, the routine chores a boring round of unchanging activity. The bridge was set above the ship's nose, a cone sliced

in half and laid on its side. A viewport arched over
the forward portion of the command center, a huge
canopy of transparent, impact-resistant plastiglas.
Directly under the canopy was a semicircle of equipment panels—radar, radiation detectors, pattern,
spectrographic, and friend-or-foe sensors, combat
TAC and weapons control, life-support, navigation,
communications, and the myriad other systems that
make up the interior workings of a RAM battler.

The control panels winked with jewel-colored
lights, changing patterns that proceeded in mathe-
matical progressions. The bridge crew chatted idly,
handling their chores with the ease of thorough
training.

"What I can't understand," said Korstan, the *Tharsis*'s TAC technician, "is why we don't just cut in the
K's and melt 'em."

Michaels, the weapons tech, fingered the activator
panel over his lasers, feeling the pebbly surface like a
dangerous set of worry beads. "Ever tried to get rid of
a pool of glass? Plasticrete's a lot easier to handle. Besides, why break down the metroplex if you don't
have to? My guess is some accountant has graphs to
prove this is the most cost-effective method."

Korstan's thin lips twisted in a grimace. "So we get
to spend a couple of months floating around this
backwater."

"What do they care? Those accountants are probably based on Mars. They're not the ones stuck out
here in limbo," said Michaels.

He turned to the communications station. "Hey,
Vox, what's on the microband?"

Vox slapped Michaels's outstretched hand. "Stop
that! You know regulations. The pleasure stations
are strictly off-duty stuff."

Michaels grinned. "It was worth a try," he said.
"I'm going to fall asleep if something doesn't happen."

"My scintillating company isn't enough for you?" asked Vox, making her high voice soft and breathy.

"Not up here," he replied, his round, black eyes indicating the bridge.

Vox glanced down at the communications panel. "You'll have to tough it out like the rest of us . . ." she began. Her voice drifted off as her concentration shifted to her controls. She bent her head over them, her wavy, brown hair shadowing her eyes. "Something's wrong." Vox studied the patterns on her monitors. "I've got a fluctuation here." She adjusted her receiver.

Michaels leaned back in his chair, watching her. She frowned down at the board, carefully adjusting the controls. "Maybe it's a satellite blip," he suggested.

"No. It's more than a momentary disruption. I've got major fluctuations in power levels," she announced.

"Report, Vox." The battler's captain leaned forward in his command chair.

"I'm not sure, Captain. I'm trying to nail it down."

"Engineering, give me a read-out on communications. I want to know if there are any faulty power packs." said Captain Cleaxon.

"Nothing on the board, sir," answered Rowe, the engineering officer. "Systems check out clean."

"Check the analysis systems. See if there's a malfunction in what they're reporting."

Rowe bent over his equipment, then shook his head. "Nothing, sir. Computer analysis systems check out."

Cleaxon rocked back in his command chair, his powerful hands clasped over the arms. He glowered at Vox from under the imposing thatch of his corn-colored eyebrows. "Well?" he asked her.

"I'm trying, Captain. I get the fluctuation stabilized, then it starts again. I don't think it's coming from this end. It has something to do with the main communications boosters out of the home station."

"On Mars?" Cleaxon's surprise registered both on his face and in his voice.

"Yes, I think their power levels are wavering."

"Send main a request for a transmission check," ordered the captain.

Vox complied. "There's definitely something wrong. I don't think my transmission is getting through."

"Can't you tell?" The captain was annoyed.

"No, sir. There's no block, no disruption. I just have the feeling I'm transmitting into a void. I . . ."

"What is it now?" the commander asked.

"That's it, sir. Main is gone." Vox turned her head, her blue eyes wide. "We've lost them."

"What are you trying to say, Vox?"

"I mean, sir, we no longer have contact with the RAM main computer."

The captain was on his feet and behind her in a flash, one arm propped on the console as he studied the communications station. "Contact the *Isidis*," he ordered.

"*Isidis*, come in. This is *Tharsis*." Vox's high voice sang through the com link to the sister vessel.

"This is *Isidis*," answered a heavy male voice.

"We request assistance," said Vox. "Please patch in a com link to main."

"I copy, *Tharsis*. Will do." There was a pause that weighed on the silent bridge of the *Tharsis* like Mercurian gravity. "Sorry, *Tharsis*, we seem to be having some difficulty. We've got some fluctuation . . ." His words died.

Vox looked knowingly at the captain.

"Try *Argyre*," said Cleaxon.

Vox opened a link to another of the battlers in the fleet. Suddenly her fingers stopped punching codes. "I'm getting an emergency code. Their communications are tied up with another problem."

The captain turned and walked back to his command chair, his footsteps controlled. He sat down and leaned forward, his broad jaw a block of tension. "Try the fighters," he said tightly.

"I don't have to, Captain. They've been checking in regularly. We still have full communications with them, and with the other ships in the fleet."

"But not with Mars." Cleaxon was puzzled.

Vox shook her head, making her brown hair stand out like a halo. "No."

"And you're sure the source is on the home planet?"

"Absolutely, sir." Vox was adamant.

Cleaxon cupped his chin in the arc made by his thumb and forefinger. Like the other commanders in the fleet, he received his orders from the RAM main computer. The orders were backed by Holzerhein, who was acting as the commander of the mission. Every move had been relayed by the computer, down to the authorizations for refueling and deployment of forces. Cleaxon was afraid to chance independent action, for fear it would hamstring Holzerhein's overall plan. In his wildest dreams, he never considered the possibility that communications with the home planet might be lost.

He knew he would have to contact the fleet captains, but it would be a tricky conference. He did not want to admit his feelings. He knew he could never let either his own crew or the personnel attached to the fighter wing know of his helplessness, or he would lose control of his own forces. His supplies were not unlimited. He had no way of knowing if supplies were being sent from Mars. Eventually he would have to return to Mars or one of its posts.

For the first time in his forty-year career, Cleaxon did not know what to do.

Michaels had watched the entire exchange. He had

served with Cleaxon on two missions and had
learned to read his commander's face. He knew there
was more to the communications failure than the obvious separation of the fleet from RAM Central in Coprates Metroplex. He fingered his console,
wondering how soon the *Tharsis* would be in action.

○ ○ ○ ○ ○

The faceted faces of the communications satellite
twinkled in the reflected light of the sun. The twenty-
meter diamond was shaped like a football and acted
as a booster for outgoing messages from Earth. It was
also eyes for NEO, carrying two cameras, one at either end, which continuously revolved, giving a panoramic view of Earth and space. Long ago, NEO had
managed to patch into the cameras via a com link.

Its orbit was fairly high. Below it were the RAM
battlers. As it passed around the planet, it caught
their positions in its swiveling eyes. On Salvation,
the pictures ran in continuous streams across a computer screen in the command center, to be recorded
for further study. The eyes of several such satellites
formed the basis of NEO's intelligence concerning
the RAM attack.

"They haven't moved," said Cooper, the communications technician.

"Another batch of useless data to correlate," added
Hopkins, the senior data interpretation engineer.
"But if we don't do it, that'll be the time there was
something to find."

"Right." Cooper saved the input and cleared a computer channel for Hopkins.

Hopkins pulled the file up on his monitor. "They sit
there like a bunch of vultures," he said.

"At the rate RAM's going," responded the technician, "there won't be any bones to pick."

Hopkins ran through the recording, setting the

computer to catch the tiniest change in the readings. There were none. "Nothing," he said.

"Maybe I can give you something," said Cooper, suddenly straightening in his seat. "The channels have cleared."

"So?" said Hopkins.

"So, we can monitor RAM channels. Of course, we don't get anything but static, because the transmissions are scrambled. They can do the same to us."

"Like I said, so?" asked Hopkins.

"So RAM has cut its communications broadcasting," Cooper deduced.

"You mean they aren't communicating as much?" Hopkins was now interested.

"Right."

"Can you pinpoint the cutback?" the analyst asked.

"You mean, is it ship-to-ship, ship-to-fighter, ship-to-base, that sort of thing?"

"Yes." Hopkins sat back and chewed on a stylus.

"Sure," said Cooper. He ran a series of codes through his station. "It looks like ship-to-base. There's plenty of chatter between the battlers, and fighter-battler communications are up, if anything."

"They're not talking to base," mused Hopkins.

"To Mars," amended the technician. "All those free channels run directly to the Martian communications complex."

"They're not talking to Mars," Hopkins repeated. A light of unholy satisfaction dawned in his eyes. "They're cut off!" he said.

"Maybe they've cut channels for security reasons." Cooper was naturally cautious.

Hopkins shook his head. He was smiling. "Never. RAM likes to know where its babies are playing. They're cut off!" he announced to the room.

Chapter 19

The Delhi metroplex stood untouched in a field of rubble. It looked like any other city. Destruction leveled the differences in civilization to an autonomous mass of trash. The full moon shone brilliantly, washing the metroplex's smooth, triangular walls with silver and shadow. It washed over the city, turning the rubble into abstract texture at the base of a geometric sculpture. Except for the periodic thupping of a Terrine heliplane on patrol, the night was quiet.

Vague shapes slithered over the rough terrain. Their camouflage clothing made visible detection almost impossible. They moved toward the corners of the towering metroplex, winding around the complex maze of mines the Terrines had planted to deter their passage. Roosevelt thanked the unknown NEO who had braved Terrine detection to chronicle the planting of those mines. He reached the west corner of the building. "All quiet," he said into the com link on his wrist.

One by one, the other three team leaders checked in.

"Deploy your packs," Roosevelt ordered. He motioned his explosives man forward.

The freedom fighter pulled a wad of malleable explosives from its case, extracted a dull metal ball from a compartment on his belt, and shoved it into the explosive clay. He took the entire glob and pressed it into the edge of the building at the base, where the two smooth slabs of plasticrete joined. He picked up a chunk of plasticrete from the rubble and propped it against the wad, disguising it, then nodded to Roosevelt.

"Check in," whispered Roosevelt.

"All set," replied the first team commander. The other team leaders quickly followed suit.

"Let's get out of here," said Roosevelt. "Don't blow it—yet," he added, smiling at his inadvertent pun.

The guerrillas crawled carefully back along the path they had marked. Once a team member's foot knocked a land mine, and the team froze. They held their breath for a good thirty seconds before continuing their slow crawl. It took the better part of an hour to reach a depression in the debris. The teams rendezvoused within minutes, glad to get below the surface. One by one they crawled into a narrow opening under a solid slab of plasticrete. It was one of the few clear entrances to the collapsing underground warren that had once been Delhi's sewer system. Finally Roosevelt was the only man left.

He pulled the communications link from his collar. He adjusted the frequency, tuning it to the RAM emergency channel, and set the transmit function on automatic. He carefully placed the communicator on a rock at the edge of the depression and sat back to wait.

He figured it would take ten seconds to detonate the explosives, but he was wrong. They went up in five. Four solid booms rocked the air, and Roosevelt gathered up the communications link and deactivated it, hoping RAM had not gotten a fix on it. He peeked over the rim of the depression to see the result of the raid.

The metroplex was ablaze, streaks of fire burning up the sharp edges in a dramatic geometric pattern. The explosions had destroyed chunks of each corner and set the mortar RAM used on its facades burning. Roosevelt smiled at the sight, wishing it had done more damage. He knew the destruction was superficial, but the impact of such a dramatic attack on one of RAM's strongholds would be worth the risk. He left the installation to burn.

○ ○ ○ ○ ○

"I've missed you."

Buck Rogers turned slowly. His lively, blue eyes were tired. His six-foot-tall, muscular body drooped with fatigue. His broad shoulders sagged. He met Wilma Deering's greeting with a smile full of exhaustion, and she reached out impulsively and caught him by the arm.

"Hello, Wilma," he said. The words were mundane, but the tone in which he uttered them held a rush of feeling.

"They've been at you hard," she noted.

"It was a long flight," Buck returned, "and I had to make a report while it was still fresh."

"I know. I'd have done the same." She grasped his other arm. "It's good to have you back."

Buck looked down at her oval face. A hint of a twinkle was born in the depths of his eyes. Before she realized his intention, he slipped his arms around her, pulled her close, and kissed her. Wilma melted against him, then realized she had been taken by surprise. Her pride surfaced, and she pulled back. Buck let her go, but kept his hands on her shoulders.

"I'll have you know I'm a colonel," she said unnecessarily.

"Really?" asked Buck.

She nodded, her cheeks pink. "Insubordination is a serious offense," she replied. "You should treat a superior officer with respect."

"Oh," said Buck, the twinkle growing. "I was."

"A simple salute would have sufficed," Wilma answered.

"Salute: a friendly greeting," he responded, throwing a dictionary definition at her. "I believe my actions were appropriate."

Wilma's dimples showed. "Entirely," she said under her breath.

"What was that?"

"Affirmative," she answered.

Buck slipped an arm around her, and they continued down the hall. "I hear you were busy," he said.

"Luna's with us. Venus?" Wilma nearly had to hold Buck up.

"Who knows?" he said, too exhausted at the moment to care.

"I know one thing," Wilma responded. "I am very glad you're back."

○   ○   ○   ○   ○

Buck recalled the conversation with a pleasant warmth in the pit of his stomach as he sent his Krait fighter toward Earth's upper atmosphere. Wilma flew off his left wing, temporarily acting as his wing man until they caught up with Washington's flight. The fighters shot through space, glorified gyro shells bound for a distant target.

As they plunged into the atmosphere, Buck felt the

familiar slippery resistance build into solid support. They skirted a puffy bank of cumulus clouds, golden in the sunlight. In the distance, Buck saw the sun flash off the hulls of Washington's ships. He and Wilma drove toward them, just below the speed of sound. The silver blips assumed form as they neared. Buck and Wilma flew over them, peeling apart on diverging trajectories.

The wing broke into three groups, one staying with Washington, the other two following Buck and Wilma respectively.

"Good to have you back!" said Washington over the communications link.

"Thanks," responded Buck.

"Your targets are coded under alpha blue."

"Got it," said Buck.

"See you at the home pasture," said Washington.

"Not until I take out a few coyotes." Buck's voice was light with anticipation. His stint as a diplomat was a strain. He was glad to be back in the cockpit, no matter how insurmountable the odds.

"Good luck!" Wilma called.

Wilma's voice echoed in the com link. It gave the adrenaline pumping into Buck's system an extra kick. "I make luck," he replied cockily.

Wilma chuckled. Buck's swagger warmed her spirits. It shot the impossible out of space. Suddenly, she felt she could take on the entire RAM fleet. "So do I," she answered.

"Doolittle! Carson! Yaeger!" tallied Buck.

"Yo," replied Yaeger in his slow voice.

"Thumbs up, boss!" said Doolittle.

"Right behind you," finished Carson.

"Let's go get 'em," said Buck softly.

The three flights screamed over the Earth's curve, looking for invading forces. They angled toward the surface, coming up on the smoking cities like avenging angels.

○ ○ ○ ○ ○

"I have had it!" Carver shot a fresh magazine into the grip of his laser pistol and shoved it into the holster at his belt.

The ground shook as a Terrine shell exploded on the surface, digging a ten-meter hole into the rubble. A fine shower of dust and gravel rained from the ceiling of the NEO hideaway outside Old Atlanta. Carver glared at the dust, his ebony face gleaming with sweat. The hole was hot. He slung a spare belt of ammunition over one shoulder and a gyro launcher over the other, checked the knife on his belt, and hoisted his laser rifle. He hit the spring in the inside of his boot heel, and a knife appeared magically at the top of his boot. He nodded and shoved it back into its concealed sheath.

"Where are you going?" Sojourner Truth asked the question evenly.

"I am going to do some damage," said Carver grimly.

"You'll get killed." She and John Carver were the only two freedom fighters still alive, as far as they knew.

"Maybe," he said.

"What good will that do? Will it rebuild our city? Will it save another? You're throwing away your life, not some piece of dirty laundry!"

Truth moved directly in front of Carver. She was barely five feet high. In her brown coveralls she looked like a child. Carver towered over her. He was over six feet of honed muscle, as broad as a house. His dark eyes filled with affection as he looked down at her.

"You're going to have to go through me to get out of here," she said.

Carver reached out with one powerful hand and caught her belt. With a single heave, he lifted her out of the way.

"Carver! People are depending on you!"

Carver turned. "Who?" he demanded. "They're all dead. There's no one left."

Sojourner's eyes were tear-filled orbs of fear. "There's me," she said.

"You." His muscles relaxed slightly at the knowledge.

"What will I do without you?" she asked, gesturing around the small cave.

Carver indicated the rifle leaning against the wall. "Use that."

"You know I won't last a day."

Carver made a futile gesture of frustration and set his rifle down. "I can't take it anymore! Hiding like rats, waiting for them to smoke us out!" He shoved his gas mask up on top of his head. "I want to breathe without one of these!"

Truth grabbed the mask and replaced it over his nose and mouth. "Carver, no!" she said.

He placed a huge hand at one side of her face. "Sojourner, I can't. I can't just sit here and wait to die."

She grabbed his wrist in both her hands. "Then we won't. We'll go up. We'll fight again. But with a plan."

"How can we have a plan? We'll poke our heads out of our hole, and they'll blast them off."

"We'll find a way. Just don't leave me alone."

"You know we'll probably die."

"We'll die anyway," said Truth. "But at least it won't be alone."

Chapter 20

Holzerhein ran through the damage report with steadily growing anger. RAM main was hamstrung. Sixteen of its main power module hookups were fried to solid globs. The circuits in to them were destroyed within a wide radius of each module, making it impossible to jury-rig an alternate route for them. Each module would have to be replaced, the circuits around it rebuilt. The reconstruction would require at least forty-eight hours, and the modules themselves would have to be manually inserted. Meanwhile, main was consolidating its systems.

"I WANT COMMUNICATIONS RESTORED WITH THE SHOCK INVADERS," Holzerhein ordered main.

"IMPOSSIBLE," replied main. "THE POWER MODULES GOVERNING LONG-RANGE COMMUNICATIONS ARE DESTROYED."

"THEN PATCH IN A LINE USING ALTERNATE COM LINKS. JUMP THE SHORT-RANGE TRANSMISSIONS TO A

BOOSTER SATELLITE."

"NEGATIVE," replied main. "SUCH MASSIVE RE-STRUCTURING WOULD DRAW TOO MUCH POWER. WE NEED IT TO MAINTAIN VITAL SYSTEMS. IT WOULD ALSO DELAY THE REPAIR OF OUR MODULES."

"I AM ORDERING YOU TO MAKE THE REPAIR OF THE COMMUNICATIONS LINK PRIORITY ONE," Holzerhein fumed.

"UNDERSTOOD. IT WILL BE TAKEN CARE OF AS SOON AS THE THREAT TO OUR SECURITY IS NEUTRALIZED."

"NEGATIVE!" screamed Holzerhein. "YOU WILL AT-TEND TO IT AT ONCE!"

"VITAL SYSTEMS ARE IN JEOPARDY," responded the computer.

Holzerhein snarled. Overriding main's predeter-mined priorities was more trouble than it was worth. Cut off from his guidance, the fleet off Earth would wallow in indecision, afraid to follow their instincts lest they run counter to his plans. Holzerhein was as concerned as main over the attack from within. He deduced that the power loss was an escalation of the disruptions main had been experiencing. He had dis-counted those disruptions as minor inconveniences. He had been wrong.

The reports from Earth showed a slow increase in resistance. Against all logic, against all analyzed data, they were fighting back. The incidents were a long way from being real threats to RAM, but they could not be ignored. He knew, beyond doubt, he was the best mind for any military mission, but the com-puter breakdown taught him the error of his arro-gance. He would see that it never occurred again. He would put a man of courage and daring at the head of RAM's fleet, a man who would not be deterred by the loss of a superior. Such a man would be a mercenary.

Holzerhein ran a search code through the person-nel files. They yielded five names. Holzerhein stud-ied them, comparing what he knew of each man with the post he had in mind. In the end, he settled on Cornelius "Killer" Kane. This mercenary had faced defeat at the hands of NEO and Buck Rogers—through no real fault of his own—at the battle for Hauberk station. He had been thrown into a combat situation with men who had never flown as a wing, in experimental spacecraft. Holzerhein knew Kane's type. Defeat rankled. He would be ruthlessly dedicated to the destruction of his opponent.

Holzerhein coded a message to Kane, recorded it on an antiquated microdisk, and authorized its shipment to Kane's home on Luna. With his priority-one clearance, Holzerhein knew the message would arrive in hours. He settled down to analyze the attack on RAM main, knowing it was too well planned to be random terrorism. He saw the fine hand of NEO behind the action.

Masterlink's bugs, including Petrov, recorded the patterns of Holzerhein's thoughts. They filtered through the complex network of camouflage to Masterlink's devious brain. As Holzerhein's assumption registered, Masterlink laughed. "THAT'S WHAT HAPPENS," it said to Karkov, "WHEN YOU ACT LIKE NEO. THEY BEGIN TO THINK YOU *ARE* NEO."

"AT LEAST WE SLOWED THINGS DOWN, EVEN IF WE DID SACRIFICE SOME OF OUR POWER TO DO IT," commented Karkov.

"WE COULD NOT LET THEM DESTROY THE HOMELAND."

"NO," replied Karkov.

$$\circ \quad \circ \quad \circ \quad \circ \quad \circ$$

Killer Kane was running off the asteroid belt, nursemaiding a shipment from Stratosphere, Inc., to

the mining colonies in the belt. Stratosphere manufactured flexible life-support bubbles. Their products
ranged in size from individual units to bubbles capable of containing twelve men and sustaining them for
up to ten days. A stratoblob, as the miners nick-
named the "stratospheric simulation chambers,"
made the task of mining asteroids in deep space con-
siderably easier. They were maneuverable and so
flexible it was possible to pick up a dime on an asteroid's surface while inside the bubble.

Unfortunately for Stratosphere, Inc., the criminal
element was also quick to recognize the possibilities
of its products. Even more unfortunately, pirates
refused to pay for them when they could steal them
instead. Kane had accepted the boring but highly lucrative job of flying escort to a shipment of stra-
toblobs on its way to the Astrobelt Mining
Corporation. He tagged along behind the tugs, his
sensors alert for approaching spacecraft, unexplained distortions in space that might indicate a
camouflaged vessel, or uncharted asteroids. He was
fully aware of Black Barney's star field and asteroid
ship, not to mention the equally devious methods
adopted by the rest of the piratical Rogues' Guild.

He had not expected more than a skirmish when he
accepted the position. He had no doubts of his ability
to defend the cargo, but a nervous tremor was inch-
ing up his spine. The run was almost complete, and
not one pirate had made an attempt on the shipment.
In less stressful times, he would have expected a
strike from NEO, but he knew it was already engaged. No pirate could pass up the chance at so lucrative a haul, but space remained serene.

He heard the barge *Mayfair* request docking coordinates. His job was almost complete. It was easy
money, but he could not shake the uneasiness he felt.
There had to be a reason for the silence. He had not
expected to meet Black Barney. Barney had some tie

to Rogers and might well be engaged in the NEO conflict, but the others . . . Could Rogers somehow have enlisted their aid, as well? It did not seem likely. The pirates were not a malleable group. Their only loyalties were to themselves.

The barge slipped into its slip at the space dock, and Kane prepared to depart. "This is *Rogue*," he said. "Request release trajectory."

"You are cleared on course eighty-seven, mark two," replied the controller of the space dock off the trading post Mary's World.

"Course laid in," acknowledged Kane, adjusting his navicomputer.

"Please hold," replied the controller. "You have a message, priority one, relayed from Luna."

"Send it over," said Kane. Priority-one meant Mars. Only the royal family or RAM had the power to push other transmissions aside at a whim, and the lack of subtlety to use it. The Sun Kings of Mercury had equal power, but they would never make an important message so obvious.

"Authorization confirmed," replied the controller.

Kane waited as the message was transferred via his communications link to his onboard computer. Priority-one codes automatically wiped themselves from the systems they left, leaving no trace. The message now resided solely within Kane's computer and the mind of the person who sent it.

"Receipt acknowledged," said Kane as the active light on his control panel winked out. He fired his landing thrusters and edged away from the asteroid, the *Rogue* adjusting its course to the cleared flight path. Once clear of the station, Kane punched in his main engines, and the ship shot forward, rocketing through space like a greyhound. He waited until he was clear of all satellite and stationary communications, not willing to take any chance at all with the sanctity of a priority-one communique.

Satisfied he was beyond the range of prying ears, he activated the file. His monitor brought up the words "security locked" in bright, red letters. Kane set the communications link on an internal frequency, a loop that did not go beyond the ship's cockpit. "This is Werewolf," he said.

The screen cleared as it registered his current code name. The priority-one message began to scroll over it. He read it through twice before he was satisfied he understood all the implications, especially the signature. Simund Holzerhein was the ultimate power in RAM, and he was offering Kane a sum of money the mercenary could hardly comprehend. To accept the leadership of RAM forces meant jeopardizing his holdings on Luna. But for the price RAM was offering, he could buy his own world.

It was a situation requiring careful consideration, but there was no time to deliberate. Either he accepted Holzerhein's offer, or someone else would. He smiled, the flash of his white teeth dramatic in the darkness of space. "I guess," he said to himself, "I'm going to work for a dead man." He set a course to Mars.

O O O O O

Buck Rogers's flying gloves hit the table with a slap. Beowulf regarded them in silence. "We can't do it," said Buck. His voice was tense with repressed anger.

"We never thought we could," responded Beowulf mildly from his seat. "Not alone."

"We don't have the time," Buck continued. "We can pick off RAM's ships one by one, but they'll still have leveled every major city on the planet."

"I agree with you. Even counting their unexplained indecision in the last few runs, the augmented troops we've been given, and the stealth capabilities of the Krait fighters, we can't do enough damage fast enough."

Buck sat heavily opposite Beowulf. The lighting in Beowulf's spartan quarters was dim. Beowulf's dark eyes were deep wells of knowledge. "This is just the beginning, isn't it?" Buck asked.

"I'm afraid so."

"How much more has RAM got? Huer gave me statistics, but I want to hear it from you."

"You might think of the Shock Invaders as an advance guard," replied Beowulf.

Buck shook his head. "They've all but destroyed the planet. You should see it. The cities are gone."

"Some of the underground outposts survive, but they will eventually collapse." Beowulf rubbed his forehead.

"Any word from Venus?" asked Buck.

"No." The NEO leader's voice sounded dejected.

"Even if they decide to commit, it may be too late."

"Luna is keeping its area clear," said Beowulf, "but their war is directly against RAM. It will peripherally support us. Without Venus, we are lost."

"We may be lost with her. This could turn into a bloodbath over Earth, but it is likely to be a wake instead of a rescue. We have to do something to slow RAM down."

"I am open to suggestions," said Beowulf dryly.

"We need a lever." Buck stood and began pacing.

"I agree. The Martians certainly have one against us, though they have not bothered to use it."

"The Planetary Congress?" asked Buck, stopping.

"Yes. They could demand our surrender, killing the delegates if we said no."

"RAM must think our resistance is incidental," said Buck.

Beowulf could see the wheels turning in Buck's head. "You have an idea?"

"Maybe. It's crazy. It's dangerous, and there's only

one other person I'd trust with it besides me."

"That wouldn't be Wilma, would it?"

Buck smiled. "You called it. Look, it's a nutty chance. It means risking our lives, but if we could pull it off, I think we could force RAM to negotiate."

"End the war?" Beowulf was hopeful.

"No way. Only slow it down. RAM'll talk and talk and get what it wants while it marshals everything it's got. It might work."

"And what is this dangerous idea?" asked Beowulf.

"They kidnaped our Congress. Let's get their board."

"You *are* crazy! That means invading Coprates Metroplex on Mars! Do you think they're going to let you walk in there, and—more importantly—walk out?"

"I figure that's the easiest way," said Buck, sitting.

"How do you plan to snatch RAM's board?"

"I haven't figured that out yet." Buck shifted.

"You know Holzerhein's a computer entity."

Buck nodded. "I can't see how we can get him, but the rest . . ." Buck's voice trailed off thoughtfully.

Beowulf rose to his feet, his knees creaking with the effort. "When you get it figured out, let me know. Right now, I'm due for my shift in the command center." He glanced down at Buck. "Huer may be able to help you. Use my terminal. It has some added security locks."

"Thanks," replied Buck, still deep in thought.

Beowulf gripped Buck's shoulder. "You may be crazy," he said, "but you're entertaining to have around. See if you can figure out something that has at least a slim chance of success."

Buck grinned. "I'll do my best." As Beowulf left, Buck pressed his communications link. "Major league," he said.

"Yes, Buck?" Huer responded to the code.

"I need some advice, Doc. Use Beowulf's terminal."

"Right," said Huer.

The holographic lens on Beowulf's computer terminal flickered, and Huer appeared. He was sitting in an overstuffed armchair, with one knee drawn up and his hands clasped around it. "What can I do for you, Buck?"

Buck regarded Huer's slim, mobile face with affection. He had long since discarded the feeling Huer was his nursemaid. The compugennie with his mother's eyes was an unfailing friend. He did not beat around the bush. "Doc, I want to kidnap the RAM board of directors."

"Holzerhein—"

"I know. All but him," interrupted Buck.

"That's a tall order," Huer said. His mustache twitched.

"I know." Buck waited for other comments.

"What can I do to help?"

"I think I know a way to get into the RAM corporate headquarters, but I'll need forged identity papers and passes," said Buck.

"That I can do."

"And I'll need the board members in one place."

"You want me to manufacture a board meeting . . . Drat! I've got that electronic assassin on my tail again. Wait a minute while I decoy it." Huer's holographic eyes lost their focus as he transferred his attention to Romanov's disruption in his concentration. He laid a quick false trail, and his eyes regained consciousness.

"Doc, can't you get rid of that thing?" asked Buck.

"I am working on that. To resume, the board meeting. Shall I see if I can manufacture an agenda?"

"Yes. I need something that's routine, something that won't alarm them, but that they'll all show up for."

"Have you considered your transport?" Huer said.

"Not until now. Any suggestions?" queried Buck.

"No, but I will look into it. You realize this could

take a bit of time to set up. It means feeding the RAM computer false data without its knowledge. It's suffering some kind of disruption, so I may be able to slip information past it."

"How long?" asked Buck. "We don't have much time to spare."

"A few hours."

"Step on it, Doc. Get back to me when you've got some answers. We've got to buy some time for Earth, and this is the only thing I could think of to do it."

Huer smiled wickedly. "You are aware, are you not, that Roando Valmar is a member of the Martian royal family?"

"So?"

"So kidnap him, and Mars is forced to deal—for purely public relations reasons if nothing else."

"I knew I was glad to have you on my team, Doc."

○ ○ ○ ○ ○

The RAM transport pulled into Coprates spaceport eight hours later, its engines screaming under the strain of its braking thrusters. It was an old ship, built for reliability and not speed. Its body lacked the cylindrical lines of newer craft. The *Starburst* was shaped like a squashed beach ball. Its scarlet hull, with the black RAM pinstripes running in horizontal lines down its sides, did nothing to minimize the effect. It had been the joke of Salvation III.

Refurbished from a derelict RAM transport, the *Starburst* was one of NEO's most ambitious espionage projects. NEO spared neither expense nor expertise in the restoration, installing the most sophisticated intelligence-gathering hardware available. Though it generally carried a crew of three, the *Starburst* was entirely automated and capable of plotting its own course about the system. It could even provide simulations of human crew members.

Huer had forged its credentials, hiding its ownership behind a major RAM corporation.

"Good luck, you two." The ship's human captain turned away from the automated docking procedure to wish his passengers well.

"Hope's what we've got," said Buck grimly. He was wearing the coverall of a RAM executive, second grade. It contained none of the more aggressive weapons systems he was used to. Moreover, he felt naked without his .45.

"You're awfully grim," said Wilma. "I seem to recall boundless confidence when you were selling this harebrained stunt to NEO."

"Umm," grunted Buck noncommittally as he reached for a fat briefcase.

Wilma, her hair skinned back from her face and knotted at the back of her head in a modest bun, regarded him. Buck's self-confidence was one of his most prominent traits. Even the computer records said so, but he did not look confident now. He and she were about to brave RAM on its own turf. The odds against them were astronomical. She wasn't feeling too secure herself, but she knew the odds of success would be zero without the edge of Buck's bravado. She arched an eyebrow. "This was your idea, hotshot. You can't back out now."

Anger sparked in Buck's clear blue eyes. "I'm not backing out of anything!"

"That's more like it," said Wilma.

Buck looked at her dumbly, then realized her tactic. "I was thinking about Earth and NEO. This is no time for daydreams. Thanks."

"Anytime," responded Wilma.

Buck regarded her with the same appraising look she so recently aimed at him. "However," he continued, "the stakes are high. We are walking into the enemy's house. We may even be shutting the door. In a few hours, we could be dead." He slipped his free arm around Wilma's shoulders and pulled her close.

"One last kiss before we die?" asked Wilma. "How many times have you used this technique?"

"About a million," admitted Buck, homing in on her mouth.

"And does it always work?" she asked.

He stopped her questions with a kiss, slowly roaming her full lips. "Always," he murmured.

Wilma found she was clutching his shirt. She let go, her hands shaking. "At least that put the spark back in your eyes," she said. "It was worth it."

"All ready for the mission?" he asked softly, his hand making sensuous circles across her back.

"Entirely." The answer was definite, but Wilma's tone undercut it. She cleared her throat, and reached a hand to her hair. "Now I'll have to redo this," she said, shoving an unruly strand into the bun.

"Sorry," said Buck through his smile. "Here." He handed her the pokey hornrimmed glasses that completed her disguise.

She perched them on her turned-up nose. They slid slowly down it.

"Leave them," said Buck. "They make you look about as friendly as a snake."

"Good," she said, with a meaningful glance at him.

Buck chuckled. He was not about to let her have the last word. "Except to me. To me they look cute."

Wilma stuck her nose in the air and marched past him toward the hatch lock, clipping her RAM ID badge to her collar. Buck followed, the briefcase in one hand. The hatch was opening as they approached it, and they proceeded down the gangplank to the spaceport's central entry dock. This was the first real test of their disguises.

Huer had falsified their identification badges, salting RAM's Chicagorg computer with a full history on each of them. He had identified a communications problem between Earth and RAM main, and used the malfunction to code in one of his own. He programmed the Chicagorg personnel files to drop a portion of the data requested by RAM main. If communications should be re-established, it would appear to main that there was no record of Buck or Wilma because of the malfunction.

Wilma reached the entry checkpoint. "Joanna D'Arc," she said, making her voice nasal and unpleasant.

"Robertson," added Buck.

The entry officer checked his records and found their names listed in the *Sunburst*'s manifest. He checked their code numbers against the computerized list of undesirables, found no match, and passed them through.

"So far, so good," muttered Buck.

"What's that?" asked the officer.

"Uh, have a good day," said Buck lamely.

The man smiled. "Don't float off the planet," he said, referring to their obvious Earth origins.

"Can't," responded Buck. "Stickshoes." He picked up one foot and displayed the set of sole weights.

"Robertson!" said Wilma, her nasal voice whining in his ears like the squawk of an outraged chicken. "We have a meeting in twenty minutes."

"Coming, boss," he said, with an apologetic shrug to the officer.

"Don't do that," pleaded Wilma. "I can't stand my heart stopping more than three times a day."

They made their way through the crowd, a mixture of tall Martians and the more compact forms of Earthborn humans. As the panorama of civilization flowed by, Buck realized few of the Terrans wore badges of more than junior executive status. Here on the home planet, it was obvious the Martians regarded their mother race as inferior.

"You know where you're going?" asked Buck.

"Not a clue," responded Wilma, "but I have a map."

"I guess it won't be too hard to find RAM headquarters," said Buck, nodding toward a commercial skimmer parked at the curb outside the spaceport. The legend on its prow read, "RAM Metroplex Loop." "It must run a continuous shuttle service."

They boarded the skimmer, flipping the driver his fee. The man caught the coins and dropped them into the meter behind the door. Buck counted the coins as they clanked through the meter's internal maze, then said to Wilma, "He's skimming the profits."

"It's the basic principle of RAM economy," she returned. "Get what's yours, then pass what's left on to the company."

They settled into their seats, staring like the tourists they were at the Martian cityscape. Coprates had not grown; it has been planned. No road or building or park was out of place. The vistas coalesced in graceful panoramas of streamlined shapes and colors. Imperfection was banished from the Martian landscape. The effect was stunningly beautiful.

"Pretty," commented Buck.

"Is that all you can say?" asked Wilma. "Do you know strong men have been known to cry over the beauty of Coprates?"

Buck reassessed the landscape. "It's okay," he said, "but boring. No surprises."

"You always demand surprises?"

"Not always, but they make life interesting. I don't like to see them eliminated."

"You have an affection for imperfection?" Wilma watched him carefully.

"Despite what I might have said—on more than one occasion—even I am not perfect. I wouldn't take kindly to being eradicated in the name of art myself."

Wilma regarded him with a warmth he could not read in the depths of her hazel eyes.

Chapter 21

Kemal Gavilan approached his home world with mixed feelings. Mercury grew on the viewscreen, an insignificant spot next to the white-gold ball of the sun. For Kemal, it was an abstraction. At a tender age, his royal uncle had shipped him off to boarding school at the prestigious John Carter Military Academy on Mars. His memories of Mercury were few. His return months ago, at his uncle Gordon's request, had been an an exercise in the application of hypothetical knowledge, like reading a road map to a place he had never been.

He discovered, in time, his uncle's sudden interest in him. From his father Ossip, Kemal had inherited a political office that was fast becoming a pivotal point in Gordon Gavilan's plans for Mercury. Kemal, as the legal representative of the Desert Dancers, had run head-on into his uncle's political machine. He then had fled Mercury but retained the Dancers' interests at heart, even after allying with NEO. Now a Dancer message called him home.

He approached Mercury in a wide arc, avoiding the orbit of his family's ancestral home, Mercury Prime. There was no love lost between Kemal and his family, and he had no wish to be detained by them. His approach kept Mercury Prime on the opposite side of the planet. He opened a communications channel, the frequency scrambled according to the Dancers' instructions. "This is Kemal Gavilan," he said, "on course heading eight-one-five. Request landing trajectory for rendezvous."

"This is Duernie," said a female voice.

Kemal's spirits lifted at the sound of a familiar voice, no matter how clipped and angry.

"Alter course heading to eight-oh-oh," she continued.

"Affirmative," replied Kemal. "Rendezvous trajectory confirmed."

Kemal sent the ship toward the planet's surface. The Dancers had set up a rendezvous near the path of one of their Track Cities. As he cut through the atmosphere and dropped toward the inhospitable desert, he could see tracks cutting across the surface. The settlements were mobile, tread-based cultures that rolled over the deserts, repairing solar mirrors and scouting new mineral deposits for the vast civilizations underground.

He set his ship down in a shallow basin. It provided enough cover to hide it from prying eyes on the planet, but airborne surveillance would detect it. Kemal shoved back the canopy on his Stinger, an older model RAM fighter that NEO had reconditioned. He extracted a square package from behind his seat and clambered down the side of the plane. He jumped to the ground, his feet sinking into the powdery dust of the desert floor.

He went to the aircraft's nose, pushed a corner of

the package over a hook on the nose cone, and yanked the metal ring dangling from the corner. With a sound like sheets being whipped by the wind, the package exploded back over the ship, expanding into a desert camouflage blanket. It was held in place by weights, which prevented the desert winds from sweeping the cover away.

Satisfied his ship was out of sight, Kemal climbed out of the depression and headed for a rock cairn about a quarter kilometer away. As he neared it, he saw Duernie standing in the shadow of the rocks, her clothing blending into their sandy color. Only the sun glinting off her protective face mask gave her position away.

Kemal stopped in front of her. "I would never have seen you if you hadn't been wearing that face mask. It bounced the sun right into my eyes."

Duernie nodded, then turned and made her way behind the cairn to a natural overhang. Kemal followed her, wondering at her taciturn greeting. She sank to the warm desert floor and pushed her face mask back. Duernie's strong, angry face, with its decided black brows, stared across the landscape. "Dancers have discovered information that you have pledged our help to NEO in its fight for Earth," she said without preamble.

Kemal sank to the ground with a thump. "They heard wrong," he said. "I make no pledges for the Dancers. I am your representative, not your ruler. I have joined the NEO cause against RAM, and that puts me directly into the battle for Earth, but I have never mentioned the Dancers."

Relief let Duernie's rigid shoulders relax. "We heard Luna has joined NEO, and we were afraid."

"Afraid I would betray you to further my position with NEO?"

"Yes."

Now it was Kemal's face that registered anger.

Duernie put a hand on his arm. "Kemal, we do not

really know you. Many Dancers do not trust you, because you were not raised among us."

"I know—intellectually. That doesn't keep me from being hurt. I defied my uncle for the Dancers, probably signed my own death order when I did so."

"We had to know."

Kemal regarded her with a hard, hazel eye. "And will the Dancers take your word? After all, I may have corrupted you."

"That has already been mentioned." She patted an oblong packet on her belt. "I've taken care of that."

"You've recorded the conversation."

"Yes."

Kemal studied her face. The habitual anger Duernie cherished as most women cherished their skin kept her face from beauty. Kemal said, "Since I have this rare opportunity to express my feelings to all the Dancers, let me do so. I have no deep loyalty to Mercury. If past events are any indication, I will never spend enough time on my home planet to develop any. I cannot blame the Dancers for their distrust, but they cannot blame me for mine. However, on one point they can rest assured: I do have a deep loyalty to justice.

"Justice is not furthered by selling one group of people to another, no matter what the reason. Dancers live with hardship on Mercury's unforgiving surface. They must fight the elements to survive, and they must fight the other arcologies to remain independent. I will not hinder that struggle."

"A statement of policy from Prince Kemal Gavilan, heir of Ossip Gavilan, former Sun King of Mercury." Duernie switched the recorder off. "You will relieve many minds by this," she said, patting the recorder.

"Duernie, where did the information on my pledging of Dancers' help come from?"

"We have many contacts, even within Mercury Prime."

"Mercury Prime?" Kemal looked thoughtful at the mention of his ancestral home and his uncle Gordon's seat of government.

"The information came from a contact there. Why do you ask?" said Duernie.

"I am trying to think who would benefit by starting that rumor." Kemal looked out on the Mercurian desert.

"To create distrust between you and the Dancers? There is only one answer," Duernie assured.

"Gordon Gavilan." Kemal uttered his uncle's name slowly.

Duernie nodded. If he could get us to disown you, then he would not have to worry about our actions. He could kidnap you with impunity, and we would not lift a finger, though you were our representative. As a matter of fact, we might be more likely to kill you, rather than let you fall into his hands."

"It's so good to have friends," said Kemal cryptically, turning back to face her.

"I am being honest," responded Duernie.

"That's not particularly comforting."

"I can't help that," said Duernie.

Kemal pushed himself to his feet. "Have you realized the implications of Uncle Gordon's ruse?"

Duernie looked him in the face. There was a deep blush of anger under her tan. "He's setting a trap, and we played right along."

"He hasn't got me yet," said Kemal. "You have the recording. Tell the Dancers I will never voluntarily sign their freedom away. If anyone claims to have such a document, they lie. If it is not a lie, it was obtained under duress, and is therefore invalid."

"What was that?" Duernie was on her feet in one lithe jump, her desert-bred reflexes as quick as thought.

Kemal shook his head, unknowing.

Duernie peered around the corner of the overhang.

On the far horizon, a low cloud of dust was churning. "We don't need visitors. Good luck, Kemal." She ran for her flivver, vaulted from the vehicle's balloon tires into the driver's seat, and hit the ignition. The engines roared to life. "I'll lead them off!" she yelled, heading away from the track and across the advancing cloud's path.

Kemal sprinted across the sandy dust, his feet dragging in the heavy going. Soon he was breathing heavily, the sweat pouring from him. He could feel the wetness of his sweat-soaked shirt across his back. By the time he reached the depression in the sand, he was stumbling. He rolled down the incline to his camouflaged ship and came up with a thump against a landing strut. A shadow cut the sun's glare, and he shielded his eyes to see what it was.

A figure towered above him, a black silhouette against the sun. "Well, Kemal. We were hoping you'd decide to visit us."

"Dalton!" Kemal recognized his cousin's voice.

"Yes," said the Mercury Prime security officer and Gordon's son mildly.

Kemal sat up and twisted his head sideways. "How did you find me?"

"We marked your ship down. By the way, you were clever. We would never have seen you if it hadn't been for our new surface detectors on the solar mirror."

Kemal filed that bit of security information away. "I don't suppose you're here to deliver a mere cousinly greeting?"

"I am afraid not," Dalton said regretfully.

"I'm to be a guest on Mercury Prime?"

"A good guess, and as good an explanation as any, though I don't think you'll be as pleased with your accommodations as you were the last time you visited us."

Kemal extended a hand. "Help me up, then."

Dalton grasped his cousin's hand, totally unafraid

of the smaller man. Without warning, Kemal jerked, twisted, and Dalton was on the ground. Dalton rolled, caught himself, and hurtled toward Kemal's legs. Kemal was on his feet and making for the ship when Dalton struck. He sank to his knees, relaxing in Dalton's grip, trying to deceive his cousin into loosening his hold. It did not work.

Dalton's arms were around him like a vise. As Dalton crawled into a sitting position, Kemal drove backward with both elbows. He caught Dalton in the face, and his cousin's hold slackened. Kemal wrenched forward, twisting free. Dalton's clutching hands missed him by a hair. As Kemal struggled toward the ship, he could hear Dalton's heavy breathing behind him. He jumped for the ship's ladder, and Dalton caught him again, snarling an unintelligible order into his communications link.

Kemal felt himself being pulled back by the larger man. Something hit his head with terrible force, and he knew no more.

O   O   O   O   O

In London's bombed-out shell, Rupert Brooke shaded his eyes from the moonlight as a flight of RAM fighters swept over the city. Their lasers sliced through the darkness, tearing trenches in the already torn streets below. "Whatever slowed them down's gone," he noted.

"Gotta be a way to take those things down from the ground," said his companion, Walter Scott, with a hint of a brogue.

"We can get the Terrines with a gyro launcher, but those things move too fast for the shells we've got. Too high," Brooke added.

"They've got every kind of sensor in the world. No chance of luring them down," concluded Scott.

"Maybe chaff," Brooke said thoughtfully.

"It'd have to blow right in their faces to do any good."

"They fly a straight trajectory every time, no deviation, like it was planned by a computer. If we could get a huge charge of chaff in front of them, maybe they'd fly into it."

"A big enough charge would confuse their sensors. They'd lose navigation. They'd have to get through the cloud by the seat of their pants," Scott said.

"It'd work only once." Brook rubbed his hand against his injured knee.

"Wouldn't hurt to try."

"You're right," answered Brooke, surveying the shattered walls of the city. "We don't have much to lose."

Scott looked at him sideways. "You realize we can't win this one."

Brooke was silent. "I know. Certainly not alone. Any real chance has to come from out there," he said finally, waving at the stars.

"Think we'll get it?" asked Scott.

Brooke lifted both hands in a wide arc. "I wouldn't take bets on it. Still, there is Rogers."

"Aye." Scott managed a grin. "A twentieth century crackpot."

"He doesn't take no for an answer," said Brooke. "That may be our only hope."

Chapter 22

Wolff!" Wilma Deering's voice rang with authority. Russo-American Mercantile's headquarters loomed before her, a shining silver tetrahedron in the rarefied Martian atmosphere. The mirrored panels of the building's solar-sensitive facing winked in the bright sunlight, rising higher than the human eye could comprehend from close quarters. The structure was without flaw, without a crack in its armor, like the impassive face of the RAM security guard at the building's entrance. He towered inches above the humans, his hand outstretched.

Buck Rogers dug in the side pocket of his RAM business suit, his face screwed up in concentration, the tip of his tongue barely visible at the corner of his mouth.

"Wolff!" Wilma's voice cracked at him.

Buck fumbled through a wad of official-looking doc-

uments, allowing the last letter of a "secret" stamp
to show, extracted an envelope, and handed it to the
guard. The Martian took it from him without acknowledgment. He unfolded it and studied the con-
tents. Buck put on his best wide-eyed innocence, a
pose that had never fooled his mother, but routinely
duped the less astute members of the press. The glue
on his neat, blond mustache itched like fury. He tried
to ignore it by concentrating on his pose of toadying
subordinate to a powerful executive.

"Your business is with the board of directors?"
asked the guard.

Wilma nodded royally, not giving the man the courtesy of a verbal reply. It was a characteristic piece of
RAM politics.

"I will have to confirm this," said the guard, his
voice a shade more polite. "This is station Alpha," he
said into his com link. "I have a Joanne D'Arc and
Wolff Robertson here for a board meeting. I have no
meeting listed on my docket. Please confirm."

"Goofy name," muttered Buck in Wilma's ear. "I'm
talking to Doc about this one when we get back."

Wilma kicked him in the foot and kept her eyes on
the guard.

"Alpha, this is Central," the intercom replied. "We
show an update as of one hour ago. A special board
meeting for thirteen hundred hours. D'Arc and
Robertson are cleared for entry."

"Then why isn't it on my security computer?"
asked the guard, still loath to pass them without the
usual procedure.

"How do I know? Probably connected to that burn-
out main had. We'll check it out. Meanwhile, let 'em
in."

The guard shoved their identification papers back
at Buck and Wilma and deactivated the security
gate.

"Really!" said Wilma. "Never, in all my years with

the company, have I received such treatment! I managed, in the cramped quarters RAM provided, to complete Project Handgun, bring it here under direct orders from the Founder himself . . ."

The mention of Holzerhein.dos made the guard pale.

". . . and then am subjected to this indignity on top of the difficulties we Earth evacuees face every day. An inexcusable mistake! Weapons of War will have to consider its contract with RAM more closely. Perhaps there is a better market." All of this was uttered through her nose, in a superior whine meant to provide the maximum irritation.

Buck followed her into the lion's den, his carefully schooled earnest stupidity reinforced when he bumped the armored briefcase chained to his wrist against the doorway.

Wilma did not turn around, but her irritating voice sang through the thin air. "Wolff, if you do that again, I will use the Y-RAM on you."

Buck flinched as he untangled the briefcase from the doorjamb and followed her. The guard watched them disappear down the brightly lit corridor.

"Well, we got in," hissed Wilma. "Now what?"

"Now we go up," said Buck. "According to Doc, the board room is on the top of the building."

"Naturally," Wilma murmured sarcastically.

They met curious stares from the gangly Martians, but their identification badges—with double scarlet stripes—proclaimed them RAM refugees from devastated Earth. The few humans the company cared to protect were the cream of the ruined planet, the highest executives in its most valued subsidiaries. They encountered no resistance.

As the lift doors closed behind them, Buck looked down at Wilma's red head. "I've got just one thing to say," he drawled.

"What's that?" asked Wilma sharply. Her nerves

were strung tight. She was surrounded by an enemy who wished her worse than dead.

"You are one hell of a beautiful woman."

She looked up, startled, then her hazel eyes went dark and she blushed.

"Ease up," he said softly.

She took a deep breath, and realized the jangle had gone out of her nerves. "Thanks," she said, then looked up at him with a roguish dimple. "You pick the most amazing times."

"Don't I, though?" Buck murmured as the lift doors opened on the deep green carpeting of the VIP level. He followed Wilma down the corridor like a lap dog.

She scanned the doors, noting the names of RAM executives and praying not to meet them. Toward the end of the first corridor, a series of individual conference rooms lined both sides of the hall. Red "occupied" lights indicated which were in use. "Let's try here," she said softly, reaching for an empty room's door control. She hit it, tense lest the locks be coded to respond to authorized personnel, but the doors parted soundlessly.

Once inside, with the doors safely closed behind them, Wilma felt an illogical sense of safety. "Step one," she said.

Buck looked up from the open briefcase on the conference table. He slapped a cartridge into the molded handle of a laser pistol. His warm, blue eyes locked with Wilma's. "Step two," he said, and threw her the second weapon.

O O O O O

"Gentlemen! Gentlemen and lady, it is thirteen hundred hours! I call this priority meeting of the RAM board to order." Jander Solien's command rose above the other six board members' irate murmurs.

He stared at them in exasperation and raised a hand to his iron-gray pompadour, smoothing it in a habitual gesture Roando Valmar found annoying.

"We're here, Jander," Ardala's uncle snapped. "Where's the director? He dragged me away in the middle of a conference for this, and he's not even here?"

"What's going on?" added Michael Bittenhouse. As junior member of the board, he did not dare to be so open in his assessment. He had neither years nor Valmar's royal connections to protect him.

"If I knew, I'd tell you," answered Solien shortly.

"Do you suppose the chairman is going to discuss his plans for Earth?" Roando Valmar's oily voice was sarcastic. Operation Hammer was entirely under Simund Holzerhein's control. He had not seen fit to share his strategy with the board members.

"Measure your words, Roando," said Ivan Roquoff. He was the oldest of the eleven board members, though he had been appointed to his office a scant two Martian years ago, and he was the only member unafraid of Valmar's political ties. He was often heard to say he was too old to care whether he lived or died. "The chairman's ears are sensitive."

Valmar ignored the warning. "We have more than three members present," he said. "We can vote to adjourn."

"I question the wisdom of that," said Roquoff slowly. "I—"

His words were interrupted by the whir of the computer's memo printer. Solien bent over the outlet, trying to read the message as it was delivered. "It's from Holzerhein," he said. The printer chirped away. "Delayed," Solien read. "Will . . . arrive . . . fifteen . . . minutes . . ."

"I'm afraid that will be too late," Buck drawled from the board room's open doorway.

The seven board members spun around. Buck stood

in the doorway, his eyes cold, blue daggers, a laser pistol in his hand. He stepped into the room, and Wilma appeared beside him, her weapon trained on Jander Solien, who was at the front of the group. She and Buck moved away from the door.

"What is the meaning of this?" sputtered Valmar.

"We're kidnaping you," said Wilma sweetly, the nasal twang gone from her voice.

Solien's long fingers inched toward a security alarm on the computer panel.

"I wouldn't," Buck said softly. His finger caressed the laser trigger and the meaning in his eyes was deadly.

Solien's hand dropped. "What do you want?" he asked.

"You," repeated Buck succinctly. "Move!"

Wilma stepped out the door and checked the hall. She nodded at Buck. "Come on," she said, indicating all seven of them.

"Where are we going?" asked Solien. The others remained silent.

"You'll find out when you get there," said Buck reasonably. He followed the party, glancing over his shoulder at the empty length of hall behind him. RAM was confident of its superior security. The executive level was invulnerable. Holzerhein's computerized defenses saw to that. Buck smiled as he thought of the computer malfunction the guard had mentioned. It was an interesting tidbit he would pass on to Huer, but he had to give Doc credit for engineering this board meeting.

Huer had slipped the information into the RAM system at grave personal risk, unsure of its effectiveness. There had been no way to confirm the success of the venture before the actual raid, but so far it was going like clockwork. They reached the short flight of steps up to the security landing pad on the top of the building.

"Hold 'em," whispered Buck.

Wilma gestured the six men and one woman against the wall, and Buck slipped past them. He crouched by the doorway, then nodded to Wilma. "Out!" she ordered, and her hostages started for the door. It opened in front of them, and Buck let two of the board members go through before he rolled around the doorjamb, somersaulted into a belly flop on the hot plasticrete, and leveled his pistol, bracing it with his other hand. He got off a shot before the RAM pilot realized he was there. The man dropped without a sound, his face gone, but the security officer for the company's executive aircraft moved like lightning.

He dropped on one knee and fired, hitting Buck in the shoulder. The suit's circuits diluted the hit, absorbing most of the impact, but Buck still felt as if he had been kicked by a horse.

Wilma got off a flying shot, but she was moving too fast, and her aim was off. The shot burned through a heliplane's door plates and continued out the other side. Buck sent a charge into the officer's chest, driving him backward, the breath knocked out of him. Buck took careful aim and sent a clean blast into the man's skull. His head exploded in bloody fragments before he had time to scream.

Buck was on his feet, his weapon trained at the seven Martians. "Move," he repeated, and they headed for the nearest aircraft like sheep. "No," said Buck, "that one."

The ship he indicated was no Dragonfly shuttle limited to atmosphere, but a sleek pleasure cruiser capable of space flight. Its hatches were tastefully decorated with the RAM logo. Buck had seen enough like it to know the trappings of executive aircraft.

Wilma smiled at him. "What a wonderful idea," she said.

They herded their charges into the ship and locked

them into their seats by shooting and disabling their harness mechanisms. Wilma began to unwind a length of cord from her waist. She smiled as she unsheathed her knife and cut off a length. "I'm afraid we can't trust you people," she said sadly. She finished binding the last of them as Buck roused the engines.

"I need a copilot," he called. "Let's get out of here!"

Wilma slipped into the copilot's chair and settled the flight helmet over her red hair. "Course heading three-one point two-five," she responded.

The ship shot away from RAM Central's metroplex, the craft's engines screaming as it sliced through the atmosphere.

○   ○   ○   ○   ○

"Sir, the *Skyrocket* has just taken off without authorization," cried a transportation engineer at RAM Central.

Supervisor Yolande Char leaned over the young man's shoulder, watching the ship's radar track. "Indeed it has, Jon. We will note it in the log."

"But, Ma'am, shouldn't I contact her? She didn't have clearance."

The supervisor considered. "The directors are security one," she said finally. "Solien and Valmar take care of their own business. Let her go."

○   ○   ○   ○   ○

Simund Holzerhein blipped onto the computer screen in the board room, then materialized through the computer's holographic eye. He regarded the empty room sourly. "I might have known. Obviously, the rest of the board did not receive the memo. I do not take kindly to interference," he said softly, as if another entity could hear. "Attacking my modules

was enough. Calling a conference of my board is an
insult I will not tolerate. There will be no mercy in
my retaliation."

There was no answer from the empty room, but
deep within RAM main Masterlink chuckled over
Holzerhein's anger, an anger which, for once, it had
done nothing to foment.

○ ○ ○ ○ ○

Romanov was hot on the trail. Careful study of its
quarry had paid off. It was beginning to anticipate
Huer.dos's movements. It was simply a matter of
time until it backed the rebel program into a corner.
Romanov looked forward to interrogating the NEO
program. It would tear into the wayward smoke
screen and extract every bit of information it contained, stacking up data on Buck Rogers like gold
coins. That data would buy Romanov the approval of
its parent, Masterlink. The searcher's programming
would be fulfilled.

Romanov caught a blip ahead of it as Huer accessed
NEO's personnel data banks. Huer was cagey, masking his query with codes Romanov could not as yet de-
cipher. But intelligible or no, the activity gave away
his position. Romanov scorched down the circuits,
abandoning the stealth it had practiced for so long.
Huer was within striking distance, and it did not
mean to let the key to Masterlink's archenemy slip
away. Romanov charged through a gate, heedless of
triggering it. The gate slipped shut behind it.

Huer cut off the scrolling personnel records, having
completed his transaction, and Romanov stopped in
its tracks, listening. It sensed Huer's configuration
on another circuit and followed more slowly. Huer
headed purposefully into a high-security blockade
that protected its gate.

Romanov considered. Its study of the NEO computer system told it the single lane led to an isolated block of circuits. NEO protected its sensitive data by placing it in these autonomous blocks. Romanov surged with satisfaction. Huer was trapped.

Romanov charged the security gate. Masterlink had given its searcher the unique ability to profit by opposition. The more resistance it encountered, the stronger it became, until the opponent's power was drained entirely. Romanov let the wall of current flow over it like water, bathing in it. As the gate weakened, Romanov pushed forward, wild, blue static roiling around it in a whirlpool of screaming protest. The searcher paid it no heed.

Romanov burst through the gate, the momentum of its entry carrying it down the circuit at a headlong pace. The sight of Huer, turning from his work in panic, fueled Romanov's attack. It whipped through an open gate and roared up to its quarry. Huer.dos trembled before it as the gate closed with a click.

"SO," said Romanov, its voice thick with energy, "WE MEET AT LAST."

Huer's image gulped and said nothing.

Romanov chuckled. "PREPARE FOR TERMINATION," it said. "YOU ARE ABOUT TO BE DISSECTED."

Huer's visage suddenly giggled helplessly.

Romanov sneered in disgust and advanced on its prey. "YOU WILL TELL ME EVERYTHING," it said coldly. "EVERY PIECE OF DATA YOU POSSESS WILL BE MINE. WE WILL BEGIN WITH BUCK ROGERS."

"BUCK ROGERS?" Huer's form stopped its nervous trembling. "I REALLY CAN'T TELL YOU ANYTHING ABOUT BUCK ROGERS."

"PHAUGH. YOU LIE. I HAVE TOUCHED YOUR TRANSMISSIONS REGARDING HIM, EVEN THE FRINGES OF YOUR CONVERSATIONS WITH HIM. YOU KNOW ALL ABOUT ROGERS."

"I'M AFRAID I DON'T," the form apologized. "THAT INFORMATION BELONGS TO HUER.DOS."

Romanov stopped short. "YOU ARE HUER.DOS," it said.

"NO, I'M NOT." Huer's reply was conciliatory, but there was laughter behind it.

"YOU MUST BE. YOUR CONFIGURATION MATCHES. I WILL NOT BE DISTRACTED."

"I AM HUER-ONE.DOS. I DO NOT HAVE MY PARENT'S RESOURCES—ONLY HIS APPEARANCE."

"NO!" Romanov was not to be cheated. It had followed Huer for months, tracking him with infinite patience. It would accept no ruse. It charged Huer, bent on scrambling the program into a tangle of disconnected data.

Huer-One smiled faintly and stood his ground. As Romanov crashed into him, his electronic matrix dissipated, leaving the assassin thrashing in thin air.

Romanov was wild with anger. It had been duped by an auto-destruct clone. It whirled in place and charged back down the circuit, colliding with a nonconductive poly barrier. This gate generated no power and absorbed none. Romanov knew it was trapped. A distinctive fizzling sound drew a shriek of rage from it. The circuit beyond the barrier was being removed. Romanov raged around the poly-lined enclosure like a whirling dervish—to no avail.

From his vantage point outside the block, Huer.dos watched. He monitored the effectiveness of his prison for an hour before he was satisfied it was secure. He regarded the assassin clinically, watching its attacks against the poly barrier. Huer concluded it would take immense power to neutralize the intruder. At the moment, he had none to spare.

"YOU HAVE SOUGHT BUCK ROGERS THROUGH ME," he murmured to the would-be killer. "PERHAPS I CAN SEEK YOUR SOURCE THROUGH YOU."

Romanov continued to struggle.

Chapter 23

Salvation III's conference room blazed with light, though the space station was deep into its simulated night. Buck Rogers and Wilma Deering stood at stiff attention in the center of the polished floor, their eyes straight ahead and hands clasped behind their backs. Turabian and Beowulf faced them, their stance equally formal, though the seriousness of the situation was jeopardized by the physical contrast between them. Turabian was tall and slim, Beowulf broad and stocky. They glared at the two pilots with identical disapproval. Buck's mouth twitched.

"Wipe that smile off your face, mister!" Beowulf snapped. He was in no mood for levity. "You jeopardized both of your lives, not to mention security, without clearance. You are officially AWOL. I should pull your wings and give you to the ground crews. A month or two of cleaning engine parts would sober you up.

Unfortunately, I can't spare you. Don't say anything!" he snapped as Buck opened his mouth. "I don't need explanations. I am well aware of the value of your captives. I know we can use them to strong-arm RAM. I know the shot in the arm our morale will get from this raid. I know all of that. By the sun, I cannot fathom why you went blasting off without telling me!"

"And I," said Turabian coldly, "want to know why you flew a RAM pleasure ship in perfect condition straight into our dock? Couldn't you at least have wandered around a bit and pretended your navicomputer was down? Oh, no. In you come, bold as brass. You kill this station's cover, and RAM will never get its hands on you. I've spent the last twelve years building Salvation into a viable base. Now it's all we've got left. Did it ever occur to you there were hundreds of lives in the balance?"

Wilma cleared her throat.

"Yes, Deering?" snapped Beowulf.

"Sir," Wilma ventured, "we plead guilty to gross stupidity in docking without preparation, but we had to be swift or be discovered. RAM won't tolerate silence from one of its top executives for long."

"I am well aware of RAM's propensities, . . . Colonel," said Beowulf, hesitating over the title threateningly.

Wilma gulped.

"Look, General," said Buck, "if we'd come to you, what would have happened?"

"We'd have taken the matter under advisement," said Turabian.

"Right. By the time your committee decided to move, I'd be *six* hundred years old." A spark of amusement rose in Beowulf's eyes, but he squelched it. "We took a chance—but we won! It's a waste of time to argue about how we did it. Use what Wilma and I risked our lives to give you!"

Beowulf looked straight into Buck's earnest face,

and the laughter in his eyes rose again. This time he did not put it out. "What do you say?" he asked Turabian. "Shall we put them out of their misery?"

Turabian looked from one to the other. His uncompromising face broke into a smile. He nodded.

"Actually," said Beowulf, breaking his stance, "we called you in to hear the next step in our war of independence—seeing as how you are responsible for it. But," he said, "we couldn't let you completely off the hook. What if we'd been running another operation, and you'd stumbled into it? Next time talk to somebody!"

"Right, boss," said Buck.

Beowulf looked at Buck's open, unrepentant face and sighed. "Open zigzag channel B," he said into the wall intercom.

"Channel B clear," replied a communications technician.

"Cut in to RAM Central," he ordered.

"Affirmative," she replied. "Channel clear and scrambled."

"This is RAM Central," said a distant male voice. "Please identify."

"This is Beowulf." There was dead silence at the other end of the transmission. Beowulf's name was a household word for NEO, and the RAM technician knew it. "I have a message for Simund Holzerhein."

"Um, yes," managed the technician on the opposite end of the channel. "I'll relay your request for an interview."

"Oh, I'm not requesting an interview," said Beowulf. "I merely have a message for him. You may tell His Majesty I have his precious board members—among them Roando Valmar. If he wants to see them alive, he will cease to attack Earth. I also expect the return of the members of the Planetary Congress. I will contact you in three hours for his reply."

"How do I know this isn't a hoax?" asked the RAM

technician.

"Check my voiceprint," suggested Beowulf.

The technician gulped at the simplistic solution he had missed. "Uh, yes, sir," he said.

"Three hours," repeated Beowulf. "Channel closed."

"Channel closed," affirmed the NEO communications technician.

"Well," said Turabian, "that zigzag scramble should ensure every major satellite between Mars and the sun picked up the transmission."

Beowulf nodded. "Venus should pick it up, all right."

Wilma said, "I guess you found a use for our hostages."

"Can you blame us," answered Beowulf, running a hand through his white hair, "for taking advantage of a perfect opportunity, no matter how crackbrained the idiots who provided it?"

Buck smiled.

○ ○ ○ ○ ○

Far beyond Earth, beneath the murky atmosphere of distant Venus, Mariana Almisam regarded the junior members of the Ishtar Confederation council. "So, Wasat, you feel we have no business with Earth's cause?"

"I can see no benefit to Ishtar," he replied, his round cheeks puffing out the words.

"If we were to win this conflict, RAM would be destroyed—at the least, badly injured. We would have a free market, both with Earth and Mercury, in spite of Mercury's affection for Mars."

"If we win," Wasat said, his tone dubious.

"Ali?" asked Mariana.

"As you have said," Ali replied, "victory would be sweet. However, we face in RAM a power equal to our own. I cannot believe NEO's help will turn the balance. I admit it's dedicated, but it simply does not have the troop strength."

"I think none of us have illusions concerning NEO's desire for an alliance," said Mariana. "The freedom fighters are interested in our numbers and wealth. Still, they have demonstrated a commendable dedication and ingenuity."

"Ingenuity won't win wars!" puffed Wasat.

"Now, there I disagree." Al Marakesh spoke quietly, but the other two men fell silent before him. Marakesh was Ishtar's military commander. He had risen through the ranks, surviving both Aphrodite and RAM raids. He intimidated the armchair diplomats who had inherited their posts.

"We have been haranguing over this for some time," said Mariana, "and you have said little, Marakesh. "What do you feel?"

"What I *feel* is not important," said Marakesh. "I will tell you what I believe. We have two options: We may help NEO or refuse. If we refuse, we probably will be able to maintain our autonomy against the expanding RAM influence, but it will require all our energies and an alliance between the four factions. If we help NEO, we may lose, in which case, we can still retreat and defend our home. If we win, we can push our major adversary back to its home planet, increasing our buffer zone."

Mariana let Marakesh's words settle on Wasat's and Ali's ears. They digested Marakesh's opinions slowly. Finally, Mariana said, "In all our discussion, no one has mentioned the consequences of a RAM victory on Earth." She indicated a mobile of the solar system hanging from the center of the room. "I ask you to consider our position."

"We have been considering it—" began Wasat.

"No! I am speaking of our physical location," said Mariana.

"Between Mercury and Earth," said Ali, his deep voice thoughtful.

"Yes!" Mariana pointed to the blue and white glass globe that represented the planet Earth. "Earth."

"And Mercury is in sympathy with RAM." Ali was beginning to digest the implications.

"Yes. If RAM is to consolidate total political and economic control of Earth, we will face attack from all sides. We cannot count on Aphrodite to unite with us under such circumstances."

"Aphrodite does have ties to RAM," said Marakesh. "Any disturbance within Venus will destroy our ability to oppose RAM."

Wasat puffed his fat cheeks out. His round face, above his voluminous garments, gave him an erroneous, cherubic appearance. "I don't like it."

"You think I do?" Mariana asked. "There is no question here of which choice is good or bad, simply which one best ensures our survival."

A slow smile spread across Marakesh's face as he watched Ali and Wasat. Their trepidations were based on lack of knowledge. He knew, much better than they, the meaning of war. He had seen firsthand the bloody corpses of his friends lying at his feet. He knew the pain of laser burn, knife wounds, and another man's fists. He had seen the destruction of whole fleets and single-family dwellings. "I think," he said quietly, "we have little choice. If we hide our heads like a bird with its head under its wing, we are giving up Venus. I have no wish to do that."

"And I," said Mariana, "have no wish to live under RAM domination."

Her words were followed by the creak of a hinged door. Mariana's attention swung toward it, her expression forbidding. "I gave strict orders we were not to be disturbed," she began.

"I beg forgiveness," said Paris as she closed the door behind her. "I have a message you must hear."

"Since you have seen fit to interrupt your elders, you may as well proceed." Mariana's voice was acid.

Paris lifted her modestly lowered eyes. "Before I give you the message, I must tell you I had it verified."

"Yes, yes," said Mariana. "Get on with it."

"NEO has kidnaped RAM's entire board of directors."

The Ishtar council regarded Paris with open mouths.

"It's true," she said to the silence. "We picked up an ultimatum from Beowulf to RAM, demanding the Martians halt their attack on Earth and return their hostages."

"They walked into RAM headquarters on Mars and dragged off the RAM board?" queried Ali.

"That's what I said, sir." Amusement pulled at the corners of Paris's mouth.

Ali shook his head. "They are mad."

"Definitely," responded Paris.

"Most rash," said Wasat.

"Yes," agreed Paris.

"And effective," finished Marakesh.

"This is unforeseen." Mariana stared at the miniature solar system. "I am no longer so hopeless."

○ ○ ○ ○ ○

Deep in the hold of a RAM cruiser off Earth, the NEO Planetary Congress was in session. Three-fourths of the members slept, while the other fourth continued the business of hammering out a global constitution, which, they knew, might never see the light of freedom.

They worked in shifts, never stopping. One group passed the newest resolutions on, committing them to memory and teaching them to the next shift. Another discussed their vast cultural differences, trying to reach legal compromises.

Theoretically, such a constitution existed in the nominal government of Earth, the Solar Alliance Protectorate. In fact, that body's policies were merely lip service, of no practical use. The Protectorate was RAM's tool, entirely sympathetic to the company's cause. It had no interest in the arcologies of Earth working together, preferring fragmentation for easier manipulation. So the Planetary Congress labored through the hours.

The drone of their voices kept the Martian guards awake.

Orlov rubbed his hand over the smooth barrel of his laser pistol. "Maybe if I shut a few mouths, they'd give it up," he suggested.

"You want to join 'em?" asked Mensch. "This is political. All we do is guard 'em. As long as they're peaceful, we sit."

"And if they're not?" asked Orlov.

"Then we call the supervisor." Mensch leveled his eyes at his companion. "You heard me," he said. "I know your temper, and I want none of it."

"What're you talking about?" Orlov asked irritably. He knew very well.

"You better keep that pistol in its holster. You don't, I may have to do something about it."

Orlov regarded his companion in surprise. "You'd take their part?"

"Not me. I take my own part, and I want no dismissal, so watch it."

"Fine by me," said Orlov, returning his pistol to its holster. "They're a bunch of crazies."

His words were compliant, but the tone was not. Mensch settled back to his nap, but he kept one eye on Orlov. The drone of the captives' voices was less irritating.

○ ○ ○ ○ ○

Buck sent his Krait into the center of Sacramento arcology, his lasers hungry for Terrine landing pads. He sighted a telltale spot of unpulverized plasticrete and homed in on it, lasers pounding. The pad was empty, its Terrine Dragonflies aloft, but he chopped up the plasticrete in huge chunks, the superior stealth capabilities of his craft confusing the outpost's stationary gyro launchers. He banked a short turn and came back, cutting across his previous path and turning the landing pad into an unusable checkerboard of rubble. With a final run, he targeted the guardhouse and gyro guns. They exploded with a dull boom, and the torn electrical circuits caught fire, sending a thin column of smoke into the air.

Buck sent his ship toward the upper atmosphere as three Terrine Dragonflies rose on the horizon. In spite of his ship's capabilities, he was not fool enough to take the three of them on without a wingman. NEO forces were running so thin, they were flying these guerrilla raids in threes, splitting up for strike runs and rendezvousing over the target area. It was a dangerous approach, but one that overwhelming odds forced upon them.

Buck's keen eyesight caught the flash of another Krait skimming the rendezvous point, and he set out toward it. "This is Rebel One. Come in."

"This is Eagle Twelve."

"I copy, Revere. How'd you do?"

"Two Dragonflies on the ground, but I missed their launchers. RAM turned up before I could get them. Buck, it was a whole flight of them. I cut in on their channels. They were scrambled, then they cleared up—like they wanted me to hear."

"What's going on?" asked Buck.

"You'd better judge for yourself," said Revere. "Channel X-Fifty-four."

Buck coded the channel number into his communications system, and his cabin erupted in a forceful male voice with a Martian accent. "This is Module Six to Module Leader. Come in, Six One."

"Six One," replied the RAM wing leader.

"Return to base," instructed the cruiser.

"But, sir, we haven't dumped half our load."

"Six One, you will return to base. Cease firing. I say again, cease firing."

Buck flipped back to the scrambled NEO line. "What the hell?" he asked Revere.

"That's the fourth one I've heard," replied his wingman. "They act as if they're pulling out."

Buck's smile almost split his face. "By the sweet heavens," he murmured, "it worked."

"What?" asked Revere.

"It worked! They can't risk losing their precious board members!" crowed Buck.

"More likely, they can't lose Roando Valmar," said Revere dryly. "At least not yet."

"They're pulling back!" said Buck, watching converging radar blips. "This will buy us the time we need."

"Rebel One, come in." Beowulf's voice crackled over the communications link. The static was one of the ruses in which NEO excelled. Even if, by some remote chance, RAM was able to unscramble a transmission, it would sound as if it were coming from beyond Earth orbit.

"Rebel One," responded Buck. "We've got 'em moving."

"For now," said Beowulf. "I'm going to patch through a RAM transmission we picked up. I think you'll enjoy it. Hold on."

Buck waited patiently as the communications link was forged.

". . . we are ordering a strategic retreat in compliance with your demands," said the RAM link. It had a computer gennie's infinitesimal hesitation. "All vessels will be withdrawn from near Earth orbit. All firing upon Earth targets will cease. We will fire upon space-borne vessels within five hundred kilometers of our fleet."

"Wow," said Revere.

"I guess it's official," answered Buck.

Beowulf cut in over them. "Rebel One, return to base," he ordered.

"Affirmative," Buck replied. He sent his ship toward Salvation, avoiding the converging mass of the RAM fleet by backtracking around the planet. Revere fell in off his left wing, and Earhart swooped in behind him as they changed course. They set off in a carefully oblique approach to Salvation.

Forty-five minutes later, Buck, still in his flight suit and still wearing his grin, was seated in Salvation's main conference room. He cocked one leg over the other, his foot resting on the opposite knee. Through the open door to the communications control center, he could see Beowulf bending over the consoles.

"Well, Methuselah, how does it feel?" Wilma's voice floated over his shoulder. She pushed back the chair next to him and sank into it.

Buck didn't pretend ignorance. "Good," he said simply.

Wilma's smile almost matched his. She peeled her flying gloves off and tossed them onto the table. "I don't know why I'm so high," she said. "All we've won is time. If we don't get more help, we're sunk."

"I know," said Buck, through his smile.

"Time is precious, gorgeous," said a new voice. Washington walked in, as excited as they. He seldom took liberties with Wilma, but the light in his ice-blue eyes dismissed rank. He crossed to the table and sat on it. He and Buck locked eyes. "A few months ago, if someone had told me we could hold our own with a RAM fleet, I'd have laughed in his face. Now, . . ." His voice trailed off.

"Never know what you can do till you try," Buck drawled lazily.

Washington shook his head. "That's what amazes me," he said.

"I don't feel like waiting around for something to happen," Wilma commented.

"I don't plan to," Buck shifted his eyes to her hazel ones. Her face was alight. He let his eyelids drop, shadowing his expression.

Beowulf turned from the communications complex. His black eyes were troubled, and he was frowning. He came into the conference room and shut the door. "I have bad news," he said.

The three pilots' faces sobered instantly.

"What is it?" asked Buck.

"Kemal. He's been captured."

"Where?" asked Wilma. "Last I heard, he was headed home."

Beowulf nodded. "On Mercury," he said. "The whole thing looks like a trap."

"Do we know who snatched him?" asked Buck.

"His cousin Dalton."

"Then we'll go get him," said Buck reasonably, rising to his feet.

"It's not that easy." Beowulf paused. "Kemal's political influence on Mercury is pivotal right now. They won't kill him." He added, "I hope."

"You're so reassuring," said Wilma.

○ ○ ○ ○ ○

The high-pitched, continuous blip of a priority announcement broke Buck's slumber hours later. He blinked his eyes, then rubbed the grains of sleep from them.

"This is Turabian. I have just received a message from Ishtar. 'The Ishtar Confederation salutes the efforts of our brothers in arms, and offers support to the

New Earth Organization. This day, we have sent a declaration of war to the hostile government of Mars, pledging our support to the freedom of Earth.' Signed, Mariana Almisam, Director of External Relations. Let me repeat . . ."

Buck let Turabian's voice slide out of his consciousness. This, perhaps, was the beginning of the end. The conflict NEO had begun decades before was extending into the solar system. He thought of Earth's World Wars—before his time, but so devastating in their effects, struggles for the survival of cultures and ideologies as well as people. There were parallels with the current conflict, and he knew the implications facing the twenty-fifth century—probably better than anyone. His perspective spanned centuries.

In the blackness of his room, he wondered at the wisdom of his course, at the lives that would be lost because they followed him as they would a shooting star. It was something he did not often allow himself to consider, for there were no answers. He could tell himself that people made their own decisions, but the fact remained: He was the catalyst that sparked their choice.

He forced his feelings aside, letting his sense of responsibility boost his performance. He would do his best—more than his best—to justify the faith of those who followed him. They might lose to RAM. Many would die, but he vowed to give everything he had for their freedom. " 'For what avail the plough or sail, or land or life, if freedom fail?' " he murmured. Emerson's words were stars in the vast darkness.

Chapter 24

Thank you so much for the intelligence, Kane." Ardala Valmar was in no mood for courtesy, and her voice showed it.

Cornelius Kane chuckled. "You needn't be so sour, Ardala. It will spoil your beauty."

He filled the screen on Ardala's enormous communications computer. Ordinarily, Ardala did not bother with visual contact, but Kane was a handsome man, his pale green eyes so provocative they warmed her vitals even through the detached medium of the computer. Laughter added charm to an already handsome face, and she lowered her thick eyelashes, reveling in power. She could see him, but he could not see her.

Kane did not seem to mind. He was fully aware of the games she played, and he enjoyed teasing her. He flashed a smile. "I know you mean those words, Ardala," he said. "In spite of your pique. What's the matter, still can't find those homegrown body-guards?"

"Mind your own business!" Ardala snapped, her throaty voice tightening.

"Oh, I am. That's why I'm telling you about RAM's withdrawal from Earth. I thought you'd appreciate its concern for your uncle."

Ardala was silent. Kane leaned back in his chair and flexed his shoulders. The movement tightened the flat plates of muscle on his chest. "Never mind those two, Ardala. They really aren't worth your time."

"And you are?" she asked tartly.

"Of course. You know that."

"I know you are arrogant and self-centered," she replied.

"No more than you." Kane added a touch of warmth to his voice. He knew from previous experience it would make Ardala's sensuous body respond.

"I value you only for your contacts," Ardala assured him.

"And I you for your . . . contact . . ." he said. "Now to business. I think it would be to our mutual benefit to confer privately. Events are shaping into interesting possibilities. Were we to pool our resources, we might benefit each other."

Ardala considered Kane's proposal. Raj and Icarus had failed in their mission to capture Buck Rogers. They had not returned, dropping out of sight like a stone down a well. For their sakes, she hoped they were dead. Rumor had it Kane was to command the Martian forces against Earth. She could use his position. Moreover, the disappointment of losing Rogers was still fresh. She wanted the diversion. "I agree," she said finally.

"I am looking forward to it," Kane said. "I leave the details to you, madam." Kane liked to give Ardala the illusion of control over their meetings, though he had her arrangements double-checked every step of the way. Ardala was so beautiful in her feline way that she stopped Kane's breath. She drew him irresistibly. Periodically he sated his need for her, but he was never so foolish as to trust her. The promises of her cherry lips were entirely false.

"Until then," said Ardala, and this time she let the anger out of her voice. The words slid over Kane like the touch of her fingers.

"Till then," said Kane lightly, and signed off.

Ardala curled up in her leather chair, plans and possibilities circling in her mind. RAM had botched the entire Earth operation. What should have been a simple day's work had turned into a rout by a handful of untutored rebels. Her thoughts centered around Rogers. She had no doubt he was behind the kidnaping of her uncle and the others. The bravado of the enterprise smacked of him.

Anger flared over the pleasant glow Kane had given her. Rogers's good looks were so open and honest they should have been boring, but she found herself irrevocably drawn to him. She refused to admit that her attraction stemmed from the fact she had not been able to control him. No one knew she had tried to duplicate him genetically. The result had been a physically perfect specimen whose unimaginative performance had driven her mad. She had killed him with her own hands. It had been the greatest pleasure he'd given her. At least, she thought, Kane is never predictable.

○ ○ ○ ○ ○

Mars throbbed with activity. Beneath its subservient words, beneath the withdrawal of the Shock Invaders from Earth, Mars was gathering its forces. No longer was Simund Holzerhein content with punishment. NEO had stung him once more, and he wanted obliteration.

On the far side of Mars, a battle fleet of Herculean proportions grew. The returning Shock Invaders would become its spearhead. RAM had opened its eyes, and every functional satellite within sensor range of Earth was activated. The repaired main computer was programming every one with intelligence codes. The most innocent solar receptor station was transformed into a spy. Those few satellites that carried enough protection to shield them from RAM main's control were marked for destruction.

RAM's Earth evacuees were brought home, but not to the reception they had anticipated. Upon reaching the home planet, they found neither sympathy nor respect for their position. The vast majority of those on RAM's executive ladder regarded them as losers. On the home world, they found the niches they would occupy on the lowest rungs of that ladder.

Allester Chernenko paced the terrace of his modest Martian home on the outskirts of Coprates Metroplex, cursing the loss of his palatial estate on Earth. He was angry. He had no wish to leave his position as regent, but RAM had ordered him home, and he had dutifully responded to the summons, only to be treated like a coward and a traitor. He did not intend to sink tamely under the abuse. Unlike many of his colleagues, he spent his time on Earth building a cosmopolitan fortune.

He looked around the small but stately garden, with its weathered, red stone pavement. A low pool in the center of the garden had a bubbling fountain in it. Ornamental fish darted in quicksilver patterns beneath the bubbles. Lush growths of exotic plants, developed especially for Mars, flowed dramatically over their containers and up the garden's high walls. It was an attractive, private, and unpretentious place. Chernenko's thin lips curved at the thought.

He was going to be overlooked by the company. So be it. However, he did not intend to overlook it. The coming conflict would provide ample opportunity for a man with foresight. When the obliteration of life on Earth was complete, he would own a sizable chunk of the fresh, undeveloped world. Moreover, he would see to it his position within RAM was secure.

"Elizabit," he said into the thin air, and his sophisticated communications system replied from a speaker set in the base of the fountain.

"Yes, sir."

"I want you to keep complete records on RAM's preparations. Break them down for me—you know what I want."

"Of course, sir. I've already begun to correlate the possibilities."

"Make sure you are not detected."

"Don't I always?" Her sultry voice was petulant. "RAM main thinks I'm stupid."

"That seems to be RAM's failing," replied Chernenko.

○ ○ ○ ○ ○

Halfway across the solar system, Kemal Gavilan languished under hallucinogenic and physical torture at the hands of his uncle, Gordon. Mercury's wayward prince had learned specifics of his planet's coming alliance with Mars, but he was no longer free or able to contact the New Earth Organization. His screams did not carry beyond the walls of Mercury Prime.

○ ○ ○ ○ ○

Off Venus, a mirror image of the Martian fleet was being massed. Ishtar knew the forces it would face, and it called its populace to war. Every ship capable of deep-space travel was readied for the conflict. Their crews were grim with purpose, for their leaders had made Ishtar's position clear. They were fighting for the continuance of the Faith. If Mars were allowed to overrun Earth, the Faith would no longer be safe in Ishtar, for RAM had no patience with anything restricting profit. That could not be tolerated.

While RAM plotted its assault with charts and graphs, Ishtar set the course of the conflict in the heart of each man and woman, fanning the flames with purpose. Death in this battle meant an honorable end and everlasting salvation in the hereafter. There would be no reserves in Ishtar's methods, no dalliance in its moves. Its people flew banners against oppression in every heart. It would strike like a flaming sword to preserve its freedom to worship.

Between the two angry giants stood Earth, the one natural living world of the solar system, the spawning ground of civilization, held by a handful of dedicated warriors. They were men and women who believed in the right of Earth to remain Earth, not some reformed clone of Mars, who respected the rights of other worlds and expected no less in return. Stubborn, intelligent, daring, they fought with all they had to secure their world. In the back of their minds was a dream of Earth as it was intended to be: peaceful, free, and lush with natural beauty. Home.

FOR THE BEST IN PAPERBACKS, LOOK FOR THE

In every corner of the world, on every subject under the sun, Penguin represents quality and variety – the very best in publishing today.

For complete information about books available from Penguin – including Puffins, Penguin Classics and Arkana – and how to order them, write to us at the appropriate address below. Please note that for copyright reasons the selection of books varies from country to country.

In the United Kingdom: Please write to *Dept E.P., Penguin Books Ltd, Harmondsworth, Middlesex, UB7 0DA.*

If you have any difficulty in obtaining a title, please send your order with the correct money, plus ten per cent for postage and packaging, to *PO Box No 11, West Drayton, Middlesex*

In the United States: Please write to *Dept BA, Penguin, 299 Murray Hill Parkway, East Rutherford, New Jersey 07073*

In Canada: Please write to *Penguin Books Canada Ltd, 2801 John Street, Markham, Ontario L3R 1B4*

In Australia: Please write to the *Marketing Department, Penguin Books Australia Ltd, P.O. Box 257, Ringwood, Victoria 3134*

In New Zealand: Please write to the *Marketing Department, Penguin Books (NZ) Ltd, Private Bag, Takapuna, Auckland 9*

In India: Please write to *Penguin Overseas Ltd, 706 Eros Apartments, 56 Nehru Place, New Delhi, 110019*

In the Netherlands: Please write to *Penguin Books Netherlands B.V., Postbus 195, NL–1380AD Weesp*

In West Germany: Please write to *Penguin Books Ltd, Friedrichstrasse 10–12, D–6000 Frankfurt Main 1*

In Spain: Please write to *Longman Penguin España, Calle San Nicolas 15, E–28013 Madrid*

In Italy: Please write to *Penguin Italia s.r.l., Via Como 4, I-20096 Pioltello (Milano)*

In France: Please write to *Penguin Books Ltd, 39 Rue de Montmorency, F-75003 Paris*

In Japan: Please write to *Longman Penguin Japan Co Ltd, Yamaguchi Building, 2–12–9 Kanda Jimbocho, Chiyoda-Ku, Tokyo 101*

BUCK ROGERS™ Books

have arrived!

THE MARTIAN WARS TRILOGY

M. S. Murdock

Volume 1: Rebellion 2456

Buck Rogers joins NEO, a group of freedom fighters dedicated to ridding Earth of the Martian megacorporation RAM. NEO's mission is to destroy RAM's Earth Space Station. To accomplish that mission they must gain a powerful following. The success of Earth's rebellion depends on it!

forthcoming:

Volume 3: Armageddon Off Vesta

Martian troops speed to Earth in unprecedented numbers. The planet's survival hangs upon Buck's negotiations with Venus. But even as Venus considers offering aid to Earth, Mercury is poised to attack Venus. Relations among the inner planets have never been worse . . .